THE NATIONAL ANTHEM

THE
NATIONAL
ANTHEM

★ ★ ★ ★ ★

Barbara Raskin

E. P. DUTTON & CO., INC. / New York

9/1977
am, Let.

Library of Congress Cataloging in Publication Data

Raskin, Barbara.
  The national anthem.
  I. Title.
PZ4.R2247Nat [PS3568.A69] 813'.5'4 76-18699

ISBN: 0-525-16417-0

Published simultaneously in Canada by Clarke, Irwin & Company Limited, Toronto and Vancouver

10 9 8 7 6 5 4 3 2 1

First Edition

TO MARC

"Everyone knows what you seem to be; few know what you are."

Niccolo Machiavelli

THE NATIONAL ANTHEM

One

"Identification please."

Nona opened her purse, extracted her press card, and handed it over to the blue uniformed U.S. Capitol guard.

"I'm going up to the periodical press gallery," she said. "To get my Watergate credentials."

The guard's gaze slid over the hill of Nona's embroidered T-shirt, skid past the hand-tooled leather belt hugging her hips, and shimmied down the Levi's covering her legs. Then he looked up into her face again, searching for some surer sign of subversion—something beyond the ambiguous act of wearing blue jeans on such an auspicious occasion.

"You got some other ID?" he asked. "So I'll know this is your pass?"

Nona's ambivalence about her assignment evaporated the moment she felt herself being politically challenged because of her clothing. Reluctantly she produced her driver's license and watched the guard's lips quiver as he subtracted 1940 from 1973. Suspicion clouded his eyes as he compared Nona's incongruously glamorous photograph with the intense, insolent woman facing him.

"Are you trying to tell me that you're thirty-three years old?"

Nona sighed. Only an occasional assimiliationist, she always felt anxious at entrances or checkpoints—uptight around guards and ushers, customs and immigration officers, registration clerks and receptionists.

11

Invariably her own uncertainties triggered official resistance, but today she felt detached enough to keep the exchange casual.

"Well, I am thirty-three," she said, leaning across the wooden table. "The only reason I look so young is because I'm still a virgin."

Startled, the man returned her ID.

"Thank you," Nona flashed him an ironic smile of false appreciation and then turned back into the crowd of tourists bottlenecked near the revolving doors.

A young student, probably the son of some generous senatorial campaign-contributor, was operating the press elevator and he tucked a finger in the center of a large red torts book to show his impatience at being disturbed. Nona entered the metal cage and met a mirror reflection of herself at the rear. At first glance she presented a slim, exotic figure, but as she advanced, proximity tightened up the focus and her face became more impassioned than pretty. Up close her eyes were more critical than conciliatory and her full lips seemed sulky rather than sultry. Nearness destroyed any illusion of easiness and Nona turned her back upon her own alien image.

On the third floor, the law student parted the elevator doors with slow theatricality to reveal a mostly male crowd of journalists lined up outside the periodical press office. For a moment Nona froze as a soul-rush of contradictions swept through her. For years the press had been part of the enemy to her—arrogant spokesmen for the establishment—and now she had come to join them. Torn between the urge to escape and the desire to make a perfect entrance, Nona stepped into the corridor and, hugging the wall a little, moved toward the rear of the line.

A ripple of swiveling heads stirred the regiment of restless reporters.

From the corner of her eye, Nona saw the men seeing her—watching and weighing her appreciatively as she passed. Feeling a little high from their blatant approval, she surveyed the crowd but could recognize only a few people: a woman from *Harper's* magazine who had covered Michael's trial and another, a man from the *New Republic* who lived near Nona's apartment. Then, near the tail end of the line, Nona saw the short bouncy form of Barry Stein, a pale intense man who had climbed his way to the top of the journalism establishment on the back of the Antiwar Movement and become Washington bureau chief of the Kinkaid Syndicate. Since he still considered Nona one of his news sources he still afforded her the same courtesies that Capitol Hill reporters offered legitimate congressional wives.

"Hey!" he called and reached out to grip her arm without endangering his place in line. Despite some silent but heavy flack from the men directly behind them, he integrated Nona into position beside him. "You really look fantastic," he said. "How come you're in drag?"

Nona laughed. In an effort to disguise herself as a trendy media type she had left her long hair loose, instead of coiled behind her neck, and had softened the challenge of her wood-dark eyes with soft blue shadow.

"I'm on assignment," she said. "I'm going to cover the hearings for Metro."

"Far out," Barry grunted unenthusiastically. "You must be broke."

Nona shrugged. It had always bugged him that she was able to ricochet between the establishment and the Left. Her uncanny ability to mount and ride any writing assignment with the ease of a good jockey who could race any horse confused him.

"Or are you going straight?" he persisted, intent on working her over a little since she upset his instinct for order. Knowing Nona as a Movement person, Barry preferred she stay put in her proper slot rather

13

than break out of form to trespass on his professional turf.

"Oh, I don't think it will corrupt me . . . if I'm careful." Nona laughed. But despite her sociable smile he knew she pegged him for an ambitious apolitical fact-collector who monitored the world without any commitment—a classic self-exile from any advocacies.

A few seconds passed in tense silence.

"Well, how have you been?" he finally asked to end the hostilities. It was an off-the-record allusion to Nona's lover Michael Daniels, a federal fugitive who still remained a recognized Movement leader.

"Oh, I've had some rough times," Nona said in a cavalier voice that reduced the horror of the past five months to an inconvenience. Then she studied the seersucker jacket of the man in front of them while fighting off the desolation that articulated itself each time her mind touched base with the fact that Michael had gone underground without her.

Several more tired-looking reporters piled out of the press elevator and started toward the end of the line.

"But I'm out of the tunnel now," she lied. Still feeling savagely betrayed by Michael's flight, she was still in active combat against the stubborn estranging anger that had caused her to retreat into the solitude of her apartment, half-annihilated by the events that had shattered her life.

"You *know*," she intoned, appealing for empathy. "I thought that working on a steady basis for a while—getting back into the big zone again—would help me straighten out my head." Her voice faltered and failed for lack of conviction.

"Sure," Barry consented. "It's just too bad Mike got convicted before this Watergate thing broke. But maybe if Nixon gets impeached, Congress will vote a blanket amnesty for all the draft-resisters and pardon the antiwar people who got convicted."

14

"I rather doubt *that*," Nona objected with a soft cynical laugh.

Although Barry had spent many long days and nights tagging after Michael and Nona, desperately trying to understand the logistics of some antiwar strategy, he had never gotten a real handle on the radical perspective and was never able to use a Movement analysis even as an academic exercise. He was, however, sensitive enough to sense the error of his optimism, and he let the subject of amnesty drop.

It took almost an hour before they were processed. Barry went inside first and then waited in the corridor until Nona reemerged gleefully clutching a handful of Senate press credentials.

"So you got 'em," Barry teased. "You passing a security check reminds me of Groucho Marx saying he wouldn't ever join any country club that would accept him. Well, come on," he took her arm. "I'm meeting some people for drinks, and I'll stand you to a couple for pulling a fast one on the feds."

Nona laughed as she followed him into the elevator. "Well, the only reason I can get clearance is because I'm a victim of sexism," she said quietly enough to exclude the law-student operator. "Since none of the men I worked with would ever give me credit for the political organizing I did why should the government hold it against me?"

It was after five when they left the Capitol and cut through the Senate office building to reach the dark cocktail lounge of the Carol Arms Hotel. Nona stepped inside, surprised to see that the tacky bar had assumed the air of an ocean liner on the eve of an exciting voyage. A crowd of the country's top political reporters, waiting to embark upon an assignment that would carry them across the summer, were busily making contacts and connections, cementing cliques to sustain them during their crossing.

"Jesus. What a scene!" Barry whistled under his

15

breath. "Every *macher* in the media's here. I'm going to have to pinch a few *tochises* later on. I haven't seen most of these guys since last summer."

"Really!" Nona hummed, feeling a flurry of stage fright.

"Well, come on," said Barry. But his tone had changed. Obviously feeling enriched and reaffirmed by the gathering of his clan, he seemed concerned that Nona might become a drag and inhibit his chance to circulate and cultivate his colleagues. Reluctantly he navigated her across the room, towing her along with jerks of his head as he skirted the low-slung cocktail tables, dodging a couple of rambunctious reporters who shoved their chairs into the aisle without any signal in a rush to greet someone.

Panic squirted through Nona's body. I'm not up for this, she thought, eying the short-haired, well-dressed journalists who found both direction and identity within the contours of a good assignment. The national political reporters were clearly aching to immerse themselves in the ongoing orgy of a story that would organize their personal and professional lives for them and legitimately amputate them from their families and nonpress responsibilities.

Nona had expected some manic behavior from the media but it was all coming at her too fast now. She was still too psychologically fragile to handle the crush of hot bodies and the raw come-ons of competitive hustling. Her legs began to cramp as her thighs tightened protectively. After half a year of hibernation she had wanted to move slowly—to take baby steps back into the real world—so she could reacclimate gradually to the frantic speed she had forgot.

"Hey, Nona, over here," Barry called, motioning toward a table where three men and a champagne-colored blond were watching them expectantly.

"Where you been Barry boy?" a heavyset gray-haired man asked as they approached.

16

"I've been waiting to get my fucking credentials, that's where I've been," Barry growled.

"You don't need any credentials to fuck this summer," the man responded. "The Senate passed a resolution."

"This is Nona Landau," Barry mumbled in a vague voice as he messed around with the chairs. "She's free-lancing for *Metro*."

Then, without assigning them in any order, he mentioned three names Nona knew only as printed by-lines in national papers. Two of the reporters shifted slightly on their haunches to acknowledge the introduction.

"You know Cindy Reynolds, don't you?" Barry asked. "She runs the Kinkaid Washington bureau."

There was a hurried shifting of chairs to make room, and Nona sank down into the vacant seat between Barry and Cindy Reynolds. Disoriented by Barry's rude introduction and the crude responses of the men, Nona turned toward the blond who was holding an empty glass out in space, signaling any invisible waitress cruising past their table.

"If I don't get another drink soon, I'm going to die," Cindy complained. A creamy smile crossed her face before she rested her pastel-blue gaze on Nona. "I know your name. Weren't you . . . Michael Daniels's . . . friend?"

"Yes." The past tense phrasing pierced Nona's heart.

"I thought so. My friend Julie Pasternik covered his trial for the *Chronicle* and she mentioned you a couple of times."

Cindy's face remained surprisingly stationary while she spoke, as though her features had been cosmetically fixed into a perpetually stylish expression. Occasionally she extended a limp-wristed hand to flick back the long front-locks of her hair, briefly exposing her brow before the pale strands fell forward again.

17

"Do you still live in that same commune they kept talking about during the trial?" Cindy asked, starting to stalk waitresses again.

"No. It broke up a few weeks after Mike . . . left," Nona answered.

Barry groaned and leaned over Nona's shoulder to insert himself between the two women. "Aw, come on, Cindy. Knock it off."

"What's the matter with you?" Cindy asked, making a strenuous effort at sincerity to offset the aura of superficiality that clung to her personality like perfume. "Is that what you call 'protecting your sources'?"

"There are some things you just don't talk about in cocktail lounges," Barry growled.

"Actually, it wasn't really a commune," Nona said, spurred by a sudden urge to erase the tension she'd created. "It was a collective."

The gray-haired man, Jack Lieutenant, slouched beside Barry, stirred to attention. "Does that mean you weren't allowed to have monogamous relationships?"

A corkscrew of anger spiraled up inside Nona's chest as she read the eager leer on the man's face. He was obviously ready to talk a little commune— to engage in a polite form of public fucking while finding out if radicals made love the same way the establishment did. Nona lit a cigarette, determined to stay cool.

"People who live in a collective work together on common projects," she said informationally. "I mean . . . *that's* the organizing principle. We used to put out a community newspaper."

"But a lot of collectives promote communal sex, don't they?" the man persisted. "To avoid private liaisons taking precedence over group loyalties?"

"Where'd you hear that?" Nona asked, trying to retard the speed of the exchange so she could stay on

18

top of the action. That much she had learned from Michael. Slow was good for dealing with people.

"Oh, come on," the gray-haired man chided. "You people consider monogamous sex counterrevolutionary, don't you?"

"Hey, Jack," Barry said reproachfully.

Nona bent over so the weight of her hair fell forward, shielding her face, as she tried to recover her purse from beneath the table.

"Aw, don't get sore. Lieutenant was just teasing you," Barry said.

There was an uncomfortable silence.

"Yah, I was just doing you a little," Jack Lieutenant agreed with a sheepish smile. "Barry's right. I guess what I really wanted to know is why the Movement's folding right now when the war's over and Nixon's on his way out. How come it's all coming unglued?"

"It's not," Nona said, sitting back again.

Although Michael's desertion had cost her a great loss of personal and political certitude and conviction, she would never admit it to any outsider. Even though everyone she cared about had fled Washington, her primary loyalties were still with the Movement and her commitment to her political past was far stronger than her current resolve to return to the slick media world in order to support herself. Although she had left her paper to go off with Michael, her professional credentials were still in order.

"Oh, come off it, Nona," Barry objected. "You know all the heavies have split. Half of them are back in law school and the other half are sitting on top of some mountain being Leninists all day."

"Well, you're the one who keeps writing all the New Left obits," Nona replied sarcastically. "You're the big authority. So what are you asking me for?"

"Oh, look," Cindy simpered, cocking her pale head slightly to one side and unconsciously beginning to preen. With her shining eyes, she flicked back her

19

hair and dipped the tip of her tongue across her lips. "There's Tony Lewellen."

A respectful silence spread around the table as the reporters looked up to pay their dues to one of the pinup stars of the liberal press elite.

Unable to resist, Nona turned, too, and though she had only seen the postage-stamp-sized photo of Anthony Lewellen above his syndicated column and society page pictures of him with his streaked blond-haired wife hurrying in or out of Georgetown parties, she recognized him at once.

It was clear that Anthony Lewellen was the epitome of the prohibited man—trouble handsomely gift-wrapped in a flamboyant style.

Startled at first by the clock of faces watching him, Lewellen produced an extravagant expression of surprise that sent a flock of laughlines racing across his face. Then recovering, or counterfeiting, nonchalance, he began threading through the crowd, coming at them with the air of a man returning from some dangerous assignment and now ready to apply his talents to more pleasurable but still daring pursuits. Although he was large, his limbs were loosely strung together so that he moved invitingly, suggesting an affinity for physical pleasures.

Parking behind Barry, Lewellen laid an affectionate hand on his shoulder—symbolically putting him on Hold while taking care of business on another extension—and looked around the table, flashing unwarranted amounts of affection from his rakish denim-blue eyes. His theatrically handsome face was framed by heavy dark hair graying stylishly at the temples.

"Jack Lieutenant! Howya doing? Reilly? Munson? How's my girl?" he asked Cindy with another expensive smile.

Recognition from him seemed to endow each individual with special status. Slowly, he turned to look at Nona for several seconds, studying her with chess-champion concentration as if psyching out his strategy before making any moves. Then, having made an enormous production of his silent, sexual intentions, he turned back to the group.

"So. Have you heard the news?" he asked.

Everyone froze.

"The FBI just admitted they've been running wire-taps on eight journalists here in Washington for the past five years. It just came in over the ticker about an hour ago."

His words triggered hoots of indignation and everyone leaned forward, passionate with protest, to demand details.

"Who'd they tap?"

"Who signed the order?"

"Who broke the story?"

"Sam was one of them," Tony said, looking at Cindy.

There was another chorus of outrage.

"Sam!"

"That's ab-so-lute-ly in-cred-ible," Cindy gasped. "Where is he?"

"I just dropped him off over at his lawyer's. He'll come by here when he's through."

Then, using the mileage he'd made with his astonishing announcement, he withdrew from his public and looked down at Barry with a more genuine brand of affection that he'd held in escrow during his performance. "So? Who's our new friend?" he asked.

"Don't you know Nona?" Barry asked. "She did that series for Metro on multinationals."

"If I'd met her before, we'd probably be in the south of France by now," Lewellen drawled softly.

Barry laughed and began to introduce them. But the ritual was only a cover for a silent conversation between the two men in which they exchanged covert information. Tony Lewellen was making mute but indiscreet inquiries about Nona's availability while Barry signaled back caution—advising Lewellen not to get involved.

And despite a hot burst of anger at their cozy chauvinist assessment of her, Nona felt a shudder of excitement.

"So you're the beautiful Marxist we've been reading about," Lewellen said.

"Is Sam all right?" Cindy interrupted.

"Well, he was a little shook," Tony responded, projecting enormous concern.

Nona smiled at the irony of Sam Kinkaid being suspected of subversion. Both of Kinkaid's national news-magazines had been soft on the Nixon administration up until Watergate, and Nona herself could have vouched for Kinkaid's loyalty since she had been with Michael on the afternoon he had called a large number of journalists to discuss publication of the FBI files Michael had stolen. Sam Kinkaid had been the quickest to refuse.

"Sam must be freaking out," Barry groaned. "Who else got tapped?"

"Walter, Dave, John, Carl, and Sid Resnick. . . ." Tony began.

Bud Reilly slapped several dollars down on the table. "I'd better report for duty," he said, shuffling to his feet. "Joe must be wild."

His departure unsettled the others, and there was a surge of restless shifting and stirring.

"I'd better call my office, too," Barry said, standing up. "Here, Tony. Take this chair. I'll get another."

"Don't bother," Lewellen protested. But accustomed to being accommodated, he sank into Barry's place and began settling in—parking his cigarettes, his sunglasses, his elbows on the table, marking out the territory beside Nona as his private staging ground. When he had finished making himself comfortable, he stretched out a little and let his eyes range around the table again as he shuffled through a deck of smiles, dealing out equal amounts of affectionate attention to each player.

Nona leaned back in her chair and listened to the

22

start of a discussion about invasions of privacy and violations of First Amendment rights.

When a waitress appeared, Lewellen looked up at her, first with irritation and then false good humor. "O.K.," he teased. "Just tell the truth. How long's it going to be before you get back here again?"

"Well, it's getting pretty rough," the woman said evasively, looking around the crowded room.

"What are you drinking?" Lewellen asked, turning to Nona.

"Nothing yet. Johnny Walker on the rocks would be nice."

"Give her a double and make me a triple of the same."

The others began to order in chorus, but even in the confusion everyone picked up on Lewellen's proprietory concern for Nona and understood that he was staking out his claim by absorbing her bar bill, putting down earnest money so as to acquire the rights of first refusal. Then, spinning off the general conversation again, he settled down to the business of putting the make on Nona.

"Well, they've really gone too fucking far this time, haven't they?" he asked, leaning toward her with an amorous curve of his shoulders.

"Oh, I don't know," Nona shrugged. "It's not any different from what they've been doing right along. There was a tap on our phone for years. . . ."

Lewellen accepted Nona's comment as a public admission of her relationship with Michael Daniels.

"Well, Watergate's going to break loose a lot of new stuff," Tony said. "You turn over the rock and . . ."

Predictably he adopted the tone liberals always used to show their academic empathy and abstract concern for civil liberties without condoning any particular political actions.

The waitress returned with a tray of drinks, and everyone helped distribute them while Nona sat

23

motionless, considering the practical significance of the FBI admission.

"Did they say how long they'd been tapping Kinkaid?" she asked, turning to Lewellen.

"Probably since 1969 or 1970."

"You know. . . ." She paused to light a cigarette and let the intimacy Lewellen manufactured gather around them again. "About a year and a half ago I was with Michael Daniels when he telephoned Sam Kinkaid. If they were monitoring Kinkaid's phone back then they must have picked up Mike's call. . . ."

Lewellen settled back in his chair and riveted his eyes on Nona's face.

"That would sort of put Mike into the Daniel Ellsberg bag . . . of accidentally being overheard on someone else's tapped phone. Anyway, it would mean the government had access to illegally obtained evidence before they indicted him. Really!" she said, suffused with a sudden optimism. "That would be an incredible breakthrough for Michael. If Kinkaid would come out publicly and say Mike had been overheard . . . I mean . . . if he swore Mike had called him . . . Mike's lawyer would probably be able to move for a new trial. Because I know that what the FBI heard was self-incriminating. In fact, that's probably how they caught up with him."

"Whew." Lewellen blew out a long sound of amazement and drew back from her with exaggerated alarm. "You sure don't waste any time do you?" he laughed. "You're sort of like that guy in *All's Quiet on the Western Front* who saw his buddy's leg get blown off and then asked for his boots." Lewellen sipped his drink, chuckling to himself. "Two minutes ago we'd never met and now you're asking me to deliver my best friend. . . ."

"Well," Nona smiled, "if I knew Sam Kinkaid I'd ask him myself. I'm not very shy."

"No. I wouldn't accuse you of that." He was eying the front of Nona's T-shirt, shaking his head back and

24

forth in slow-motion wonderment to show the impossibility of reconciling her soft shape with such a tough stance.

Nona let her lips flutter into an affirmative smile.

"But what makes you think I'd get involved in something like that?" he asked, with a mocking macho tone that challenged her politically while coming on to her sexually—putting her down while putting her on.

Nona stiffened. "Well, I *don't* know. Georgetown gentlemen journalists hardly have big reputations for being heroes, but—"

"Now what the hell is that supposed to mean?" he snapped in a sizzling voice that destroyed the cozy sensuality between them and aroused the interest of everyone else at the table. "You mean the lefties are still pissed off at me? You mean I'm still on the Movement's shit-list? Me and Dick Nixon? Is that it? You gotta be kidding, lady. Or don't you people ever forgive or forget? Even after a guy's been rehabilitated. . . ."

"Rehabilitated?" Nona echoed him with incredulity. "You bum-rapped McGovern every day of his campaign. You ran that phony peace-is-at-hand story Kissinger peddled right before the election as if it were gospel. You guys set up Nixon to be reelected and now *you're* talking rehabilitation!"

"Listen," Lewellen said after a quick gulp of Scotch. "I don't mind taking a few punches from you, but at least let's get the record straight. I came out against the war early in 1970. I supported all the McGovern party reforms, and I endorsed him for the presidency. I know it was pretty late in the game, but I did it."

"With friends like you he didn't need any enemies," Nona scoffed.

"Hey, Barry!" Lewellen pleaded. "Your guerrilla friend here says I'm still considered an en-e-my of the pee-pole. Tell me—is that fair?"

"Oh, Nona's very tough," Barry said, vicariously enjoying the highly charged performance. "Ve-rry militant."

From their exchange Nona gathered that the Left had been retroactively redeemed by the greater sins of their adversaries and that the liberals were now ready to take it on the chin for some of their mistakes. But caught behind enemy lines, she felt compromised and could engage only in some fragging from the rear.

Then suddenly Lewellen shifted around in his chair, effectively excluding the audience he had garnered, and dropped his jocular air. Behind his elaborately injured expression, he looked genuinely hurt.

"Tiger," he said wearily. "You didn't have to run that number on me. That's what I'd call a prime example of New Left overkill. All I wanted to do was to make a little time with you and right away you whipped out the old nuclear hardware."

Nona's confusion was increasing. The antagonism between her and Lewellen was having the same effect as a fast-acting aphrodisiac.

"So tell me," he said, leaning closer to her and invading her psychological territory, "why didn't you go underground with Daniels?"

Nona stared at him, stunned. Afraid of unraveling, she took several long drinks from her glass before answering. "Well," she said slowly, "usually when people jump one hundred thousand-dollar bail they don't take a lot of their friends along."

No one but Nona knew the truth—that Michael had left without any warning, had silently fled the commune in the middle of the night. It had been easier to pretend such a thing could never have happened to her so she encouraged some people to believe she had known Michael's plans and allowed others to assume it.

"And you mean you really don't know where he

is?" Lewellen asked cynically, smiling at her negative head-shake.

"No."

"What a crock!" he laughed.

"No. It's not. It's true. He just took off. He never even told me he was planning to skip." She said it in the well-practiced way that gave the lie to her words.

"And you've never heard from him since?"

"Look, you can believe what you want to," she shrugged, looking across the table at Barry. "And if you don't believe me you're still in good company. The FBI thinks I know where he is, too, and they're always dropping by to ask how he's doing and whether he's interested in a deal yet."

"I'm sorry," Lewellen said quietly. His hand crept crablike across the table toward hers, extending a silent apology.

Nona wavered briefly between weakness and withdrawal before putting her hands in her lap.

Don't touch me, she thought bitterly. Because you're right. If I knew where he was I wouldn't be sitting here with you.

Then, suddenly afraid that she had unconsciously exposed the truth, she began to laugh. "The only thing that bugs me about the FBI dropping over is that they've gotten younger than I am. When Michael and I started out we were always ten years younger than they were but now . . ."

Then she couldn't tease anymore because she'd started remembering the days right after Michael left when she had worn one of his huge stretched-out sweat shirts over her paint-splattered jeans and padded around the commune in a pair of his yellowing woolen socks, cooking or cleaning or lying about reading—unable to work. She had lost ten pounds in the first two weeks so that her jeans seemed to dribble off her and she was unable to finish anything she started—as if she were acting out her anger at

27

Michael for not letting them finish their lives to-gether.

"Well, tell me," Lewellen said gently. "Do you really want me to talk with Kinkaid? If you think it could help . . . I'll arrange it."

For the first time Nona let her eyes meet his. This stranger, this affected but affectionate man, was in his own funky way committing himself to her and she felt a soft soundless erosion of resistance.

"Yes," she said, looking away. "I would like to meet with him."

"I suspect he'll be pretty freaked out when he gets over here," Lewellen said. "But maybe we can set up something for later tonight."

Without asking, Nona snared Lewellen's pack of Salems and helped herself. Then, unsuccessful in a hunt for matches, she turned to him, confirming their claims on each other by silently waiting for him to light the cigarette she'd taken without permission.

Slowly Lewellen extended his lighter.

And in that moment of trivial need and service, their eyes met again, and Nona felt the click occur between them. In the mute idiom appropriate for barroom negotiations, Lewellen had provoked her into a sexual entanglement just as he might have lured a quarrelsome sailor outside to settle some dispute with a fistfight.

Now they were clearly on, and Lewellen pocketed his lighter and settled back in his chair, satisfied with the knowing.

The timeless afternoon that had stretched out so elastically snapped into nighttime. In the dimly lit room, the throng of drinkers sensed that outside there had been a natural time change and that night had happened. Everyone began to spark. Reporters staggered to their feet and began scrambling for their checks, itching to move on—to pick up their telephone messages, to check back with their offices, to confirm or cancel appointments made earlier in more sober hours. Drunkenly, they began drifting outside encountering newcomers who passed on the fresh rumors they had collected in lieu of after-dinner mints at some swank restaurant.

Mellow on two double Scotches, Nona relaxed while Lewellen initiated a where-should-we-eat discussion, bargaining collectively for both of them, presumptuously subsuming her as if she were a child who automatically accompanied her parents. When the check arrived, he picked it up and tossed a credit card on the prim brown tray.

"Treat's on me," he said to the group.

"Fat city," Nona clucked, finally connecting with her purse.

He looked at her with a slow indulgent smile. "Do you like Italian food?" he asked.

"Yup," she said, standing up. "But I've got to meet someone, I'm ten minutes late already."

Caught totally off-guard by his own arrogance, Lewellen was stunned. His first rush of anger seemed directed at Nona but then he turned it in upon himself for having assumed too much.

Quickly Nona said good-bye to the collection of surprised faces and darted off into the milling crowd.

Two

She walked through the early evening dusk past the new Senate office building, the Supreme Court, and the Library of Congress watching young self-important congressional aides hurrying past. A May wind was blowing, caressing her skin, stirring her hair, and reminding her of other times on Capitol Hill when she had been with a crowd of demonstrators trying to shake the American government up or down. Now the Hill seemed placid—a collegiate kind of community cloistered within the city. When she reached Pennsylvania Avenue, Nona began to walk more quickly past the tacky shops and restaurants still to be restored by energetic Hill investors.

She was thinking about Anthony Lewellen, wondering about his reaction to her exit. It had been a calculated risk—an act that would either turn him on or off. But she had felt compelled to show her seriousness since it was clear he was a classic playboy—that he had the city of Washington in his pocket and the national press corps between his legs. For years she had seen Style section photos of the Washington journalists at play—Lewellen with his photogenic children at Ethel Kennedy's annual pet show and Art Buchwald's Easter egg hunt and all the other festivities traditionally attended by the liberal establishment and their groupies. Still, remembering how Lewellen's smile faded as she walked out, she wondered if she'd been so harsh that he wouldn't call and wouldn't introduce her to Sam Kinkaid after all.

It was with a sense of uncertainty that she pushed open the swinging doors of the Fourth Estate. Behind the Victorian façade was a carbon-copy crowd of the one that had jammed the Carol Arms. Although congressional reporters had always frequented the gay-nineties'-style saloon on the House side of the Hill, the enormous influx of foreign and out-of-town journalists covering Watergate had swelled attendance and created a chic kind of congestion.

Nona twisted through the forest of human trunks looking for Jay and Patsy among the journalists who were crowded amorously close together, rubbing bodies as well as egos. Newcomers advertised their arrivals with loud greetings, oozing with excitement. Egocentricity hung like the smell of dope in the air. Nona slithered onto a plastic barstool and listened to the reporters standing around the bar energetically testing themselves against their colleagues, exchanging alcoholic challenges and compromises—priming themselves for their prize assignment. Unsuccessful in trying to attract the bartender, Nona listened to the conversations and began to remember the structure and strictures of her own careerist years, when she had been the most promising young journalist on the Minneapolis *Star Tribune*. But even the memory of those hungry years put her out of harmony with herself and she tried again to catch the bartender's eye.

"Nona, Nona!"

Jerking to attention Nona looked toward the door where Patsy Bator, a tall standout beauty wearing a sharkskin pants suit was vigorously pointing toward a vacant table in a far corner of the room. Nona slid off the stool and pushed her way through the crowd.

"Well, this is the last time I'll ever come in here!" Patsy said, sitting down with an indignant flounce

31

that sent her long auburn hair flying. "It's wall-to-wall New York new journalists. I can't stand these creeps!" Her prim rimless glasses, which she self-mockingly claimed she wore to distinguish herself from Vanessa Redgrave, slid forward and she sent the polished tip of a languorous forefinger up the haughty bridge of her nose to edge the spectacles back into place.

Nona smiled, feeling inexplicably indulgent toward the daughter of deceased but long-time national vulgarity symbol, movie-mogul Morty Bator. Among the crowd of *Metro* magazine writers and groupies, Patsy was the only one to whom Nona could relate. Although Patsy worked hard at creating a flippant style, essentially she and Nona shared a sensibility that superseded their stylistic differences.

"Jay phoned me right before I left the apartment and said he'd be late," Patsy announced. "But I'm glad because it gives me a chance to talk to you." She began to rifle her purse, ruffling the flame of hair flung over her shoulders as she excavated cigarettes and matches, slid an ashtray into position, jacked up her eyeglasses again, and looked around the room. "Oh, miss," she yodeled above the din. "Over here, please. I have to belt down a couple of fast ones," she explained to Nona. "Jay's dragging me to one of those grotesque Georgetown dinner parties tonight, and I can't hack those things unless I'm smashed before I get there."

A harassed waitress in a short gay-nineties' costume arrived, took their orders, and disappeared.

"Listen," Patsy pleaded, "I'm wigging out, Nona, I really am. I think this thing I've got going with Jay is bad news. I mean—I've hardly worked at all since I started living with him. And it's a real Gaslight number because he keeps *noodging* me to write more articles while he keeps *hokking* me to make perfect little dinner parties."

Nona lit a cigarette and settled back in her chair to listen to one of Patsy's unsolicited, uninhibited

32

career-and-love laments, remembering a year-ago when Patsy had sprawled out on a couch in the *Metro* reception office, intent on establishing her claims on Jay and her staff position. She had hung around the whole time Nona was there reading galleys. Even then Nona had sensed that Patsy's interest in Jay Lazar was ambivalent and that she disapproved of the very qualities that drew her to him.

The waitress returned and served them their drinks with a special sneer reserved for unaccompanied females. Patsy wrinkled her nose in response and then began sipping her Scotch with odd furtive motions— one of many mannerisms from a large repertoire of vulgar gestures that somehow never detracted from her innate glamour.

"Really, Nona, Jay's big trouble," Patsy persisted. "I haven't finished a single article in the last six weeks. He's forever sending me out on errands. Every time they advertise a new little *chotchke*, I have to go buy it for him. And he's a nut about ice cubes. I spend half my time filling up little Baggies with ice cubes so we won't run out when his fancy-ass friends come over. Shit!" She raised her brows above the rimless edge of her glasses, making her hazy myopic eyes almost as large as the lenses. "Oh, I don't know . . . I suppose it isn't really the ice cubes. It's just that . . . he's such a society junkie . . . that's all he ever thinks about. Half the time he publishes articles just for the shock effect they'll have on people he wants to meet. And he loves all the *Post* people and he's always sucking around Joe Alsop and Joe Kraft and Rollie Evans. If you ask me, that's why he bought *Metro* in the first place—just to get next to the Kennedys and Birch Bayh and Tunney and those guys. And of course he'd sell his soul to sit next to Eric Kessler at a dinner party." Patsy shook her head with amazement. "Or to get invited to Kay Graham's for dinner. He still hasn't made it over there yet, and he goes bananas every time she has a party. I don't even know how he hears about them because none of the *Post* reporters are allowed to cover her private parties, so God only knows how he finds out. Probably the same way she finds out she's not invited to the real upper-class wing-dings with the cliff-dwellers she's after."

With four and a half Scotches under her belt, Nona felt brave enough to interrupt. "I just met Anthony Lewellen," she said.

Patsy looked up, as easily distracted as she was digressive. "Oh, yeah? He's heavy into that scene, too," she said. "Actually, he was my dinner partner a couple of weeks ago, and he's not as bad as most of the other guys. You know he was in Saigon for a couple years, so he's got a little more soul than the rest of them. Everybody really likes him. Kissinger adores him, and so do Richardson and Kessler."

"I know," Nona said wearily. "I've seen a million pictures of him partying with all those heavies."

"The thing is," Patsy said, returning to her original track, "I got Jay, for whatever that's worth, by writing sexy features every month, and I know for sure that if I slack off too long he'll just get the hots for some flashy new writer he'll find. But by the time I make those dinners—go down to the wharf to buy fresh fish and back to the French Market to get the pâté and over to Larimers for some goddamn artichokes, I can't do anything else . . . I'm wiped out. Oh! Here he comes! His nibs!"

The sarcasm of Patsy's last words was spiked with sexual spite and Nona felt an empathetic anger as she looked over at Jay Lazar who was stalled several tables away from them, blocked by a waitress bending over to take orders. Jay was studying her shiny triangular crotch with an unscrupulous expression, as if getting ready to goose the bright target, and it wasn't until the waitress finally straightened up and liberated him that he strolled on over to their table.

A fleshy man in his early forties, Jay had receding

baby-fine blond hair that accented the heaviness that smudged his features.

"Didja hear the six o'clock news?" he asked, pulling out a chair and sitting down to survey the room with satisfaction. "Lotta action around here tonight. Nobody knows whether to shit or go blind about that FBI admission."

He kept watch over the action of the crowd as he spoke, seldom looking directly at either Nona or Patsy.

Always at a disadvantage with Jay, Nona decided to pull some bogus rank and drop a few names to arrest Jay's attention and gain some leverage.

"Tony Lewellen said Sam Kinkaid went over to see his lawyer right away."

"Where'd you see him?"

"Over at the Carol Arms."

Jay swiveled around on his chair to check out Nona more closely. "You got something going with Lewellen?"

Nona crocheted her face into an enigmatic expression. "No." she said, implying a cover-up.

"Well," Jay shrugged, "if you don't mind getting screwed by married men, Tony's the best gun in town. Actually, come to think of it, he would go for someone like you . . . he likes women with lots of bread or bad reputations." Then, clearly unsettled by the notion of rejecting a woman whom some superstar found interesting, he changed the subject. "Listen," he said in a serious voice, "I've been thinking about what I said over the telephone to you. I think it'd be a mistake to let you just rehash the hearings every month. I don't want any dried-up review of the testimony because you know as well as I do that the *Times* is gonna run every frigging word. So by the time you'd get to it—with our fourteen-day lead—that stuff would be dead as a doornail." His peevish expression suggested it was Nona's fault he published a monthly magazine rather than a daily newspaper. "Nobody's going to want to reread the same stuff again and I sure as hell don't want to run any of your half-baked Marxist analysis. I want some local color, something with pizzazz and sex appeal for July, August, and September." He spoke in an intimidating tone preferring to coerce rather than convince his writers and since he operated exclusively on vague verbal arguments he could squirm out of any arrangement or assignment if the subsequent scenario didn't please him.

From the moment Jay began talking, Nona knew what was coming. Indeed she had been expecting it ever since the day a few weeks ago when she had opened the windows of her apartment and watched the green leaves of her plants stirring in the wind willing her back to life, calling her into the world again, demanding that she look down at the Spanish people playing out the TV dramas of their lives on the stage-set street below. She had suddenly felt alive again, juiced up and hungry. Old cravings started to stir for the first time since Michael had left, and she had experienced an urgent desire to lunge at life and risk involvement once more. When she had finally telephoned Jay, he had agreed immediately to let her cover the Senate hearings for *Metro,* but Nona had known him long enough not to trust him completely.

Still—she had begun to fix her desk that day. For the first time since moving into the apartment she felt a sense of potentiality, and she had attacked the box of writing materials still stashed, unopened, beside the windows and with a rush of energy began arranging the contents on the desk. Energetically, she had collected all the disposable cans of Lo-Cal soda, Big Mac wrappers, and old newspapers that filled her studio. Systematically she had gathered up the clothing she had flung around during months of blurred days and nights, slowly restoring order and integrity to her home and her soul, manifesting her first life signs since the New Year began.

In the weeks since the phone call Nona had spent many conflicted hours arguing with herself about her motives for calling Jay. She debated whether she had wanted to cover the Senate investigation because Watergate was a public confirmation of her personal politics or because she wanted to find out if the assimilated life was still an option open to her. She wondered whether she'd asked for the assignment simply to earn the money she so badly needed or because she wanted to infiltrate the world of winners once again and play the Washington power game. Sometimes she accused herself of selling out for money, respectability, and social acceptance. But other times she knew she was simply using the only craft she had—writing—to begin taking care of herself once more.

But now, on the night before the hearings started, Jay Lazar was reneging on the deal. Nona sat perfectly still waiting for disaster.

The waitress arrived, and Jay ordered a drink, looking into her face with a petulant leer. Then he turned back to Nona. "Since it's already too late for anything for June, on July tenth I want a six-thousand-word piece on how the hearings change the lives of the committee members. You know . . . how eight hours on TV every day turns them around, all the ill-effects of celebrityhood. Because after tomorrow people are going to know Sam Ervin and Howard Baker and Senator Montoya. They're going to be folk heroes, and I want you to find out how they take it. Check out their office staffs, see what kind of mail they get, how their personal schedules change. For August I want a hellofa-good piece—it might even be the lead or cover story —about all the journalists who cover the hearings, both the broadcast and print journalists, all the media personalities and newspaper heavies. I want to know how these guys live while they're on a long assign-

ment, where they hang out, what they do at night
. . . what happens at the Capitol Hill Quality Inn on
the weekends." His eyes brightened as he envisioned
the sensational possibilities of the story, and he
scanned the room again as if trying to envision the
entire Washington press corps caught with their
pants down. "You could do a couple of takes on the
New York hot shots, Mailer and Mary McCarthy and
maybe a Hunter Thompson-lifestyle thing. This is
going to be like a national political convention for the
press, and it's good copy. I want you to find out
who's into what and who's into who, who gives the
good parties and where people drink. You can throw
in some serious stuff." He blew a stream of cigarette
smoke menacingly in her direction, daring her to
resist. "So whatya think?"

Nona drained her Scotch. "You mean you don't
want me to deal with the hearings at all? I'm supposed to sit in the caucus room all summer and then
write about everything except what goes on in there?"

"Christ, Nona, the *Post* is going to take care of all
that. I want something no one else has. I want a
little dirt—something about the network anchormen
and the big by-liners. You know . . . some inside
poop about the press."

Who gives a damn, Nona thought furiously.

"I think it sounds like a great idea," Patsy said.
"I wouldn't mind doing a story like that."

"Look. You just finish up the piece you're doing,
wouldja?" Jay snarled. This time he blew his smoke
into the empty space between himself and Patsy.

"Well, I know it's running a little late, Jay," Patsy
said pointedly. "But a couple of things came up that
sort of interrupted my work schedule."

They exchanged belligerent accusatory looks. Their
anger and ardor reverberated across the table and
Nona felt rattled by the cross fire of their fight for
supremacy or survival. Nervously she slipped the

cellophane off her Winston pack and began crackling it between her fingers.

"Now, look! If you're not interested, there's some other people I could ask," Jay said, insulted by Nona's lack of enthusiasm. "Betty Allentuck was in this week looking for an assignment."

"Oh, yes . . . there's always Betty Allentuck," Patsy mocked.

"Well, I don't want to write a gossip column," Nona responded with her last reserve of bravery. "I mean, I don't mind doing some profiles . . ."

She needed the money. She didn't want to take any more loans from her parents. Jay paid $750 for a six-thousand-word story and, besides rent and food money, she had to keep some cash in the apartment in case Michael needed it or in case he asked her to join him.

"Shit! Don't give me any more of that high-type crap. It would be easier for me to write all the articles myself than deal with you Jewish prima donnas."

"I'll give it a try," Nona said, feeling all her editorial integrity floating away. But she had no bargaining power with Jay—she didn't write enough for *Metro* to accrue any chits. Working on a free-lance basis meant each article was a new beginning—a renegotiation of her right to work, another tryout for which she had to come on and put out.

Frustrated, she sank back into her seat, hating herself and Jay and Michael Daniels who had unknowingly set her up for this irony by leaving her broke and desperate with Jay Lazar as her only alternative to bankruptcy and isolation. Since Michael was deaf to the siren call of social or professional approval he saw no danger in flirting with commercial success, and he had been the first to encourage Nona to return to journalism, insisting that she write the story of his trial for *Metro* magazine. Since they had needed the money, Nona had done the article. Despite the fact that rage had permeated it, Jay Lazar liked the

39

piece enormously and ran it as his lead, insisting Nona write more until she eventually produced a half-dozen feature stories.

The waitress delivered Jay's drink, and he applied himself to his glass as if to douse his anger with Scotch.

Nona lit another cigarette. The room was vibrating now from the raw-edged competition. Everyone seemed intoxicated by the unannounced, unofficial intramural contest of the Watergate sweepstakes.

"Well, do you want to do it or not?" Jay asked, balancing his chair on its back legs.

"I said yes, didn't I?" responded Nona sullenly.

Jay continued rocking on his precipice, dissatisfied with Nona's attitude. Out of sorts, Jay radiated aggravation and emphasized his impatience by eying various parts of Nona's body as if to keep himself amused.

"I'm on," Nona repeated.

"Good. I'm sure you'll give me some dynamite stories," he said, finally satisfied. "If you can get enough juicy details to do a real hatchet job everybody in town will want to read. All you need is a couple of hard facts and a lot of innuendo." Then he turned to Patsy. "Finish up, babe, we have to be at dinner at nine."

Nona sat in silence until they were ready to leave and then followed them outside. Jay had parked illegally in front of the entrance, and he stopped beside his car, laying a hand on Patsy's shoulder to prove physical possession.

"Give me a call next week and tell me how it's going," he said.

"O.K." Nona spoke through frozen lips. "Have fun." Then she turned and started the long trek back to the parking lot behind the Teamster's building on the Senate side of the Hill.

She drove the Volkswagon she'd inherited from

40

Michael down North Capitol and up Columbia Road toward Adams-Morgan, one of the few half-conscious, if not totally intentional, integrated communities in the city. Movement people who had stayed on in Washington still lived in Adams-Morgan where, despite some formal community organizations, the neighborhood was held together by strong, but unstated, communal feelings, a sense of embattlement shared by the social and political exiles who lived there. The Cuban refugees, white radicals, poor blacks, and east Indian émigrés, all had the attitudes of misfits—alien souls in an affluent society.

Fifteen minutes from the Capitol, Nona reached her battered and besieged block. Columbia Road was a grim, grimy, congested street, crammed with apartment buildings, ethnic restaurants, tawdry shops, and disheveled crowds. The entrance to Nona's building was squeezed between a dry-cleaning shop and an Italian delicatessen. She let herself inside the dark rancid hallway and ran upstairs to open the various hardware-store locks that crusted the door to her apartment. Although she had lived there alone since January, she had never become accustomed to the silence that confronted her each time she came home and still felt surprised at the tentative, between-tenants look of the place. Because she could never let herself believe that Michael had permanently abandoned her, she continued to struggle against her aloneness, pretending that it was only of limited duration—a temporary interlude until he returned or summoned her to join him.

Nona walked through the large front room and set down her purse on the kitchen table. After years of communal living, she essentially felt ashamed of being alone, painfully self-conscious in the eerie unfamiliar silence. And it was at night that she most missed the clatter and clutter of commune life. A flush of loneliness stirred her as she thought of all the years when the shared vision of her friends had

41

buoyed and sustained her. Even if they quarreled or fought, ripped each other off or screwed the wrong people, for a brief euphoric time they had all believed in something finer than themselves and had given their individualities to a grander scheme.

Nona opened the silverware drawer, took out the tin-foil-wrapped pack of marijuana, and rolled a joint, wanting to forget the commotion of the day and her confrontation with Tony Lewellen, which remained with her like the after-sting of a sharp astringent on her skin. It was impossible to pretend that she had been immune to his hype or invulnerable to his flattering infatuation with her.

When she finished smoking, she walked down the hallway to the little alcove she used as a bedroom and impulsively flung open her closet door. Intent on keeping her mind occupied, she began to research her wardrobe for various outfits she might wear to the Senate hearings, combing through the Levi's and denim shirts, flowing caftans, and Indian print dresses.

Aimlessly she began to retrieve from the back of the closet clothes from earlier ages and stages of her life and vainly tried to remember herself in the mini dresses she had once worn as front-and-rear sandwich-board-advertisements for her originally ambitious self. Feeling a trifle spaced out, Nona began to drop and develop several different groups of garments on the floor, piling up heaps of previous identities to wash, iron, or sew.

When the telephone rang, she knew who it was and sat down on the bed before answering.

"Hello?"

She could hear him breathing. The receiver slid against her cheek, slipping in the perspiration on her skin.

"How are you?" he asked.

Nona sighed, "O.K. I picked up my credentials today. The hearings start tomorrow."

42

"Oh, you're going to have a ball there, Nona. I'm going to try to find a TV to watch."

"How are you, Michael?"

"Good enough."

This is the last time, she promised herself. I'll never ask again.

"I don't have to start tomorrow," she said. "If you can get word to me, I'll come and join you."

Dead silence.

For a moment Nona thought her arm might take independent action and replace the receiver.

"You'll be the only fresh eyes there," Michael said. "It's important for you to do it."

She didn't answer. The old familiar rage was traveling through her body, scratching against her nerves. She wouldn't beg him anymore.

"Did you hear about the FBI admitting they wiretapped a bunch of reporters?" he asked.

"Yes. I bumped into Barry Stein over at the Capitol, and he took me out for a drink. Tony Lewellen was there—he's a friend of Sam Kinkaid's—and I asked him to set up a meeting for me with Kinkaid. I was thinking maybe if he said you'd called him over his tapped telephone, Dave might be able to move for a mistrial or something. Or get you a new one because of new evidence."

Michael was quiet for a moment. "That's interesting," he said slowly. "That's a possibility. I didn't think of that. I'd forgotten I'd called him. Who else is on the list?"

"I didn't see the paper yet," Nona said. "But I'll check it out tomorrow."

"Have the feds been bothering you?" Michael asked.

"Not for the last few weeks. I'm pretty sure the phone is tapped though."

"It doesn't matter. I'm moving on tomorrow. As a matter of fact, I probably won't be able to call for a couple of weeks. Maybe longer."

"I could meet you," Nona repeated. "We could drive to Canada or go to Europe. I can get some money."

He didn't answer.

"Tell me why, Michael. Please. Just tell me why."

"I've told you why. Because it's crummy living like this. I don't want you to live this way."

"But I don't want to live like *this*, Michael. You don't have the right to assign me a life I don't want just because you think it's better for me."

"Look . . . do you want to talk or do you want to hang up?"

"Talk," she said.

When she remembered Michael's face it was never from life but from newspaper photos, grainy wire-service shots of him at the front of a protest line or speaking to a crowd. Her only physical memory of him was of his hair, which she often remembered falling through her fingers like long-stemmed flowers.

"So . . . how are you?" he asked.

Nona didn't answer. Because of her love for him she had given up neutrality and become a political person. He had drawn her into an obsessive love that obliterated reason and irrevocably alienated her from an easy life.

"Barry Stein said he thought Congress might pardon all the antiwar people if Nixon gets impeached."

Michael laughed bitterly.

"I can't stand all those . . . flacks, Michael," Nona complained, thinking of the crowd of reporters at the Carol Arms. "I don't want to commute between . . . me and them."

Michael put on his sermon voice. "You're going to have to learn how to live with the contradictions, Nona. It's the only way you'll be able to make it."

"What do you care?"

"I care," he said gently.

"Well, Lazar already told me I can't cover the

44

testimony. He wants me to do local color stuff about the circus."

"What do you mean?"

"You know. I'm supposed to cover the carnival part of it." She put on a falsetto gossip-columnist voice. "The attractive UP photographer who wears a chain of camera straps over his Cardin sport jacket has been seen lunching with Senator Shmuck's secretary." She took a breath. "Lazar's a pig, Michael. I told you that a long time ago."

"Look, you're just going to have to cool it," Michael said.

"But I don't want to be in that world again. Those people mix me up. They turn me around." She thought of her infatuated encounter with Anthony Lewellen. "It's like before I met you, Michael. As soon as I get into that plastic world of theirs, I forget who I am and start wanting a piece of the action. I know it's going to happen again."

"Don't be silly, doodle," he laughed. "You understand that scene. You know how it works. Just do your number. If you write decent stuff Lazar will run it. Don't forget he has to fill in the spaces around the ads."

"Michael, I have to write what he tells me to write or he'll get someone else who will. He told me that."

Ever since September when the judge imposed sentence, Michael had been coaching Nona on how to live alone, trying to prepare her for when he went to jail. Every night after she ran through her litany of despair he would respond with a catechism of faith urging her to be brave, insisting that it was personally and politically correct for her to become a journalist again, assuring her that she could make it financially. But Nona had never absorbed any of his certitudes and had remained unreconciled to his imprisonment or her own life without him. When he skipped town without her all of his arguments had become irrelevant.

45

"I'm going to end up writing about who's sleeping with who," Nona repeated.

"Hey, Nona! If you have to write about the press, just show what groupies they are. Let 'em have it for all their copouts before they became big Watergate heroes. Just remember what they were really like for the last ten years. Forget the past six months. Don't let them get off so cheap. Just remember that weekend we called everyone to get them to look at the files. They were all scared shitless, and you know it. They're all a bunch of presidential groupies; and they'll all be back in their same old crease again a year from now. You should really blow them out of the water."

Nona felt her fingers curl up angrily inside the purse of her palm. "Well, if you're so fucking down on the media, how come you kept telling me they'd publish the files? You should have known they wouldn't. If you were so hip to their number, why did you bother ripping off the stuff in the first place? Those files just ended up being government exhibits against you. You wasted a whole year planning that number, and you got yourself a five-year sentence and ruined everything we had going—all because you were so sure some newspaper would print the stuff. And now you come around with this big new heavy-duty theory. Shee-it."

He always waited for her to blurt out the anger so he could cast about in the swamp of her emotions to help her find something positive to grasp.

"Look, just write what *you* want to write, Nona. Talk about the kind of press Nixon got off those guys before he got caught red-handed. It'll be all right, Nona. I know it will. But I'd better get off now. We've been on too long."

"Michael!"

"Yah?"

"Michael, please let me come with you. Please."

"I can't, Nona. I love you. Don't worry if you don't

46

hear from me for a while . . . it might even be more than a couple of weeks. I've got to hang up now, honey. I love you."

"You shouldn't have skipped, Michael," she said. "You should have gone to jail. Five years is better than forever."

He hung up.

"I love you, too," she said into the dead telephone. "I love you, Michael."

She lay back on the bed, waiting for the love to revert back into fury, waiting for the resentment that would smother the pain. After a while she got up and turned off the light, but she couldn't fall asleep.

She remembered the day Michael had telephoned Sam Kinkaid.

It had been an afternoon that grew dark so early that they had to turn on the overhead light in the living room. At irregular intervals a sudden rain would start up against the windows, tapping urgently for several minutes before stopping in a desultory, disheartening way. A damp chill filled the house leaving only islands of warmth around the tall rusted radiators. Bare tree branches scratched against the screens blotting out the sounds of traffic or children playing on Mintwood Place. Nona lay beside Michael on the couch, feeling his woolen shirt rub her face each time he drew a breath. Earlier she had moved inquisitively against him, but he had ignored her rummagings so that eventually she just lay still beside him, thinking. Her face was pressed against a patch of his chest where it fit as securely as an ear against a telephone receiver, and she could hear the hammer of his heart drumming out the rhythm of his life to which she unconsciously measured and matched her breathing.

"When are you going to start calling them?" she asked.

"Pretty soon." It was a grunting request for silence.

Nona closed her eyes and let the silence descend

again. The commune was relatively quiet. Sara had taken her baby back home for a visit to her mother's. Jeffrey was in the dining room typing an article, and Robb was puttering around upstairs. On Saturdays, when the paper was at the printer's, no one had specifically assigned work tasks but that day was special because Michael had hidden the files he stole from the Pennsylvania FBI office on the top shelf of the broom closet.

"What if no one will publish them?" Nona asked, despite her resolve not to disturb him again.

"Someone will. I've got to get them out there, Nona. It's important."

"None of those reporters would ever tell the cops . . . would they? Say that someone had offered them hot documents."

"No. A reporter's sources are privileged."

With her ear pasted to his chest she could hear his words start out from the secret source of his conviction and move up until they turned into warm implosions of air against her face.

"But you could still get busted even if the files never get printed. I mean, they could lock you up and throw away the key without anybody but you and me ever seeing them. And for me, you didn't have to bother."

"That's not quite true," Michael laughed gently, and ran his finger along her lashes, brushing them in the wrong direction so that her eyelids fluttered.

She slid her leg between his, tying them together. Through the long Victorian window she could see the familiar roofscape across the street, phony turrets, pointy towers, and false attics pasted on top of the skinny row of houses.

"O.K. Let's get up," he sighed. "I'll start calling."

They walked to the kitchen at the rear of the house. Other than the old-fashioned appliances, the huge drafty room held only a badly scarred table and mismatched chairs. Nona sat down with the list of journalists and Michael started dialing off the top, working his way down the list. Each time he made a connection he walked to the backdoor, trailing the long intravenous tube of telephone wire behind him so he could look out through the barred window as he spoke. Staring into the yard at the three garbage cans chained, top and bottom, to the ginkgo tree that dropped its vile bilious smelling pods to the ground soiling the air with their stench, he delivered his pitch over and over again to each of the reporters.

He was arrested—three days later—indicted, tried, convicted, and sentenced.

Three

When she awoke the next morning in her stuffy little bedroom, ravished by the insomnia that had thrashed about beside her during the night, she instantly felt the emptiness of the apartment envelop her. Deprived of company, Nona suffered a loss of equilibrium. A lush longing for Michael seeped through her system. Quickly she got out of bed to take a shower, hoping to counteract her mood by some external stimuli. But when she walked out into the studio, cozily wrapped in a huge bath towel, her self-conscious movements reminded her of an awkward astronaut swimming through space.

Habitually Nona initiated each day by filling the kettle and placing it primly on the stove. Then, gliding along the kitchen counter, she spread open the white flower of a Melita filter, measured some coffee, and gently watered it with the same motions she used for tending her plants. Only then did she open her front door, wary of the dangers of her hallway, to collect the *Washington Post* and *New York Times*.

Sitting at the table, allowing the bath towel to fall open when the strain of her breasts unloosed its knot, she read both accounts of the FBI wiretap stories. Below the banner announcing opening day of the hearings, the *Post* carried the FBI wiretap story. Sam Kinkaid's neat WASP face smiled brightly on the front page. The article stated that there was no knowledge of who had leaked the story about the

tap or who had signed the original order for surveillance of the eight journalists. The FBI had acknowledged that the taps began in 1971 and had
continued until the recent months. There were careful responses from more than half the victimized
journalists, but Sam Kinkaid's statement reeked of
indignation and threatened retaliation.

As far as Nona could remember, Michael hadn't
made contact with the other seven reporters, although, without her knowing it, he might have seen
them in person. Sam Kinkaid was still the only person
Nona knew for certain Michael had telephoned. Carefully she tore out the list of names to double-check
when Michael called the next time. Then she cleaned
the breakfast dishes and returned to the still steamy
bathroom to station herself in front of the mirror.

A believer in her own chameleonlike properties,
Nona applied make-up with the same patience she
applied to early drafts of any article she wrote. Stu-
diously she began revising her face, erasing errors
and obliterating flaws as if covering a typo with White-
Out. Carefully she reworked her image—minimizing
the width of her lips, underlining her eyes, and high-
lighting her skin—redrafting her identity until she
came up with a more conventional version of herself.

Back in her bedroom she thoughtfully edited an
outfit to wear—a tight-ribbed T-shirt, hip-high bell-
bottoms, and a wide Indian belt that looked literate
together and made a clear, confident statement that
the wearer was a winner. Then she reorganized her
purse, selected a notebook, and ran downstairs to
find a taxi, afraid she would be unable to find a
parking space on such a sensational day. Although
she was wearing sandals, Nona could almost hear
the tap of high-heeled shoes hitting on the uncovered
steps, a ratatattat of castanet cleats announcing the
arrival of a woman on the make.

Riding in the back seat of a Yellow cab, feeling
like the woman she had long ago been or thought of

becoming, Nona watched the traffic speeding down Massachusetts Avenue. The city seemed to have shifted on its axis, as if the focus of world attention on Capitol Hill had weighted Washington eastward, tilting it so that everything tipped up and away from the White House, which psychologically centered the city. Despite the anxiety she always experienced when she passed the clump of municipal buildings where Michael had stood trial in the federal courthouse on Fourth Street, she felt almost happy—aroused by expectation.

When the cab finally reached the Hill, Nona saw a large herd of Colortran TV vans corralled on a side street and a line of people, who had obviously camped outside all night, sitting on the curbs holding their sleeping bags and blanket rolls. A throng of tourists, strung ticket-line-fashion around the Senate building, were fighting to glimpse the superstars descending from government limousines, as if at a gala premiere.

Vainly trying to screen out the media carnival, Nona ran inside the building and upstairs to the Senate caucus room.

"May I see your identification, Miss?"

Nona presented her pass to the Senate guard.

UNITED STATES SENATE
AND HOUSE OF REPRESENTATIVES

ADMIT UNLESS OTHERWISE ORDERED
EXPIRES JANUARY 31, 1974

NONA LANDAU
METRO MAGAZINE

The man nodded. "O.K., go in," he said, opening one of the heavy oak doors.

Nona smiled, grateful that he hadn't hassled her, and walked inside the caucus chamber only to be

52

instantly overwhelmed by the falsity of the scene.

An enormous glimmering chandelier transformed the room into a Broadway theater lobby. Beyond the recessed alcove, scores of overwrought journalists were milling about in the narrow margins between the press tables. Nona stopped, stung by the flash of the scene and the frenzy that walloped against her.

Triumphant reporters, too revved up to take their seats, stood near the doors auditing each new arrival —checking out winners of the Watergate sweepstakes. Around the room, reunions took on the look of pre-game skirmishes, warming-up exercises composed of feigned jabs to the midriffs of fellow reporters and ambiguous hugs for the few women journalists who appeared.

Slowly Nona edged into the crowd and began walking along the tables, reading the names scribbled on the yellow sheets of copy paper Scotch taped in front of each chair. *Time* . . . *Newsweek* . . . three spaces for the *Washington Post* . . . the *New York Times*. . . .

Aware of an army of curious eyes tracking her progress, she hurried to find the *Metro* placard. It was at the foot of the last table beside the blanket-shrouded windows, trellised overhead by TV scaffolds and cluttered underneath by spools of electrical cables. Realizing she had been relegated to the worst location in the room, Nona dispatched a deprecating smile to a man seated behind a *London Times* sign across from her and slipped into her seat.

Most of the men seated around her were quietly leafing through various press releases, apparently saving their energy until a gavel signaled the start of their battle for news.

Behind Nona, at a table set horizontal to hers, was the New York contingent of seasoned social critics sparked by Mary McCarthy and Norman Mailer. Speaking smugly and exclusively to each other, they occasionally rose to greet some other insider whose briefcase still bore an Eastern Airlines' carry-on baggage tag.

Behind the out-of-town magazine journalists, sitting in a reserve-seating section, the Senate wives sat primly, while up against the rear wall rows of standing-room-only tourists, dressed in Day-Glow-colored spring cottons, wilted like fake flowers, weary from trying to identify celebrities.

Nona swirled around on the hard folding chair and looked up at the green head table where seven senatorial nameplates rose like pin flags on a golf course. There, administrative assistants hustled about distributing papers to empty chairs, as self-conscious as amateur actors unexpectedly exposed by a premature curtain.

Impatiently Nona reached out to pluck a press release from the shrinking pile of copies and began to skim the statement of Robert C. Odel, Jr., CREEP staff director, just as the noise in the room shifted in its course and changed directions. She looked up in time to see the Senate Committee members entering the chamber through a door behind the head table, most of them cloaking their excitement behind bored, bureaucratic faces. Instantly the press began to take their places, and there was a loud increase in commotion followed by quick diminution.

A few minutes later Sam Ervin cleared his throat, wound up his eyebrows, and unleashed his features so they went skittering around his face as he began to address the nation. From the corner of her eye Nona saw the men across from her lift their pens into battle positions. She opened her notebook.

"We are beginning these hearings today in an atmosphere of the utmost gravity. The questions that have been raised in the wake of the June 17 break-in strike the very undergirding of our democracy. . . ."

For Nona it was hard to handle Sam Ervin's lofty rhetoric since he had for so long led the anticivil

54

rights fight, but she tried to smother her cynicism so as not to upset the karma of the hearings.

". . . it is clear that the Committee will be dealing with the workings of the democratic process under which we operate a nation that still is the last, best hope of mankind in his eternal struggle to govern himself decently and effectively. . . ."

Nona felt her throat tighten as a rush of patriotism brought a blur of tears to her eyes. Looking around, she noticed that most of the reporters were carefully looking nowhere, adopting the evasive tactic used by moviegoers suddenly caught by bright lobby lights after a sad film and pretending not to see any witnesses to their weakness. The prestigious national press corps was busily pushing their emotions back into the cages of their self-composure.

"The founding fathers . . . knew that those who are entrusted with power are susceptible to the disease of tyrants. . . ."

Enough, old man, Nona begged, determined to tough it out. Just get on with it now. You should have blown the whistle a long time ago. You should never have let it go so far.

"This nation and history itself are watching us. We cannot fail our mission," Senator Ervin said.

Nona felt an enormous relief when Robert C. Odel was finally called forward as the first witness to testify. Then she uncapped her pen and riveted her attention on him.

"I joined the staff of the Committee for the Re-Election of the President more than two years ago because I believed in President Nixon and in his hopes and dreams for America. I still do."

It was a little before noon when Anthony Lewellen strode through the doorway ushered in by a guard whose deference trumpeted the arrival of a recognizable member of the Washington establishment. Just past the vestibule, Lewellen stopped to lean casually against the wall immediately grabbing the spot light with the lazy signature of his style.

He was wearing a tan summer-weight suit, expensively tailored but sufficiently rumpled to give him the reckless look of a foreign correspondent suffering jet lag. His left hand, jammed deep inside the pants pocket, pulled his jacket open, exposing his lean torso and hiking up the collar so that it creased his longish hair when he shifted to look upstage.

Not quickly enough Nona turned toward the head table to see which of the senators acknowledged the columnist who controlled a major share of the nation's public opinion. The owlish Mr. Odel was still droning on, offering a fulsome explanation of his innocence with the piety of a high school valedictorian delivering a prize-winning "I speak for Democracy" speech. Nona looked back toward Lewellen.

But this time he was waiting for her.

His faded blue eyes, embroidered by the stitching of past smiles, dug into her face.

I've come for you, he was saying. I've come to get you. I want to finish what we started.

Nona reeled beneath the impact of his silent presumptuous offer of himself. Unable to break the bondage of his stare, Nona threw him a flash-fire smile.

But Anthony Lewellen was determined.

This is it, he repeated silently. We're going to get it on now. I want you.

Then, with stunning showmanship, he produced a lavish smile that pleated his leathery features.

Weakened by months of unrelenting deprivation, Nona felt herself succumb, overwhelmed by Lewellen's insistence and her own monumental loneliness. Nervously she lowered her eyes back to her notebook, hoping to restore her self-control through the discipline of transcribing Robert Odel's testimony, but a moment later Senator Ervin suddenly rapped his gavel to make the ominous announcement that the Watergate hearings were adjourning for lunch.

Nona felt the scene splinter into motion, shattering into bits and pieces of sound and movement. Quickly she stood up and stepped into the aisle, intending to hide herself among the raucous crowd of speeding reporters.

But then she saw Lewellen only a few feet away, bucking the crowd to reach her, coming to claim her in full view of his colleagues.

Nona's heart hurried.

"Hi," she said, breasting her purse and studying a button midway down his iridescently white shirt.

"Howya doing?" he asked softly. His eyes narrowed with affection, deepening the battlefield trenches of his face. "I've come to take you out for lunch."

And with that Nona realized she was virtually defenseless against any act of kindness, completely susceptible to even a fraudulent offer of affection. Desertion had toughened her to deal with hostility but had left her unfit to stave off any overture of friendship. Lewellen walking over to fetch her, quietly and matter-of-factly deciding to claim custody of her, was too much to resist and she experienced the relief of a refugee being offered sanctuary after a long arduous exile.

"Looks like they're going to put on a pretty good summer show, doesn't it?" he asked.

She could tell he was trying to jolly her up, hustle her into shape so they wouldn't become a spectacle standing together amid the frenzied reporters exploding down the aisle. But she was paralyzed by the sheer sudden pleasure of being subsumed by a man again.

"Let's go," he mumbled. His voice sounded tremulous, a sponge that had absorbed his other feelings. Automatically he kept acknowledging greetings from various reporters bustling past them while continuing to encourage Nona to move on.

"Ready?" he whispered.

So very slowly Nona began to walk. Straightening her back and raising her head she silently sold out abstinence and independence for a piece of Anthony Lewellen.

If he touches me, she thought, if he puts his hand on my shoulder or on my back, I will start to cry. Right here in front of NBC and CBS I'll break down and make a public spectacle of myself.

But he was too tactical to touch her. Even though he was willing to put himself on the line in front of the major network cameras, he was cajoling her into motion without any body contact, propelling her forward by the sheer weight of his will and the amiable authority of his sexual determination.

Outside in the brightly lit corridor technical personnel and news-staff people were shouldering each other as they fought to nab the movers and shakers streaming out of the caucus room.

"Mr. Lewellen!" A young man emerged from the crowd to block their path. "Could you speak with Mr. Cronkite for a minute or two? Just a few quickie comments about the opening?"

"Sorry, I'm tied up right now." Tony smiled, pushing Nona ahead of him through the crush of tourists surrounding the TV correspondents.

"Who can Walter ever find to replace you?" Nona asked teasingly over her shoulder.

"Don't worry about it," Lewellen answered.

But suddenly Nona experienced a flashback of the courtroom fatigue she had felt during Michael's trial. A residual exhaustion began edging through her body draining away her strength. The noise in the hall seemed inordinately shrill as the reporters rushed past, shouting out their hypothetical leads.

Tony began to guide Nona down the steep cliff of marble stairs, leading her past the rotunda, where passive tourists were pinned back behind a silk rope, and on down to the basement. There, in the wide empty corridor, he gripped her elbow for the first time.

Months of celibacy had so sensitized Nona that Tony's touch made her feel a spill of desire.

"What did you think of Odell?" she asked, trying to ignore the carnal shivers sliding through her body.

"Not too much," he drawled, moving his hand higher up on her arm so his knuckles grated her breast. "Except that he has a lot of chutzpa."

Nona looked up, surprised to hear Yiddish slang strangulated by a ruling-class accent. She could feel his nearness glamorize her and unconsciously she moved in closer to him so that her shoulder touched against his forearm as they walked past the robot rooms where automatic machines were typing letters to congressional constituents and pens, extended from crooked metallic arms, descended at rhythmic intervals to forge senatorial signatures.

Outside the building an unseasonably early heat folded around them, zipping them inside a sleeping bag of humidity. Instinctively trying to look inconspicuous, they walked quickly through the white-on-white sunlight past the Carol Arms and around the corner to the Monocle. Inside the restaurant they were momentarily blinded by the dimness, and Nona stood motionless at the edge of the black abyss, hearing the smart chatter of china and voices as Lewellen slid his hand over her shoulder and pressed himself flush against her back. After a few seconds she felt the soft dough of his sex starting to stir beneath his clothing. Mesmerized by the unfamiliar flesh, Nona remained perfectly still, vicariously experiencing his surge of urgency. Physical promise pulsated between them until a disembodied voice shattered the darkness.

"Hello, Mr. Lewellen. Will it be just for two?"

"Yes," Tony said. But his voice snagged on the ragged edge of his own excitement and he cleared his throat in an effort to sweep away any congestion of emotion.

Again Nona began a curious, self-conscious walk. But now, umbrellaed by the canopy of desire Anthony Lewellen cast over her and advanced by a fawning maître d', she realized she was being primed for the put-on of an expense-account seduction, set up for a touchless fuck across a cluttered, crumb-strewn table. She was being paraded down the center aisle past an audience of diners as the dessert that came with the meal.

The maître 'd seated them at a corner table, presented them with menus, and departed with an overdose of discretion. Contentedly Tony settled back in his leather chair, stretching out so that his shirt creased across his chest.

"Now then, let me make one thing perfectly clear," Tony said with an infinitely slow, relaxed smile. "I am into this caper for highly immoral purposes. I am not now, and have never been, an altruist. I did talk to Sam last night, and he said he'd be willing to see you some time in the next few days. But my role as middleman between you and him is only a cover story. You want Sam, and I want you." Tony's eyes patroled her face as he spoke. "The truth of the matter is that I'm only after your ass."

"Thank you for arranging things," Nona said, ignoring his blatancy and wondering whether Lewellen's discomfort steemed from political or personal shyness.

The waiter appeared. Tony ordered drinks. Then he lit two cigarettes and passed one to Nona.

"Jack Lieutenant came back again after you'd left and asked me to apologize for his performance last night. It sounded like you got caught in his Bella Abzug backlash. He doesn't like political women, and he doesn't have any kids, so he takes the New Left much more seriously than I do. I have a son not too much younger than you, so I think I know where you're coming from."

His mention of a son was intended as a show of good faith, an open admission of his age and his marriage, but Nona felt an explosion of anger rip through her.

"I'm almost thirty-four," she responded coldly. "So I rather doubt that you have the slightest idea where I'm coming from."

"Jesus Christ!" Lewellen's face went slack from surprise. Finally, he sighed. "Well, I guess Marxism must be good for the skin or something. You look like you're around twenty-five . . . twenty-seven maybe." Then needing a moment to recover and reassess his approach he said, "Well? Is there anything you want to know about me?"

Nona laughed. "Not any more than I already do. I mean, I know you're married and have a bunch of kids. And since I read your columns, I'm quite familiar with your politics. That's about all I can handle at the moment."

The S-curved smile lines carved into the valleys between his nose and mouth deepened defensively. "So, I'm just permanently a shmuck, is that it?" he asked. "Just an effete Eastern establishment snob?"

"No . . ." Nona protested lamely.

"Come on," Tony persisted. "Admit it. You just don't like liberals, do you?"

"Well, I might be a little bit prejudiced," she conceded. "But last night really blew me away—seeing you guys getting so exercised about those eight wiretaps. Everybody I know's been tapped and tailed and hassled and harassed for the past ten years, and nobody ever gave a damn."

"That's not true," Lewellen protested.

"Yes, it is. When we use to call the newspapers to tell them what the government was doing to us, no one would believe it. They thought we were paranoid nuts or something. But as soon as Nixon played his dirty tricks on you people, on the Democratic National Committee, or on some of your journalist buddies, then you believed it and got pissed off. But you never cared when it happened to us, because in this town if you're to the left of the Democratic party, the press doesn't give a damn about what happens to you. It's only when Sam Kinkaid gets stung that the shit hits the fan." The hammer of anger pounding inside her head pummeled her onward, pushing away every practical instinct trying to silence the flow of her words. "And now you're all going to act like these buggings and burglaries just started with Nixon. You're all going to pretend he was the first prez to hit up corporations for political contributions or to sell ambassadorships or fix cases in the Justice Department. You still don't want to believe that Kennedy and Johnson did it too. You guys have been on such power trips you never saw what was really happening."

Tony stared at her for a long moment, his face loose instead of arranged into one of his carefully composed expressions. When the waiter delivered their drinks, Lewellen drained half his glass before responding.

"O.K. Now you listen to me," he said in a quiet determined voice. "I've been around Washington for twenty years, and one of the first things I found out was that people's politics usually relate to their psychological problems. To be perfectly honest, I think this whole political shtik of yours is just a cover story because you're afraid to play in the real ball game. You're on this radical trip because you don't know how you fit into the big picture. And you're laying it on me because you're afraid you might like making it with me if you ever tried."

He lit another cigarette, crunching up his face to avoid the smoke.

"The fucking truth is that we don't know a goddamn thing about each other. Now you didn't catch me writing you off as Mike Daniels's old lady or some Maoist crazy or anything like that when we met, did you? I respected you as an individual, and I took you seriously."

Nona didn't answer.

"But right away you had to pin a label on me and start predicting my behavior, right? Whether you had any facts or not. Well, it just so happens that I'm not one of your basic everyday Georgetown gentlemen journalists, as you call them." He was watching her sternly, demanding she pay attention. "It just so happens that I'm a closet maverick, so I don't fit into any of your canned categories. The truth is that I'm from a family that's so fucking rich I never had to work a day in my life. I didn't have to bust my ass newspapering all these years or doing two years' time in Vietnam. I had it made, lady, and I did everything I did because *I wanted to.* I went to the Columbia Jay School because *I wanted to,* and I joined the army because *I wanted to.* That was dubblya-dubblya two," he added considerately. "And I worked with ERP—that was the European Recovery Program—after the war because . . ."

"Don't tell me you were CIA *too,*" Nona gasped.

"No, I won't. Because I wasn't."

They stared at each other suspiciously for several moments before Lewellen slammed his glass down on the table.

"Godamnit! Don't you lay that goddamn rhetoric on me. I don't like it. Now, do you want to eat or do you want to split?"

Do you want to talk or do you want to hang up? Talk, she had said.

"Eat," Nona answered.

"O.K. Then relax for Chrissake. Nobody's keeping score on whether or not you enjoy yourself. I promise I won't squeal on you after the revolution."

"You won't be able to."

He laughed so infectiously that Nona smiled.

"You know something? You have a smashing smile. It's really very classy. It's sort of like a nice slow fuck. You should do it more often."

Slowly, Nona smiled at him again.

Then he leaned back in his chair and punched out a tough-guy expression.

"All right. Now tell me why you quit writing articles. Last night it occurred to me that you just might be one of those pseudoliberated ladies who's scared of success. Because right when you were getting good you just upped and quit, and it very well might have been so you wouldn't have to cope with being successful."

"Oh, Christ," Nona moaned. "The man I lived with for five years jumped a hundred thousand dollars bail and you tell me I quit writing because I was getting too *successful!*" She felt a scorching sensation behind her eyes. "For a big-time political analyst you're pretty fucking dumb."

"Hey, I'm sorry," Tony said softly and helplessly. "I wasn't thinking about that. Look at me, Nona. I'm sorry, I really am. I was just trying to make some small talk."

She turned away to scan the room, skipping past the reporter types to study some of the well-kept Capitol Hill assistants, the congressional staffers who controlled most of the legislative action. There were only a few women in the room, and she could pigeonhole them easily: several wives, a couple of secretaries, and some older GS-14 types, probably congressional liaison personnel from some federal agencies lobbying for the day. She continued canvassing the crowd while waiting for the tears that were forming to evaporate.

"Do you want to tell me about it?" Tony asked. "What it's been like for you?"

The last raggedy remnant of Nona's pride resurrected itself, and she sipped her drink, stalling for time to work up some acceptable version of herself.

"Well, let's see," she said lightly, tapping a fresh cigarette on the table. "Michael left on New Year's Day, and our commune broke up a few weeks later because we couldn't make the rent and because . . . well . . . most of my friends decided they wanted to move to the country."

"Some friends," Tony said wryly, lighting the cigarette she held forgotten between her fingers.

For a moment Nona wanted to defend her people who had been soul-sick and weary when they fled, convinced that Nixon's landslide victory would mean a fresh assault of repression making Washington an impossible place to live. But it was all too complicated to explain to a stranger—how the ties that had held them together for so many years had come apart after Nixon's reelection and how the Christmas bombing of Hanoi and Haiphong had finally broken their spirit.

"So I had to find an apartment," she said evasively, "and I moved in the middle of January and that took a lot of time." Reluctantly she remembered the day she had carted most of the furniture out of the Mintwood Place commune, all the rejected objects from other defunct communes and Movement offices with which they had always furnished their lives. "And I had to fix up the place, build some shelves, and put up a medicine cabinet. You know, stuff like that."

He looked at her incredulously. "You mean you've been decorating your apartment since January? You sound like one of those Georgetown ladies with whom I presumably consort."

"Well . . ." Nona smiled shyly, embarrassed by her fake flippancy. "Actually, I took off some time to do some thinking."

"So?" Lewellen prodded, buttering a roll and breaking off half to put in her hand. "What did you think about?"

"Nothing in particular," Nona said lamely, looking

at the piece of bread she held. "I was just sort of . . . waiting."

"For Daniels to come back?"

"No." She shook her head, unsure of the truth. Because never during those long lonely months had she ever known what she was waiting for, although she didn't think it was a man—not Michael or any previous or future lover. In actuality, she had only thought of herself during those long winter days and nights when she lay in bed, seldom bothering to change her clothes as she waited for deliverance in some unknown nonhuman form.

"I guess, maybe, I was waiting for . . . Watergate to break," she concluded and that sounded true when she said it aloud. For it wasn't until late in March when the dirty frosting of winter began to melt off the rooftops of neighboring buildings and debris began floating past her windows in gusts of sprightly spring air that the morning newspapers broke through her numbness with their screaming accusations of crimes and cover-ups. The momentum of the press closing in on Nixon had made her feel alive once more, eager to follow the irreversible logic of the accumulating evidence. Each new exposure jangled her awake until she had finally felt restlessness gunning her body, like a hot rod revving up for a race.

"Actually, if the *Post* hadn't cracked the Watergate story, I'd probably still be sitting at home. I was beginning to think that the world was sane and *I* was crazy." But the daily headlines had assured her she hadn't been crazy after all, that the Movement had been correct in its analysis and that Michael had been right about the perilous political state of the nation. The fact that others now accepted truths that jibed with her own angry sense of reality liberated her so that she no longer felt totally out of sync with the rest of the world.

Unthinkingly, Nona had finished her drink. Instantly Tony signaled the waiter for another round.

66

"What do you feel like eating?" he asked, opening a menu. "Would you share some quiche with me for an opener?"

Nona sighed and nodded. His smoothness was so instinctive and impartial that it tired her.

"And how about a salad, too? I'm starving," he claimed. But he was making love to her over the top of the menu, inhaling her with his eyes, substituting solicitude for sex.

Nona nodded and looked away when the waiter came to take their order. Lewellen's overdramatization embarrassed her, and she used that fact to resist him and to stop herself from being submerged by his flashy style.

"So?" Tony prompted, coming onto her perfectly now. "Did you call Lazar and ask to cover the hearings or did he call you?"

The fact that Tony understood her writing was contingent upon her psychological condition caressed Nona into temporary submission.

"I called Jay," she said, trying to hide how deeply his question touched her.

"What took you so long?"

"I don't like him," she answered. "He reminds me too much of a cartoon-strip capitalist."

"Say," Tony interrupted as the salad was placed before him, "speaking of capitalists, I got your article about the multination corporations out of the library. Very classy. I never knew those companies actually coordinated their congressional lobbies like that. You did a good research job."

"You took it out?"

"Sure," he said, beginning to hunt bits of blue cheese among the vegetables in his salad bowl. "I took out all your stuff to read. You were really getting good when you quit."

She looked up, overwhelmed. Pride discharged a rush of pleasure. She was amazed that he had gone to the library to read her, and wanted desperately to

67

know which of her other articles he had liked, but she didn't ask because she was afraid that his praise would turn out to be a ploy, a patronizing pretense that he considered her work as important as her being a good fuck. Essentially it could be a far-fetched joke similar to an adult asking a child which cocktail she'd prefer before dinner, a patently absurd equating of unequal objects.

The waiter delivered their meals.

Nona stared down at her plate feeling too tired to deal with the food. Fatigue began to flood her again and eventually she gave up trying to eat and just watched Anthony Lewellen enjoy his meal, alternating bites of quiche with salad and wine.

"You know what you look like?" he asked.

"What?"

"Like you just got laid. Don't get sore. That's a compliment. That's a very good way to look. And you know what else?"

"What?"

"Everything's all settled . . . I'm going to fix up that meeting for you with Sam, and I'm going to try to take care of you a little."

"I don't need a manager," Nona said coolly.

"How about a lover?"

She drank some wine to defray desire. The temptation to refuel herself on privilege and pleasure by getting next to someone like Tony Lewellen was almost irresistible. Off him Nona could glom some effortless access into the scene. With him, she could avoid scrambling along the sidelines of the Watergate story, inching along the margin of events or inserting herself like a scribbled afterthought between the lines of action. Linking up with Lewellen meant automatic inclusion in the elitist inner circle.

"What about your family?" she asked with a sudden swell of sarcasm.

"They're going up to Martha's Vineyard for the summer."

"That's nice."

"You mean that's convenient, don't you?" He looked down at his hands cupped on the table. "Well, you don't have to be Jewish to be lonely," he said. "Even with wall-to-wall kids and a pair of matching Airedales, a guy can get lonesome."

Nona tried to suppress a smile.

"Even way up here in the one-percent tax bracket." He signaled the waiter to bring the check. "And who knows? Maybe I can help you stop chainsmoking."

"Please, don't try to organize me," she said.

"What organize? Don't tell me you're an anarchist, too, for Chrissake?"

Nona shook her head, knowing that her shaky emotional truce with herself could never survive a flesh encounter with such a flashy lover.

"Also I happen to have visiting privileges in one of the best nookie rooms up on the top floor of the Capitol building. I bet you've never used one of those rooms, have you?"

Nona stared at him.

"Don't tell me you're part of the unwashed electorate who think the Senators use those rooms for caucusing?"

Nona smiled disbelievingly.

"So . . . let's see . . . well, things are going to be a little bit tight for a while. I don't think school lets out until the first week of June. But traditionally my wife departs at dawn the very next day. . . ."

"I don't want to hear about it," Nona said putting her hands over her ears. "I don't want to know any of the details."

The waiter appeared to return Lewellen's credit card. Tony found a pen and flipped over his American Express receipt. "O.K.! Your number, please?"

She told him.

Then he looked at his watch. "I have to get going. I've got an appointment."

Outside on the street he plucked a pair of sunglasses from his jacket pocket and put them on.

"Now, that's what I would call a very successful lunch." He smiled down at her. "As they say on the Hill, I'll get back to you as soon as I can."

"Aren't you going back to the hearings?"

"No. I've got to be downtown."

The panic that recently accompanied all separations shook Nona's voice.

"Well . . ." she shrugged, "thanks for lunch."

He reached out to stroke the top of her head, snaring several loose strands of hair to twist with a crescent curve of his fingers back behind her ears where they belonged. For a moment he seemed ready to say something else, but then he turned abruptly and walked away. Since she remained standing in front of the Monocle for several more minutes, Nona knew that he didn't look back.

Four

Wearing a bathing suit under a loose Mexican dress, with her gear in a canvas bag slung over her shoulders, Nona came out of the dark tunnel of her hallway into the street. The Spanish ladies, tucked inside tight navy-serge skirts and black cardigan sweaters, were already crowding the sidewalk, filling their nylon shopping bags with groceries. Nona walked quickly up toward Nineteenth where Columbia Road turned into the svelt curve of Connecticut Avenue and where the mammoth white fortress of the imperial Hilton Hotel imperviously turned its back on the neighborhood huddled behind it.

Nona had never been inside the hotel before and for years she and Michael had made resentful jokes about the striped beach umbrellas visible above the cement retaining walls. But having waited a week for Lewellen's telephone call, she had greedily accepted his invitation for a Saturday afternoon swim at the Hilton with him and Sam Kinkaid and had spent much time preparing to lobby on Michael's behalf.

She entered the hotel through a Florida Avenue entrance and, feeling slightly criminal, hurried into the first powder room she saw to exchange her dress for a beach shirt she had brought along. Despite the fact she was invited through unknown but legitimate auspices, her clandestine change of clothing recalled various Movement capers when she had penetrated some posh hotel to clean her feet or shampoo her hair in a wash basin or make off with a reserve roll of toilet paper or a purseload of Kleenex for use back at some demonstration campsite.

Anticipating a house detective to ask for proof she was a registered guest, Nona hurried out to the terrace where she took off her shirt and used her enviable figure as a passport into the leisure scene. Experienced at trespassing, she swept past the lifeguard station and then strolled slowly along the swimming pool, snobbily inspecting the sunbathers laid out like corpses on the chaise lounges.

"Hi, Nona! Over here."

Nona clutched at the sight of Cindy Reynolds in a Barbie-doll-sized polka-dot bikini, waving to attract her attention, but she continued walking casually toward the circle of lounge chairs Cindy had reserved with a clutter of personal possessions.

"Tony had to go inside to make a telephone call. He'll be right back," Cindy said reassuringly, while assessing Nona's figure, measuring hips and weighing breasts with her baby-blue eyes.

"I didn't know you'd be here," Nona smiled. "Are you staying at the hotel?"

"Oh, no. But Bob—Senator Dempsey—belongs to the tennis club so he invites us over to swim on Saturdays." Cindy selected each word carefully as if choosing slightly melted chocolates from a boxed assortment. "Didn't the lifeguard ask whose guest you were? He's supposed to," she said, nodding toward the courts behind the pool. "Bob's playing tennis. Isn't it hot for May?"

"Really!" Nona agreed inanely.

"You'd better put on some oil," Cindy advised.

The little scullcaps of Cindy's bikini top nodded emptily on her chest as she reached out to hand Nona a bottle of suntan lotion, stretching her navel into a comma between the parenthetical curves of her hips. "Did you read Sally Quinn's article about the opening day of the hearings?" she asked.

"Yes," Nona answered, obediently beginning to grease the skin not covered by her tank suit.

"Leslie Stahl's covering it for CBS," Cindy said.

"Yes, I saw her there." Nona recapped the plastic bottle and set it down on the ground.

"She's really going to get off on this assignment," Cindy predicted, reaching out to reclaim the bottle and replace it in the bag from which she then excavated a vinyl-covered traveling mirror. "Actually, I think she's moving up faster than Cassy Mackin now." Cindy opened the mirror as if it were a book and studied her reflection. "The moral of Watergate is that you damn well better be out front all the time or you won't be ready for big opportunities like this one." She began combing her hair, splintering the ale-colored locks into sections and holding the long strands at arm's length above her head, to backcomb them. "I mean, people are really freaking now. You know Eastern had to put a bunch of extra sections on the shuttle to haul all the fancy ass down here. None of the BPs would dare miss a big do like this, and I heard that Barbara Walters is going to originate a whole week's worth of shows out of Washington this summer. For once the weather isn't going to scare anybody away." Cindy produced a bitter laugh as she lifted a shiny layer of unteased hair over the thicket of snarls. "Even the ladies who usually go to the beach every summer are afraid to miss the action this year." Suddenly, she buried her comb and mirror back in her purse and aimed a sequined smile past Nona. Bob Dempsey, the Lincolnesque senator from Arizona, dressed in tennis whites was approaching.

"You look hot, Bob," Cindy crooned. "Did you win? Can I introduce you to Nona Landau?"

"How do you do," Dempsey said. He bent down to take Nona's hand and held it firmly as he checked out the quality of character in her eyes. Then, seem-

73

ingly satisfied, he let a soft smile cross his thin tanned face. "I've heard a lot about you."

It was the same hesitant, halting voice Nona had heard live and recorded throughout the sixties when Dempsey broke Democratic ranks to support the antiwar effort.

"Did Tony tell you the whole story?" Cindy asked.

"I don't know any stories," Bob Dempsey drawled, sitting down in a chair and looking at Nona approvingly. "I just know about the work Nona Landau has done."

Nona felt an involuntary little-girl rush of panic and pleasure that occurred whenever some awesome adult condescended to recognize her. But when she looked back shyly at the senator his smile had begun to flicker, and she saw a fierce facial tic trace its way beneath his features. Silently Nona protested his affliction as she watched the contorted grimaces furl his face.

The senator looked up at the sky. "I'd say it's getting to be about that time," he said solemnly. "We can start drinking as soon as the sun is directly overhead."

Suddenly Tony was standing high above Nona, blocking the sun and smiling down at her with excitement, almost unable to coordinate a greeting because of his intense pleasure at seeing her.

And looking up at him, Nona felt a tumultuous motion start up inside her chest and cast giddy reverberations throughout her body. Their bodies were communicating in the silent language of animals alternately exchanging yearnings and urgings.

"What would you say," Lewellen asked, very quietly, as his mouth slid into a careless smile, "if I told you that there is a very important message waiting for you in a room I just rented?"

"I'd ask why you rented a room."

"I took a room," he answered softly, "so you could change your clothes before we went out for dinner."

74

"A cabana!" Nona exclaimed, sitting up. "How cute!"

"We're going to grab some lunch in the dining room," Tony announced to the others with super nonchalance.

Very casually, Nona picked up her possessions and followed him back into the hotel.

But once inside the cage of an elevator, she began to feel uncomfortable about the stark speed of her sexual consent. Embarrassed, she began casting about for some way to camouflage her capitulation, seeking an alternative impression to counteract the rawness of the scene and to procure a temporary suspension of personal accountability.

"You know I never told you exactly what I'm writing for *Metro*," she said teasingly while concentrating on the control-board panel as if her attention assured an additional safety factor. "One of the stories Lazar wants me to do is about the press people covering the hearings. A real inside thing about their lifestyles. You know, how they work and . . . play."

Lewellen looked down at Nona with a quizzical expression.

Four turned red. Then five.

"So what?" he asked.

"Well, I just thought I should tell you that."

Six. Seven.

"So, you can kid yourself that you're going upstairs with me for some ulterior motive? For some business reason? You want me to think you're getting into this so I'll put you in touch with the big enchiladas?"

"Well," Nona shrugged. "I thought you might think that."

Eight. Nine.

"You mean you wanted me to think that. You just ran that up the flagpole as a convenient little alibi, didn't you?"

Nona watched the mounting numbers flush.

Ten. Eleven.

"Well, to tell the truth, I'm a little disappointed in you," Tony said coldly. "I thought you were part of the new generation who can screw when they want to without making any excuses."

The elevator opened, and Lewellen stalked out into the hallway.

"And here you are pulling a very tired old number on me, a psychological con that's no better than pretending to be drunk."

Humiliated, Nona followed him down a corridor of closed doors, an endless series of cells that shut people in and out and apart from each other. The Hilton personified her worst phobias. It was a divisive, derisive, spacial insult that separated people and activated Nona's fears of being cut off and isolated.

Lewellen unlocked one of the rooms and motioned her inside. A small suitcase set beside the bed indicated he'd been there before, but he began prowling around the room, a worried expression scribbled across his face, as he opened the closet and bathroom doors.

Nona positioned herself in front of the bureau and looked at her slightly sun-flushed face in the mirror. Now she was desperate to choreograph the scene, to create some positive and concrete impression that she could later retrieve in the aftermath of their experience.

"Do you," she began impulsively, "happen to have any . . . rubbers on you?"

He had been looking out the window, and he paused a moment before turning toward her and shrugging his shoulders in a loose, negative twist. "On me?" he repeated. "Or do you mean on IT?"

"Well, that would be asking too much," Nona laughed. "Even SAC only keeps a third of its forces airborne all the time. No. I mean do you have any *with* you?"

"Jesus," he said apologetically. "No. I don't." He looked as if he had just yanked a tight sweater over his head, rumpling his face into a messy expression. "But I could probably get some. There's a drugstore down in the lobby."

"Well, you don't have to bother," Nona said briskly. "I have some." She reached into her canvas bag, excavated three Trojans from the cosmetic section, and tossed them onto the dresser as if she were producing a reserve pack of cigarettes late at night when the regular supplies had run out. Then she watched Lewellen struggling to deal with the fact that she carried male contraceptives in her purse.

"Well," he finally said, moving up behind her so that his body framed hers in the mirror, "that's convenient."

"It's more than convenient. It's, as they say, essential." She laughed, satisfied she had rebalanced the scales of their incipient relationship after the unexpected advantage he had chalked up in the elevator.

"Actually, this is a first for me," he said, cupping his fingers over her shoulders. "I hadn't heard that women had started carrying condoms around with them. Where do you buy them? Gas stations?"

Then suddenly understanding what was pitifully small and nasty about his character, Nona turned, hitched her purse over her shoulder, and started toward the door.

He grabbed her from behind with hard hands, his fingers biting into her forearms. "You're not going anywhere," he said more out of pique than passion.

Nona began to struggle, but he was as impervious to her thrashing as to her feelings.

"Come on," he yelled, pinning her arms above her head. "What kind of a hype is this anyhow?"

"Screw you," Nona screamed, trying to pull away as hot tears of rage splashed down her face. "Let go of me. You have to put down everything you don't understand, don't you?"

77

His fingers burned her shoulders. "I was teasing you for Chrissake, Nona! Why should I give a damn if you bring the equipment? That would be pretty stupid of me, wouldn't it? If I really thought there was anything wrong with it, I would have kept my mouth shut."

Very slowly he released his grip on her and she leaned back against the wall.

"Well, I'll tell you why I brought them," she said very slowly. "Because men like you just expect every woman they meet to be on the pill. You expect that little courtesy, don't you? You thought it wouldn't have to be mentioned, that I would just take care of that little problem so you wouldn't have to hear about it, didn't you?" Her breath began clotting in her throat as an unexpected landslide of self-pity turned her fury into sobs.

"Oh, come on," Tony groaned, pressing her head against his chest to quiet her. "Don't cry. I was wrong. I'm sorry." He began to rock back and forth in a nervous effort to soothe both of them. "Forget it now. It doesn't matter. Come on, let's go have a drink."

"I don't want a drink." Sickened by the cultural gap between Lewellen's amorous style and her own, she returned to the bureau and lit a cigarette, seeing her overwrought reflection in the glass. "See, guys like you can strip and ball fast enough, but you can't talk about it. You don't want to hear about any of the nitty-gritty stuff, do you?"

"Look," Tony said penitently, appearing in the mirror behind her. "It just seemed a little far out to me —you producing rubbers like that. Jesus, three little Trojans. I didn't know if that was supposed to be the minimum or the maximum—if you were giving me my druthers or my orders, and it just so happens I was feeling a little uptight at that moment anyway." He busied himself lighting a cigarette. "You know what I was thinking right then?"

78

"No. And I don't care."

"Now you just shut up for a minute and listen to me," he said roughly. "I mean there I was, pacing around feeling like a shmuck because I had this incredibly gorgeous sexy woman up in a hotel room and I didn't know what to do. That's the God's truth, Nona. I was thinking what the hell am I supposed to do now? What do all these fantastic feminists expect in the sack nowadays? In fact," he smiled, "I was trying to remember if I'd read anything about some new etiquette that says men should just ask—right off the top—what the lady would like to have done, you know? Because, Jesus, I've been out of circulation for so long there might be a whole new way of doing it, some incredible transcendental meditation position or something. For all I know, you people maybe like doing it hanging upside down off a mimeograph machine."

"You just can't talk about contraceptives, can you?" Nona repeated stubbornly.

"What's to talk? You're right. I'm not interested in Public Health or the Delivery of Prophylactic Services."

"I'm not talking about any HEW policy," Nona said. "I'm talking about me."

"For Christ's sake, he groaned, "I don't need a speed course in female anatomy or modern methods of population control."

But looking back at him through the mirror, Nona felt a hard sense of resolution.

"I can't use any of the 'her' products," she said in a matter-of-fact tone she might have used to give some hospital intern her medical history. "I have to use the 'his' brands because the pill gives me pigmentation spots on my forehead and the intrauterine coil makes me bleed like a pig. That happens to a lot of women who haven't had children."

"Oh, come on," he groaned impatiently.

"And I can't use a diaphragm," she continued,

79

too wound up to stop, "because I can't find the damn cartilage it's supposed to cover that all the Ob/Gyns say feels exactly like the tip of a nose."

"Stop it," Tony said hoarsely, splaying his fingers through his hair.

"And in case you think it's a psychological hang-up that's stopping me from feeling that cartilage—you're right. It is. And I know where it came from—the fact that seven male interns watched me being examined and fitted for a diaphragm at the Student Health Service because I was a nonpaying gynecological patient."

"Oh, shee-it."

Nona looked at the stranger standing behind her in the mirror and felt a sharp stab of futility at the impossibility of explaining herself to him. In the midst of an amorous afternoon adventure, there was no time or space for honesty. To Lewellen, Nona's body was a foreign object of potential pleasure for which he assumed no responsibilities. The anatomical properties, which she had once shared with Michael as a matter of mutual concern similar to the Movement and the commune and the delicate stereo system they had built and treasured because it afforded them equal pleasure, had become her own personal property again. Her barren womb had inadvertently reverted back to private ownership once more so that the maintenance and repair and servicing of her invisible internal organs would have to be hidden for the sake of propriety. All of the gross inequities of sexual intimacy with a stranger suddenly revealed themselves to her.

Nona put out her cigarette, took a deep breath, and turned around to confront her first sexual partner since Michael had left.

"Well," she said with a phony little chuckle, "I really do think condoms are sexier than any of the female equipment. At least you can see them. They're not just tucked away in some dark corner or swal-

80

lowed down like an aspirin with absolutely no erotic properties whatsoever."

Lewellen laughed, surprised and pleased by the unexpected restoration of her humor, but he kept his distance, afraid to interrupt her recovery.

"And actually I like rolling them on," Nona said as she removed her blouse and slipped the straps of her bathing suit off her shoulders rolling the soft Quiana tank suit down the length of her body so she could step out of it. "I mean unrolling them." Then she walked to the bed, pulled back the spread, and lay down, crushing the cool uncrumpled pillow so that it caved in and curved about her head.

Tony followed her and sat down on the edge of the mattress, wedging his buttocks into the space where her body curved.

Nona looked up at him, gallantly determined to obscure any obscenity by embroidering bits of humor onto the rough fabric of their physical union just as one might appliqué daisies onto the bottoms of Levi's.

"You're my very first syndicated columnist," she said.

Bent over to kiss her, Lewellen suddenly got a startled expression on his face and burst out laughing.

"You're incredible," he complained. Then he stood up and undressed, tossing his clothes onto a chair before lying down beside her.

But as soon as he pulled her toward him, arranging the upper half of her body across his chest so he could stroke her back, Nona experienced a shattering swell of resentment that reinforced her determination to resist him and his easy sexual initiatives. Paying tribute to his skill by exaggerating her struggle not to succumb, Nona submitted to his caresses with shy evasions and soft disclaimers. Occasionally, for piquancy, she contradicted herself with sounds or stirrings that suggested an inadvertent rush of sexual excitement, a spiraling of emotion that slipped past her self-control and predicted the probability of a passionate breakthrough.

"Tell me what you like," he whispered into her ear.

"I like . . . your style."

"No," he laughed again, pleased both with himself and with her, "I mean, what should I do?"

"Whatever turns you on."

But it took him a long time to get hard, and he wouldn't let her touch him. When he finally covered her body with his own, kneeing her legs apart to move into the V of her body, she was still tight and dry. Methodically he began to force himself into her, and though she speeded up with pleasure at the feel of his unfamiliar form, she remained passive.

Methodically, Lewellen worked her over, but Nona never relented. She never pressured the small of his back or pulled down upon his shoulders or clutched the round hills of his buttocks. Instead she kept a wary palm pressed demurely between them as if to ward off some unexpected violation. She initiated nothing, receiving him while refusing herself.

Then, when he was deep inside her, Lewellen stopped moving and lay stubbornly still.

"I think I'm on to you now," he said.

She felt his words against her face and laughed from beneath the heavy blanket of his body.

"I think so, too."

But when he raised his head to look down at her, his face was knotted with anger. "You like to ball without balling, don't you? You like to let it happen without getting involved. You think you can turn off your head like you can turn off the sound on a TV set and just watch the picture so it doesn't count against you." He moved even more deeply into the center of her. "Well, this one counts, sweetie," he said. "I'm counting it, even if you aren't."

"Wait." she said. "You need something."

"No, I don't. This one's on the house. Save your booties for someone else."

And then she felt him forsake reciprocity and succumb to frenzy before withdrawing to spasm against her stomach. After, when he rolled away from her, Nona heard the same sticky sound made by an adhesive bandage being pulled off a patch of skin.

He lay beside her, relieved but unfulfilled, silently knitting them together with skeins of discontent. The complicated failure of their union was bothering him and he seemed to be juggling views of the experience to extract some understanding of it, hunting to remember their original intentions. Then, glumly, he swung himself off the bed and reached out for his clothing. "You ruined that," he said after a pause. "You owe me another one."

He walked into the bathroom. When he reappeared a few minutes later, he was fully dressed. "I've got to go down to the pool and wait for Sam. Do you want to stay up here or come along?"

"I'll go with you," Nona said. Turning away from him, she rubbed a corner of the sheet across her belly and pulled on her bathing suit. Then she gathered her purse and beach bag and hurried after him down to the pool where the senator and Cindy were still sprawled out in the sun. As discreetly as she could, Nona repossessed the chaise she had originally occupied beside Bob Dempsey. An intense, childish shyness pervaded her, and she wondered if she could brazen through a social reentry after such high jinks at high noon, how she could handle the uncomfortable accommodations people made to reintegrate sinners back into innocent society.

"The restaurant must have been very crowded," Dempsey said with droll sympathy.

Tony laughed at the common knowledge of their carnal encounter.

"What'd you have to eat?" the senator continued in the same casual voice.

Tony shot a sheepish glance at Dempsey. He unzipped and scuttled his slacks, exposing the outline of his sex coiled inside red-knit swim trunks, and collapsing onto the chaise beside Nona.

Sandwiched between the two men, Nona looked up into the sky. The quiescent circle-jerk jocularity between the two men and their airs of well-being silenced her. They were joshing in an easy way. Their genuine closeness outflanked any temporary transient involvements, and somehow Nona felt transformed into some reckless prank Lewellen had pulled during a drunken escapade of no more significance than if he had been stealing hubcaps.

She lay perfectly still, exploring the internal contradictions of the moment. She could not deny she was getting a rush off the scene or that she was enjoying lying between two attractive, powerful men who seemed to be sharing and enjoying her in common. But at the same time Nona felt a streak of discomfort developing from the fact that she wasn't, as she had always assumed, immune to such obvious seductions.

Suddenly Cindy, who had been pretending to read the *Star* on a chair several yards away, stood up. Clearly chaffing from neglect, with great theatricality she twirled a towel about her head into a high-rise fashion-model turban and began to advance upon them.

"We're going to waste the whole afternoon just waiting for Sam," she complained, stationing herself near Tony. With the petulance of a spoiled child, she tilted her pelvis upward just as she might raise her nose to snub someone. "I knew he wouldn't be able to break loose before dinnertime."

"Don't worry, he'll show soon," Tony reassured her. But he was watching Nona, recycling their experience again and refining his original response to it. After a long thoughtful pause, he smiled, and Nona received the sign as a show of forgiveness for her earlier sexual politicking.

"You're right," Cindy squealed, her sunburned face

84

flushing even pinker from excitement. "There he is now."

Nona looked up to see a small wiry man in white slacks and a navy blazer bound into the pool area. Ignoring an olympic-sized guard who reached out to stop him, Kinkaid progressed along the archipelago of sunbathers until he spied a group of people he knew. Then he stopped to shake hands with each of them, extorting acknowledgment and acclaim for his new notoriety. With the style of an old-fashioned fight-promoter, Sam was flashing his politically perse-cuted self as if it were another enviable socialite at his side.

Shee-it! she thought.

"That's Sam," Tony grunted. "Sam the Man."

Cindy tore off her turban and began to run, her yellow hair jetting out behind her golden body. Al-though she slowed down when she reached Sam, trying to suggest only friendly enthusiasm, their embrace quickly became provocative as her slim body fit and fused familiarly with his. But a moment later, Sam began to disentangle himself, systematically peeling Cindy's hands away from him with the casual air of an ocean swimmer absently pulling seaweed off his body.

Registering the fact that Sam was Cindy's lover, Nona looked away so she didn't see Sam when he broke into a trot and come from behind to plunge down roughly on Tony's stomach.

"Oh, it feels terrific," Sam Kinkaid squealed with a simulated simper, swiveling from side to side and looking back over his shoulder at Tony. "Oh, it's fuckingfarout."

"Get the hell off me, Kinkaid," Tony roared, strug-gling to escape without capsizing the chaise. "You bastard. Get the hell off." But his struggle was un-dermined by floods of laughter that incapacitated him. "Cut it out," he yelled, gasping for breath. "Get up, Sam. Get off."

85

Grinning, Sam Kinkaid held his pinioning position, enjoying their reunion, while Cindy stood nearby basking in the residuals of their expansive high spirits.

Having got a good sense of her antagonist, Nona turned onto her side, producing a flurry of flesh as her right breast pitched down heavily against the left, and seized the initiative to establish some proprietary rights.

"Hey. Be careful."

"Well!" There was a formal pause as Sam absorbed Nona's warning. "If the little lady's got a vested interest, then I'll just have to get up." Accommodatingly, he rose with burlesque caution to preserve the treasure he had so recklessly crushed.

Freed of Sam's weight, Tony groaned and sat up to avert any other attacks. Then, retrieving his crushed pack of Salems, he shook loose a cigarette while eying Sam with ancient affection.

"I'll bet you wouldn't believe me if I told you this lady right here is Nona Landau."

Sam looked down gravely at Nona, his overly bright brown eyes shinning as he estimated the extent of damage she might cause him. Clearly aware of Tony's interest in her, maximized by the fact that he'd brought her to the Hilton where their incestuous circle of media friends gathered every weekend, he knew he had to move cautiously.

"That's ver-ry in-ter-est-ing," he grinned. "And she's not even carrying a rifle."

"It's under the chaise," Nona said.

Their eyes met, acknowledging each other as inevitable but worthy adversaries.

"I thought you'd look very different," Sam said seriously.

"It's just because I'm out of uniform," Nona reassured him.

He grinned back at her while the entire spectrum of sociopolitical suspicions Nona invariably provoked in uptight liberals flashed across his face. Despite his coolness, Nona could feel his authentic aversion to her.

"Nona's covering the hearings for *Metro*," Tony said uneasily, sensing the natural antipathy between the two.

"Yah? Great." Sam composed an inscrutable expression. "And here I thought I knew all the good-looking women writers in Washington."

Fitfully, he jerked back his head to toss a splash of graying hair off his forehead. Then, straddling one of the chaises, he flattened out beside Bob Dempsey. Quickly Cindy sat down on the hot cement beside Sam, stretching her arms out behind her and turning her body into a sleek triangle uninterrupted by any fleshy proturberances.

"So, what's our agenda?" the senator asked. "Business or pleasure first?"

"Always business," Sam answered, stroking the top of Cindy's head.

"Listen, Sam, I need a drink," Cindy said. "It's damn hot today, and I've been out here for hours."

"Well, where would you like to go?" Sam asked dryly. "Denver or L.A.?"

Everyone laughed. It was clearly an old joke about where the lovers would be safe.

Angered at Cindy for injecting frivolity at a moment when Sam was prepared to talk business, Nona felt spite spring to life inside her.

"Why don't we all go over to my apartment and have some drinks?" she asked wickedly. "I only live a few blocks from here."

They all turned to stare at her.

"We could even walk over," Nona insisted, intent now on flaunting her awkward environment and uneasy existence. "It's right on Columbia Road."

They could feel she was putting it to them, demanding the confrontation on her own turf.

Tony was so tense that he stood up. "Where's Columbia Road?" he asked.

"Aw, come on," Bob Dempsey groaned, winking at Nona conspiratorially. "It's obviously on the wrong side of Rock Creek Park or you would have heard about it before. I speak at a lot of Gay Liberation meetings around there."

There was silence. It was a temporary stand-off. Nona waited, strong-arming the group with her injured silence, knowing that they would knuckle under.

"Hell, why not?" Sam said. "It's got to be less crowded than the Rive Gauche on a Saturday night."

There was laughter and then a flurry of discussion about the address of Nona's building. Tony began to pull on his slacks and shirt again.

Then he and Nona walked off together through the terrace toward Florida Avenue where he said he'd parked his car. Right outside the exit he stopped beside a Mercedes. Nona bit her tongue so she wouldn't make any comment as he unlocked the door to let her in.

"There's a liquor store," he said, scanning the shops on the other side of Florida Avenue. "Should I pick up some Scotch?"

"You better!" Nona smiled, realizing for the first time that she had only vodka in her apartment. She started to warn him about the hotel trade markup in that area, but then remembered the cushion of money that allowed him to be imperious.

"Do you need any mix?" he asked.

"Yes."

"What?"

"Everything."

He feigned a sock to her jaw and walked away. Nona lit a cigarette and stared out the window. The contradictions besieging her were beginning to seem unbearable. She was undeniably enjoying the gaming quality of her relationship with Lewellen, the constant

88

sexual contest between them. She liked the caressive comfort of his world, and being with him and Bob Dempsey had made her feel rich and affluent. But the hard core of her conscience kept accusing her of a self-indulgence. By the time Tony reappeared to jam a large carton into the back seat, Nona was feeling simultaneously defiant and defensive.

He got behind the wheel.

"Take a left turn up at the corner there," she said, looking straight ahead.

Five

They drove behind the Hilton, leaving the northwest sector of the city where the white population
huddled in tense affluence, and crossed the frontier
into the ghetto where unemployed blacks sat on
their stoopfronts guarding the wretchedness of the
inner city. Predictably, Nona felt Tony begin to
tense with wariness as he pulled into a parking
space near her building. A Chicano gang, pasted up
against the glass window of the Giant supermarket,
watched Tony remove Nona and the box of whiskey
from his Mercedes before locking and double-check-
ing the doors.

"You think it's O.K. to park here?" he asked doubt-
fully.

"Would you rather bring it upstairs?"

Tony grimaced unhappily, clasping the liquor-
store box to his chest, and followed her inside the
building and up the first two flights of stairs.

"I'm going to have a coronary," he panted, as the
bottles rattled against his chest. "I'm going to die
here and end up as a nasty headline: 'Nationally
Known Columnist Croaks in Sordid Love Nest of
Third-Floor Walk-up.'"

"Fourth," she corrected him.

Breathless when they reached the top, Tony set
down the box while Nona undid the locks. He was
still laughing as the door swung open. Then he
stopped.

"Jesus Christ," he said completely stunned.

90

This time Nona felt the musty heat seep out through the doorway and saw her studio from Lewellen's eyes. For a moment she wondered if he would misread the scene and mistake the scroungy furnishings as Nona's problem rather than only a symptom of her winter-long alienation.

"For Christ's sake, Nona! Can you explain to me why the hell you have to live in a horseshit place like this?" he roared, roused to anger by the battered furnishings, the Salvation Army rejects, secondhand giveways, and GSA government office surplus equipment.

"It's not that bad," she said looking around again. "I've got what I need. Besides, the landlord at our commune said if I didn't get all our stuff out of there he'd charge me for having it hauled away."

Lewellen hid his face beneath a fan of fingers. "For God's sake, Nona. It's a dump!"

"You sound like Bette Davis," she sneered.

"No, seriously, tell me why you live here." He was walking around the room studying her belongings. "What are you trying to prove?"

"Nothing. I'm just from here," she said, not wanting to sound corny but believing that the neighborhood was part of her base and place in the universe.

"Wouldn't you like a modern apartment? Something in Georgetown or Foggy Bottom?"

"You mean a building with closed-circuit TV and all that shit?" she asked defiantly, feeling racked by a sense of their separateness and the enormous distance between their lives. Tony's ignorance of her world belittled her and destroyed any illusion that an affair with him could be either idle or innocent. Being with him meant that Nona was stepping out of character into a dangerous charade. For love affairs, like any other behavior, revealed intentionality.

"What's the matter? Did Mao outlaw upholstered furniture? What do you sit on?"

"My ass," she said, walking toward the ceiling-high

91

windows, which she thought uniquely handsome. She felt defensive: Tony was touching upon a bit of her integrity that even she couldn't comprehend, something at the center of her being—some crazy code of geographic loyalty that grounded her more firmly than any personal or political commitments. She turned around to face him again with her arms akimbo.

"Look, don't fuck around about my cave," she said. "This is where I *live*. I like it here. I like . . . the people."

And this is where Michael will look for me if he ever comes back, she thought. If he ever has to find me fast, he'll look for me in this part of town.

"So, where do you sleep? Standing up in the refrigerator?"

She led him through the kitchen down the hallway to her bedroom. He looked genuinely bewildered as he observed the bed and dresser facing each other across a ten-foot space. "Lady, I can't lie in that bed with you," he said. "It's too skinny. You'll come back to the hotel with me for the night, won't you?"

Nona shrugged and then she led him back to the studio where he began prowling again, this time zeroing in on the board atop two filing cabinets that formed her desk.

"Are these your notes from the hearings so far?" he asked looking down at an open notebook.

"Yes. But don't read them, please."

"I wasn't going to," he said defensively, glancing up with an injured expression and moving a few steps away to show his innocence. "Is this an elite or a pica?" he asked touching her electric typewriter.

"Pica."

"I'm buying a new portable next week," he announced solemnly. "I've always had an elite, but lately I've sort of been thinking about maybe getting a pica this time. What do you think? How do you like pica?"

92

Nona stood perfectly still feeling pleasure at h
childishness streak through her. "I like pica fine," sh
said feeling laughter tickle her throat. "But, now tha
you mention it, I think elite probably fits you better.
You know what I mean?"

He whirled around, determined to see whether she
meant to tease or insult him, but then a smile cracked
his face as he saw her happiness and he began walking toward her, affection pressing him forward with
the force of a hand upon his back.

Nona waited without moving. It was a good moment. Something had happened between them that
injected friendship into the equation of their affair,
purifying the physicality and erasing ulterior motives.

"You know something, Lewellen? I think you're
starting to get a crush on me."

"Now, why would you say that?" he asked, moving
up solid and hard against her. He wrapped an arm
around her waist and arched her backward so that
her hair slid behind her shoulders.

"So, these are your notes," she mimicked him
gently. "So, this is your little desk, and this is your
little tablet . . . and let's see . . . hmmmm . . . this
is your little portable with your little pica print . . .
very cute . . . very sweet. . . ."

He looked down at her for several seconds before
lowering his head to kiss her, holding her still as he
inhaled her breath and tasted her mouth. Their bodies
fit comfortably together. Nona clung to him as an
enormous need rose up and roared through her.
Then, alarmed by the simultaneity of their sudden
desire, she pulled away.

"I've got to wash out some glasses," she said to
hide her confusion.

"Why'd you invite everyone up here, anyway?" he
asked. "I bet Sam will freak out when he sees this
place."

Stationing herself at the sink, Nona turned on the
hot water and began washing glasses, self-consciously

93

rejecting the jelly jars, while Lewellen went off to retrieve the box of whiskey.

"Damnit, I forgot to get vodka."

"I've got some," she called out over the rain of water.

He came up behind her suddenly. "How come? You don't drink vodka?"

"Well, I don't use rubbers either, but I keep them around for people who do."

Outraged he twisted her hair into a rope and pulled it until her head arched far back enough for him to kiss her mouth again. Then he released her and began to put the bottles on the counter.

The doorbell buzzed and Nona reached up to press the release button above the stove. Instantly Tony closed in on her again, cupping her breasts from beneath her uplifted arms.

"I could fuck you in the time it'll take them all to get up here," he offered.

"Go open the door," Nona begged, wiggling away. "They won't know which apartment."

Senator Dempsey, Sam Kinkaid, and Cindy Reynolds swept through the doorway.

Tony welcomed them with a broad sardonic sweep of his arm into the studio.

"Well, this is quite a spread," Sam said dryly.

Cindy stood in the center of the room, dressed in a smart polka-dot sundress that matched her bikini, and politely pretended not to notice the shabby surroundings. "Can I help you with anything?" she asked Nona nervously.

The senator headed directly to the kitchen counter and poured himself a full glass of Scotch, genuinely oblivious to his physical whereabouts.

Tony made the others drinks and then they all sat on the floor atop a tattered Oriental rug that someone had once donated to the Mintwood Place commune and passed around a bowl of potato chips as if trying to transfer their discomfort on to the next person.

Nona looked around the circle of fashionably handsome faces and noted, with perverse cheer, that Sam's distress was the most visible.

"Would anyone like a joint?" she asked in a hybrid hostessy voice.

"God, no!" Sam groaned. "That's all I need now —an open-and-shut drug case."

"This place sort of reminds me of the first apartment Margot and I lived in after we got married," the senator said assuming a lotus position and looking around for the first time. "It was really sort of nice," he chuckled, rattling an ice cube around his mouth. "But Margot got used to the good life just like that." He snapped his fingers with brisk bitterness and spat the ice cube back into his glass. "In fact, she still thinks that if I hadn't come out against the war, Lyndon would have asked me to run as his vice-president, and we might be living in the White House right now." He looked over at Tony with a rueful smile. "Can you imagine anyone wanting to live in that den of iniquity?"

"Yah. A lot of people," Tony chuckled.

"There are even a lot of people who just want to eat dinner there," Nona added.

Dempsey looked over at her and laughed. "That's true. And you know something? If Congress could ban White House dinner parties we'd eliminate a major source of corruption in the country. It would sure cut back corporate political contributions . . . and it might even help the Washington pundits keep their feet on the ground."

Tony groaned and shook his head warningly at Dempsey with a let's-not-get-into-this-now expression.

The tic that trembled Dempsey's face was beginning to reactivate. He drained the Scotch from his glass. "Actually I do believe that your currently self-congratulatory press corps owes a lot of people a lot of apologies. . . ."

"Oh, no!" Tony clutched his head and then ducked it behind the barricade of his raised knees. "That's Nona's thing . . . how the press does PR for the president—any president. Don't set her off."

"But it's true," Nona said dryly. "You let Nixon get away with murder until Woodward and Bernstein blew him out of the water. You guys never laid a glove on him. And you did the same for Kennedy and Johnson. Nixon just didn't have enough smarts to romance the press. He could even have got away with Watergate if he had just been a bit more charming and had a few more dinner parties." She flattened out on her back and studied the ceiling feeling the gin and tonic Tony had fixed her escalate her resentment.

"Stop!" Tony begged, raising his arms in surrender. "Please . . . don't start in again."

"You let them dupe you on the Vietnam War for ten years," Nona charged.

"Hey!" Sam thumped his glass down on the floor framing the rug. "That's not fair. It was fucking tough getting any news out of the Nixon administration. They wouldn't give my White House reporter the time of day. I had Petti, my best man, over there. That was his permanent beat and he could never break anything loose."

"Oh, come on!" Nona pleaded. "When Ziegler said it was high noon at nine in the morning, the entire White House press corps raced out to report that as straight news. Every time Nixon announced he had nothing to do with the Watergate break-in all the reporters put that out over the wires, and it made front-page headlines."

"She's right," Dempsey said, returning from the kitchen with another full glass of Scotch. "And that's how he got elected. By the guys spreading his bullshit all over the front pages. Except then nobody knew

96

he was lying." The senator exposed a sufficient amount of hard feelings to suggest how much more he was keeping under wraps. "You guys don't have to print bullshit or if you do you should say today the president said blah-blah-blah, but John Dean, his former attorney, says he's full of shit. *That's* objective journalism—reporting all the contradictions to the official line. I can't understand why you don't do that automatically."

"I know why," Nona volunteered quickly, sitting upright again. "Because there are a lot of power junkies in the Washington press corps who don't want to criticize the government muckie-wuckies because they're afraid they won't get invited to the next big dinner party." She looked at Sam and Tony. "You guys wouldn't be so gung ho about objectivity if you didn't feel compromised by fraternizing with the politicians you cover." She set down her glass on the old trunk that served as a coffee table in front of a stiff hand-me-down Victorian sofa. "Virgins usually don't have to worry about whether or not they're pregnant."

Tony was intent on developing an easy nonpartisan expression, but Sam was raring to do battle.

"Look," Sam said fiercely, "you free-lance people think you can zero in and take pot shots at the working press and then flit off again because you don't have to write regularly. You don't have to turn in copy every day so you can come on acting morally superior and then buzz off again while the regular reporters have to earn a living. What kind of baby talk is this, anyhow?"

"Oh, come on," Nona complained. "The White House reporters are a bunch of flacks."

"Look, do you know what happened to the guys who asked tough questions during presidential news conferences?" he asked. "They got punished so damn fast their heads spun. They got bumped off the next presidential trip, and they didn't get notified of the next scheduled press conference and, in fact, they didn't get any more news *at all*. But they still had deadlines and wives and kids and mortgages and egos . . . the whole bag of tricks. Sure they took government handouts—because they didn't have time to dig up juicy little scandals every day. The national newspapers aren't like your little underground rags that don't publish unless they have some sensational scoop . . . some hot-to-trot ex-FBI agent."

"Wow," Nona whispered. "When management comes on with a labor pitch, it really blows me away. Who's talking labor conditions?" she asked in a sudden fury. Then, shaking her head at Sam's audacity, she walked into the kitchen and turned on the cold water.tap, holding her wrists beneath the spigot to wake herself up and offset the soporific gin.

When she returned, the group was watching her with mixed expressions of expectancy and apprehension.

"The main problem is that you guys use government officials as your news sources. You go sucking around them until you're so in hock you can't write anything critical—even if it's true."

"We see political people because that's one way of getting the news." Sam said with patronizing patience.

"Yah, and all you got for the past ten years was their national security jive," Nona argued. "And you swallowed it because you're always going to parties with those guys, or giving parties for them."

"Now look," Sam said angrily. "The fact that I've been wiretapped for the past few years would suggest that the government didn't think they had me in their pocket. It's a rather shocking thing. . . ."

"Oh, it's always a shock when you first hear the government's been spying on you," Nona said lightly. "But you get used to it after a while, and then you just go about your business again. I know—because Lyndon Johnson did it to us all the time."

Everyone looked at her blankly.

"What the hell are you talking about?" Sam roared. "I'm a journalist. I publish two national magazines. What do you mean I'll get used to it? That's an infringement of my First Amendment rights."

Nona adopted a tender therapeutic tone of voice. "Gee, Sam, Michael Daniels was tailed for years. And I was, too, off and on. They broke into our commune three different times and ransacked every one of our offices, and they opened our mail and messed up our files and broke our mimeograph machine and tapped our phones and reconstructed our typewriter ribbons and kept an unmarked squad car parked in front of our house and ripped off our mailing lists and hired people to disrupt our meetings. And they stole my typewriter, and they put an agent in our Mayday steering committee, and once they planted dope in my purse at a party, but I got sick and went home early—right before there was a big police bust. But you get used to those things. . . . I even ended up smoking the dope they laid on me, and it was very good stuff."

Tony laughed nervously but didn't say anything. Sam was watching Nona with the concentration of a man facing serious surgery, eager to hear any accounts from a patient who had survived the same operation.

"Didn't you ever report any of that to the cops?" Cindy inquired.

Nona sputtered delicately with laughter. "Talk about putting a fox in the chicken coop! Most of the time it was the D.C. Police Internal Security Squad doing surveillance for the FBI."

Cindy had gone through several changes while listening and now donned an impatient expression that dismissed Nona's comments as irrelevant since her hardships were warranted while Sam's were unjust. Slinging her blond hair away from her face with an efficient shrug, she turned toward the others.

"Come on," she complained. "Let's not get into this now. Let's go out for dinner."

Nona walked over to the windows and looked outside. In a moment Tony was standing behind her, his hands on her shoulders and his mouth against the crown of her head. "You better cool it, little lady," he whispered. "Or you'll have to write off Sam helping you."

Nona didn't stir.

"Go get dressed," he whispered. "Let's get out of here. We'll go have dinner someplace."

Nona looked at the people moving in and out of the Giant supermarket. Columbia Road always looked its tackiest around dinnertime on Saturdays.

"You can talk to Sam alone later on," Tony said. "Go on, do what I tell you."

Nona turned, walked past the trio still sitting on the floor, and went back to her bedroom where she put on a fresh shirt and blue jeans. When she came back out again they were all waiting for her with freshly minted smiles of forgiveness, and she knew that Tony or Bob had sung the blues about her involvement with Michael Daniels.

With forced gaiety, Nona began to describe the various restaurants along Columbia Road where no one would possibly recognize any of them since no one knew or cared who they were. Laughing, they descended the four flights of stairs and moved out into the street, flooding across the sidewalk like an enormous empire oozing across the countryside, overrunning the native population. Even the senator seemed unaware of the impression they made as they climbed into their cars and sped away.

There was a large rowdy crowd of reporters getting drunk at the Class Reunion, and Tony embraced several friends at the bar before they went upstairs to the dining room. Nona sat between Lewellen and Dempsey drinking Scotch and watching people amble over to greet Sam and Cindy who were clearly the social favorites.

When their dinners were served the men began a brittle political discussion about the chances of Nixon being impeached. They spoke in phrases that had the same pontifical tone as the cynical sentences they pecked out on newsroom typewriters. To Nona it seemed as if she were hearing copy being simultaneously spoken and printed; she half expected to hear a margin bell ring out after each slick judgment snapped to its smug conclusion.

The men spiced their certitudes with intimate allusions to powerful people and inside information until eventually Nona realized, despite her drunkenness, that she was letting outrageous statements pass unchallenged because they were camouflaged in old-boy-club dialect. It was only the mens camaraderie and commonly shared assumptions that gave authority to their opinions.

Occasionally Lewellen would turn toward Nona with desirous eyes to reassure himself that she was still in tow. Then he would flood the space around her with his presence, and Nona would experience a drowning sensation from the rush of seductive flattery that splashed over her. Again and again Tony would make some whispered comment about his incredible show of olympic restraint in curbing his lust to remain at the restaurant so she could speak with Sam.

But even after they had drunk and eaten and drunk again, snuggled cozily inside the heavy shadows thrown by the phony Tudor candelabra, even after their headiness had homogenized the entire group into a single gluttonous creature, Sam still wouldn't let go of the night and made no sign of being ready to talk.

Eventually, the mutual admiration around the table turned the group into a huge masturbatory monster, and Nona sat silently, in a post-drunk down, watching the manic performances of egocentric peo-

101

ple feeding on each other. Mindlessly, she listened to jazzy renditions of "Raindrops Are Falling" and "Little Green Apples" from a speaker near their table.

It was midnight when Tony finally signaled her.

"Sam wants you to go downstairs to the bar. He'll meet you there."

Nona excused herself and walked down the crowded staircase.

A moment later Sam joined her, briskly ordering two more Scotches from the bartender.

"O.K.," he said turning to her without giving any clue as to his mood. "Shoot."

For a second Nona was silenced by a familiar feeling of helplessness. Instantly she felt fatigued—too tired to convince anyone of anything, too weary to quarrel with the facile judgments and easy platitudes that Sam would deal her. She looked at the superficial, supercilious man who had refused to meet Michael and saw instead the still-life scene of Michael standing at the kitchen door pleading over the telephone. That moment had, apparently, become a permanent acquisition in the picture gallery of her mind. She sighed, unable to speak.

"Tony told me a little," Sam said encouragingly as he paid for the drinks. "What's the story?"

"Well," Nona began, "The *Post* says that you've been tapped since July of nineteen seventy-one. Michael called you during that period because he called in September of seventy-one. So if the FBI was recording all your phone calls they probably picked up his call, too. But during his trial the Justice Department testified that there hadn't been any electronic surveillance of any of the four defendants —so if Michael was overheard, even accidentally on your telephone, that's new evidence. It might even be grounds for a mistrial. I mean, that's what got Ellsberg off—being accidentally overheard on Mort

102

Halperin's phone." Nona took a sip of Scotch and composed one of her slow, sulky smiles that she knew men found sexually appealing. "So, I was thinking that if you would be willing to tell someone in Archibald Cox's office or someone at the Justice Department, or maybe even just issue a press release or run a story in *The Week* saying that there's fresh evidence concerning the D.C. Four case, the judge might order a new trial. I don't think it would be very hard to convince people that the D.A. lied since now everybody knows that Nixon's people perjured themselves all the time. If ever there was a right time for Michael to get another chance, it's right now."

Sam was smoking with studied concentration.

She thought he would recoil at that point, dismiss her with some slick put-down that would block any further negotiations, but he didn't. He seemed to be savoring her proposal as a personal opportunity for penance, an act of redemption for his own lack of bravery or foresight.

"Well," he said, pausing to extract as much psychological leverage as possible, "at the moment we don't know that that particular phone call was actually recorded. I don't know much law, but it sounds pretty circumstantial to me—my coming forward and saying someone called my house during a time when there may or may not have been a tap on my line. Hell, at this point, anybody could say he'd called me during that period if he wanted to accuse the government of illegal surveillance. And anyway it's pretty hard to prove your case when the evidence is in the hands of the people you're bringing charges against."

"But the court can order the FBI to produce their records," Nona said.

"Look, on this particular issue you and I happen to be on the same side," Sam said. "I'd like to get whatever tapes they have of my phone conversations, too. But if they did tap, tape, and transcribe my calls

103

they're not going to release the tapes as evidence of their own illegal activities. Besides," he added slowly, "the question will come up why Daniels was calling me in the first place. People are going to ask what our connection was."

Nona smiled. "Well, it doesn't matter if you tell them. The point is that the verdict can be thrown out because the government used illegal means of obtaining evidence against him."

Sam's forehead began to furrow. Nona sensed that some new angle had occurred to him that was cooling off his interest.

"Well, listen," he said, picking up his drink to carry back upstairs. "I've got to talk to my lawyer about all of this and he's out of town until next week. Then I'm going away for two weeks. I can't do anything about it before then. Do you think you can hold tight that long—until I get back?"

Nona shrugged and smiled faintly.

"Good girl." Sam stood up. "Should I tell Tony to come down here?"

"Yes, please. And thank you."

He put a paternal hand on her shoulder and disappeared.

By the time Tony drove back to the Hilton, Nona was so drunk that her limbs felt rubbery and her knees buckled in a way that reminded her of a pink eraser bending as it rubbed across a piece of paper. Once inside the hotel room, Tony took her into his arms, arching her into a bow against his torso and Nona absorbed the stone wall of his chest against her breasts and the hard trunk of his thighs along her legs. She rested her face on a safe plateau below his shoulder as his hand spread across the diameter of her back, regulating their closeness, rubbing her body into his until his sex started to swell and fill the lowlands beneath her belly. Softened by alcohol and brinking with feeling, Nona met his hardness, plying herself against the solid mass of his body.

Tony lowered his head so that the rock-hard edge of his jaw ground against her cheek.

"Come to bed," he said.

The strokes of his breath sent shivers of desire scurrying and skittering into the darkest corners of her body.

"O.K.," she nodded. Weakly she moved away to walk toward the windows.

"What are you doing?"

"I'll close the blinds. The people across from here can see in."

"That's terrific," he said roughly. "Leave it alone."

Nona turned around, unbuttoning her shirt and unzipping her jeans as she walked to the bed. "You like *that*, Lewellen?" she asked wrinkling up her nose. "That's pretty kinky for a bourgie guy like you."

When she awoke the next morning, naked beneath the blanket with its prim white-sheet collar tucked below her neck, he wasn't in the bed. Feeling manhandled and hung over, slightly sunburned on the outside and skinned raw on the inside, she looked beyond the wide left-hand margin of the empty bed to see Anthony Lewellen sitting in an arm chair near the window watching her.

"Good morning," he said.

"Good morning." She intended to dispatch an easy grin with her words, but an enormous shyness suddenly shattered her composure and unexpectedly she made a monster face and pulled the covers over her head. From inside the pungent smelling cave of blankets she heard Lewellen chuckle and then the creak of the armchair as he stood up. Certain that the carpet was muffling his march toward the bed, Nona waited in ticklish anticipation for him to pounce upon her. But when the suspense became intolerable, she lowered the blankets and saw him standing innocently beside the desk studying a large elaborately embossed menu.

105

"What would you like for breakfast?" he asked.

He was wearing lean white slacks and a new blue knit shirt that still bore the sharp-edged creases of its packaging. Posed as he was, holding the telephone receiver angled away from his face, he looked like a *New York Times Magazine* ad for himself—a man for women who like men—a sop to the ladies after endless pages of bra and girdle ads strategically placed along the finger-turning margins.

"Juice," Nona cleared her throat. "A double orange juice. Please."

"Eggs?" Lewellen began to dial.

"No. No. Thank you." She reached out toward the bedside table to snare his pack of cigarettes with the matchbook tucked primly inside the wrapper. Then she turned his gold watch to see the time.

"Do you know it's only seven o'clock?" she asked.

Lewellen patted his palm against the air to silence her as he began to explain in great detail exactly how he liked his eggs. When he was finished, he walked to the bureau and looked back at her through the mirror. "I have to leave soon," he said slowly, turning so Nona received a rear view of wide shoulders triangling down into handsome buttocks hitched atop the rim of the dresser. "You know something?" He was studying her in a very serious way. "You got very tan during the night. I think you got tanned from making love. I think I gave it to you."

"Man-tan," she said, cuffing the blanket more securely beneath her armpits.

But he didn't smile. Instead, he reversed all the laughlines of his face into a frown and went back to the window.

"It's a nice day," he said. His slacks drew tight across his backside as he loaded the front pockets with his fists. Suddenly Lewellen whirled around and punched a clenched fist into his open hand. "That was really a fucking stupid thing I did," he said.

"What?"

106

"It was stupid of me to order breakfast, that's what." Irritation ruffled his voice. "It'll take hours before they get it up here." He headed toward the telephone on the desk and then stopped. "Oh, what the hell! It doesn't matter . . . there aren't any more left anyway." He turned to look at her.

Nona stared straight ahead at a watercolor print of a Parisian café hung on the wall.

Rubbers, she thought. Jesus, he's talking about the rubbers again.

"You don't . . . you wouldn't . . . I don't suppose you have any others around anyplace . . . somewhere in your purse or someplace?"

"No. No, I don't," she said firmly, putting out her cigarette while trying to devise an escape route to the toilet without streaking directly past him. She wanted to brush her teeth and eat some toothpaste to rid herself of the brown tobacco flavor in her mouth. She wanted to take a shower, get dressed, and go home so she could remember and reconnect with her real self.

The drum of a knock on the door triggered her into motion. In one swoop Nona rolled off the bed, grabbed her clothes and purse from the chair where she had dropped them, and fled into the bathroom. When she was showered, made up, and dressed, she came back out. Lewellen was sitting near the window at a mobile breakfast table covered with a linen cloth and cluttered with knobby-nippled silver dish lids.

"Well," he said suspiciously, lowering the *Washington Post* into a shield for his chest. "You certainly look loaded for bear." Then he stood up and moved forward to loop his hands loosely about her waist, leaving a margin of space to look down at her.

"I'm sorry we can't spend the day together," he said.

Nona smiled.

"But you're not," he continued suspiciously. "And you know something? I don't think you're going to see me again. You don't think Sam's going to come across and that was the only reason you had for seeing me. Wasn't it?" His tone was teasing, but his insecurity and pain were authentic.

"Look," Nona said, "to tell you the truth . . . I'm not really used to being with people so much, I mean, so many people for such a long time. I'm just feeling a little twitchy this morning. I want to go home and unwind and be quiet for a while."

"That's not it," Tony charged. "You don't want to have anything to do with me if Sam won't help you. Isn't that the truth? Isn't that what you're laying on me?"

"Please," Nona protested. "I'm just hung over. I haven't eaten or smoked or drunk so much for a long time. Not to mention fucking. I haven't balled anyone for half a year. I feel glutted."

"Well, when will I see you again?"

"I don't know," she said impatiently. "I just want to go home now."

"Should I call you?" he asked. "I mean before Sam decides what he's going to do?"

"I don't know," Nona lied. "I just need a little space right now. O.K.? I mean, don't lean on me right now."

She looked away. She thought Tony was trying to line her up in advance because he knew Sam was going to refuse to help her.

She shook her head. "Look I think I'm suffering from culture shock, or something. It's just too much for me all at one time . . . making love, switching from grass to booze. The whole bit is just a little too much."

"And what am I supposed to do?" Tony asked in an ugly, twisted voice.

His pain speared her.

"I don't know. What you always do I suppose." She slipped out of his grasp.

"Wait," he said, reaching out for her. "Look. Things have changed. I mean . . . since yesterday. Everything's different."

"Not for me," Nona said.

He didn't try to stop her as she left the room.

Six

On the next Monday, June 5, the Senate Investigating Committee heard testimony from Sally Harmony, secretary to Gordon Liddy, and Nona sat motionless on her gray-steel folding chair in the caucus room listening to the defiantly defensive woman. Although during the first weeks of the hearings, Nona had been totally absorbed by the political atrocities being recited, by now she had become somewhat immunized to the stories told by the president's honchos, and only occasionally did any disclosure jar the seismograph of her soul. Information that apparently shocked the liberal journalists seated around her only certified truths she had intuited or known for a decade, and gradually the low-key accounts of illegalities ceased to interest her.

She did not see or hear from either Tony Lewellen or Sam Kinkaid during the first three weeks of June.

Although Nona knew many journalists watched the proceedings over TV, to avoid the hassles of attending in person, she egotistically and pessimistically assumed that Tony Lewellen was staying away from the Senate Office Building because Sam had come down on the wrong side of the fence. Since she stayed home almost every night, she sacrificed the illusion that people might be trying unsuccessfully to reach her. Her parents telephoned long distance from St. Paul several times, interested as always in her welfare and her work. But they never asked about her personal life, since they were afraid she knew where Michael was and didn't want to know she knew.

Sara Dundee, an ex-nun who had lived in the commune for several years, returned to visit Washington with her baby and spent several days at Nona's apartment. Late at night after the baby fell asleep on the couch blockaded by two kitchen chairs, the women would lie on the floor beneath the front windows and talk—often of Michael. Although Nona hated herself for doing it, she pumped Sara to find out if there was any gossip from underground that Michael had hitched up with some female fugitive, but Sara had heard nothing at all.

On Saturday and Sunday they walked around the neighborhood together, pushing the baby in a cheap, clumsy cloth stroller, dropping in on old Movement acquaintances Sara wanted to see. Nona found the visits painful; everyone treated her like a widow, and she suffered both guilt and gratification from accepting their sympathy.

After Sara returned to West Virginia, Nona felt totally isolated and forced herself to plunge back into her work. For the June 20 deadline she had allotted herself two weeks for leisurely research on the senators-as-culture-heroes, one week for personal interviews with them and members of their office staffs, and one week for writing up the six thousand-word story. During her days in the caucus room she kept copious notes on the proceedings planning to write, at the end of the summer, a dense and definitive summation of the entire investigation to peddle to some national magazine.

At night when she returned home she would force herself to cook a hot meal so as to generate enough energy to sit at her desk for several more hours, transcribing her scribbled notes or scanning newspapers and magazines. On her beat-up old television, she would watch both the seven and eleven o'clock newscasts to check out the show-biz aspects of the

111

hearings, watching the senators' on-camera behavior and analyzing the coverage. Since her first assignment was an easy one, Nona quickly collected more information than she needed, and began collecting material for her August story about the Watergate press corps.

Sometimes, after the hearings adjourned for the day, Nona would stop in at the Class Reunion or the Quality Inn Tavern, where the out-of-town press people congregated, to eavesdrop on their conversations. Occasionally an overly enthusiastic admirer would start to romance her, but she finally developed a certain ephemeral expression, an air of urgency that allowed her to disappear quickly and quietly if things became tense or difficult. Often she struck up conversations with anonymous reporters from the Washington bureaus of midwestern newspapers and listened to their Watergate tales and jealous analyses of the Washington press corps. Apart from the people covering the hearings Nona saw no one and by the fourth week in June she was living her life in rhythm with the rest of the Watergate reporters. The familiar roadsigns of their faces placed around the caucus room had become a permanent part of her psychological landscape—as immutable as her seventh-grade homeroom class. The intimacy among the journalists became so intense that it hovered between consensus and incest. Weekends were the only breaks in their heavy hearings habit, and many reporters experienced those brief separations as disruptions that broke the narrative flow of their real lives—unedited digressions that they automatically deleted from the ongoing plot of their Watergate summer.

The days were long, inert, and intense. By mid-June regular members of the Watergate press corps could decode dialogues conducted completely in grimaces— Isn't that a crockashit? Why the hell can't Inouye ask a straight question? When the hell do we get to have a drink?

112

During lulls in the testimony Nona would study the faces at the press tables watching boredom spirit reporters away so that their expressions became as blank as siesta shades lowered over windows of Spanish shops on hot afternoons. Often she would watch the wandering gaze of some reporter land briefly on a favorite pair of friendly eyes that waited to greet him like a good-natured waitress at some roadside truck stop. Many of the eyings were intensely sexual, almost indecent, but for the most part Nona felt befriended and secure among the press corps.

Her nights alone were much less pleasant.

Late on a Thursday in the middle of June, the telephone rang and woke Nona out of a heavy sleep. Drenched with sweat and shaking from excitement, she picked up the receiver, expecting to hear Michael's voice.

But it was Patsy Bator in tears, asking Nona to meet her for coffee in the Senate cafeteria the next morning. Nona agreed and sleepily reset her alarm clock.

She left the apartment an hour earlier than usual Friday morning and walked down Columbia Road through the early-morning heat. Although the days didn't unleash their real forces until after noon, a plague of sunshine was already descending upon the city, and Nona could feel the hot sunlight tickle the top of her head, scratching along the line of her center part, on the back of her neck, and on the backs of her knees below her short cotton skirt.

When she unlocked her VW, the air inside was dense and putrid. She unwedged the car from its parking space and drove down to U Street, cutting through the ghetto where erratic lane-switching drivers acted out their futile protests. Shy about her locked door and miserly opened windows, Nona averted her eyes from the weary black men who sat like sentries on the stairs of their wretched slums hopelessly waiting for the day as if it were a bus that had been officially rerouted without any public notice. Driving above the speed limit, Nona skimmed past Fourteenth Street where burned out buildings left their shadowy outlines on adjacent walls that still bore posters of anti-poverty programs—nostalgic souvenirs of the sixties. Once at the Capitol, Nona began a long irritating search for a parking place while the hot arms of the city tightened harshly around her.

She reached the enormous cafeteria in the basement of the Senate office building a little before nine. The restaurant was filled with Senate staff people scoring their second cups of coffee, and Nona entered the food line from the rear to avoid the breakfast crowd. Awkwardly she poured herself a cup of coffee while juggling her purse and her *Post*, paid the cashier, and sat down at a table near the main entrance.

Sipping the dark, evil-tasting liquid from the thick porcelain cup, she watched an army of anonymous Senate secretaries coming in and out of the cafeteria. Most of the middle-aged women were drab and tired, worn from self-sacrificing service to their senators, but there were also a few young beauties recently recruited from distant states to start compromising careers on Capitol Hill. The newest secretaries, who had not yet resigned themselves to obscure servitude, brightened only by occasional sparks of reflected glory, announced their innocence by wearing three-inch platform shoes and rib-tight T-shirts designed to seduce senators.

The scene, and its implicit scenario, made Nona sad. She finished her coffee and smoked a cigarette before Patsy exploded through the doorway, breathless and braless in a white muslin overblouse and skin-tight Levi's. Unconscious of the effect of her entrance on that conservative crowd, Patsy looked around the room and then, seeing Nona, hurried toward her, windblown but beautiful in her disarray.

"Oh, boy! Am I glad to see you," she said, slumping into a chair, tossing her long limbs in different direc-

114

tions and unloading various paraphernalia from her purse before contracting into a glamorous sulk across from Nona. "It's all falling apart," she announced.

"Do you want some coffee?" asked Nona who was used to the role of patient listener when Patsy was falling apart.

"No." Patsy pulled out a cigarette. "I've been up all night . . . I really have to leave him, Nona. I mean, I would have done it a long time ago except that I was so fucking stupid I let my whole career get mixed up with this goddamned affair. Oh, Nona, he's sooooo bad!" For a moment tears brinked in Patsy's eyes as she recalled some private roster of humiliations and hurts. "So I guess I'm just going to end up back on the streets free-lancing again— waltzing around looking for someplace to park my butt and sell my soul."

Her hair was in perpetual motion, falling forward and back as she bobbed her head. "Oh, I know he won't fire me if I move out," she amended herself judiciously. "But I'm sure that as soon as I split, he'll start fucking me over at the office, giving me bad assignments and cutting the hell out of my stories or burying them in the back, and I'll be Patsy Bator the former girl-superstar so fast my head will spin. And I know the whole scenario because he brought *me* in to replace Betty Allentuck. I mean, she worked her ass off for him, and then when I came along he just threw her over for me! He squeezed her dry and threw away the peeling—because, really Nona, he's more of a pimp than an editor. He just wants to ball all the good women writers, and he hooks them because he's got the bread to pay top prices, and he can turn someone into a superstar in a couple of months' time, and then he starts balling them. I mean, that's what he did to me, so I know. When I first started working for Jay he gave me all the sexy assignments and let me run up huge expense account bills, and he edited my stuff into shape and let me

115

stretch out and do my own thing. And after I'd done a couple flashy pieces for him he started taking me around town and showing me off as his hot new property, and all the trendies and groupies started rushing me, and pretty soon I was hooked on that old by-line high." She snorted contemptuously at herself. Nona watched her rearrange her chiseled features into a Hollywood brat grimace and twist her lithe body into an angry, but still alluring, position. Nona's affection forgave Patsy everything.

"I mean, I saw him do it, Nona. The whole thing—the minute I began producing some good articles he started using me as a threat against Betty, and she got so uptight she could hardly write anymore. He kept playing us off against each other, and when he finally asked me if I would move into his apartment, I did it because I was afraid that otherwise she would. And from what Betty told me later on, she felt like a piece of shit because he took away her expense account and took her off retainer, and since they'd been sleeping together, too, it ended up being a big sexual rejection on top of the rest. I don't know why or how he does it, but Jay makes women think it's their sex appeal, instead of their talent, that they've got going for them."

Nona lit a cigarette.

"You know writers like Betty are terrific," Patsy continued, "but if they don't have a magazine to publish in regularly, they're nowhere. And so when he started pushing me up front, he started getting real tough with Betty about her deadlines and how much space he'd give her, and when she started acting like a sulky wife around the office, you know, pouty and pissed off, he got disgusted and let out the word that she was all washed up and that I was taking over. And I let it happen," she said pensively. "I let it happen because I loved it." She slumped back in her chair again. "So now I'll just get what I deserve. Now it's going to happen to me. He'll

116

pick up some hot new writer who wants to be a star, and he'll start promoting her, and I'll be out of the ball park." She lit a cigarette.

It was the classic backlash of the personality cult of new journalism. Since style was more important than subject, a writer was tortured by vulnerability. The threat of banishment from the center of the action caused instant panic.

"And then there's the fucking sexual jealousy," she said in a soft rhetorical tone. "I think jealousy sucks."

"You won't get any argument from me on that one." Nona laughed.

But she felt a pang of sympathy as she flashed on Michael. If he called and sounded cold, or impersonal or impervious, Nona would wait for his next call to release her from the bondage of the last. But as summer progressed Nona felt him fading. Either he was purposefully trying to let her off the hook or he was defensive because he was hurting badly or he had finally found a woman to comfort and abet him in his flight.

"I know it's just the old replacement panic." Patsy shrugged. "The nobody-but-me syndrome."

"Well, I know someone you don't ever have to worry about," said Nona. "Me. I'm only working for Jay because I'm broke and I certainly don't want to be his leading lady."

Reinforced by Nona's reassurances, Patsy bounded off to buy them coffee. When she came back she said to Nona, "That wasn't very cool of me to talk about jealousy to you. I'm always ego-tripping. I just realized how awful it must be for you with Michael away."

Nona flinched as white-hot anxiety lashed her.

"I mean, don't you wonder if he's still alone?" Patsy continued.

Nona sighed. "I can't let it matter, Patsy. He's probably lonesome and afraid, and there's probably

117

women around wherever he is. I mean, I try hard not to let it matter."

She finished her coffee and excused herself. The suspicions that constantly lured her toward despair reappeared in all their trappings. She hurried out to the corridor to take an elevator upstairs. Now that she had let down her guard she was being invaded by a ravenous jealousy. Michael's image kept reappearing to her, and she saw dissolving angles of his face wearing a poignant expression, a pinched pleading look of loneliness. Walking into the caucus room, Nona's hand twitched with a desire to reach out and touch the apparition, to wipe away the pain from Michael's face as if it were a speck of dirt. The more time that elapsed between phone calls from him, the more jealous she became, certain that he had found another woman.

Entering the caucus room, Nona saw Cindy Reynolds in the chamber for the first time standing near the senator's table, talking to Dan Rather.

Impulsively Nona hurried over to Cindy, touching her shoulder lightly from behind, stopping the cascade of chatter.

Cindy whirled around. "Oh, hi," she said. "How are you? I haven't seen you in ages." She lowered her voice. "They're both up in the Vineyard, you know. Unloading the families." Then with a quick smile, she looked back at Rather and introduced him to Nona.

Unconsciously tightening up her face into an unmistakably distant expression, Nona shook hands and then turned back to Cindy, hoping to get some hint as to whether or not Sam had made any decision yet. But Cindy had already turned away and, inhaling a heady whiff of the excitement being generated by the press, lost any interest in Nona. Murmuring only a vague good-bye, Cindy drifted away, with the air of a prom queen arriving at a homecoming dance, toward a small crowd of reporters.

Nona returned to her table.

Shortly after Senator Ervin opened the hearings, the Senate call bell rang three times announcing a floor vote. The press disregarded the summons, acting as if it were a college roommate's alarm clock ringing for an early class, conspicuously advertising their bored familiarity with Senate procedure. But the break in the proceedings caught Nona off-guard. Depressed from her talk with Patsy and irritated by Cindy's departure, some of Nona's shallowly buried feelings began to surface. The image of Tony Lewellen vacationing on Martha's Vineyard with his family, untroubled by Nona's dilemma or her fear that Michael would telephone to ask what progress she'd made in his behalf, angered her.

Feeling used and abandoned, Nona experienced a great sense of despair. She no longer believed that Sam Kinkaid would help her. She did not think Tony would risk coming onto her again after failing to deliver his friend. She felt that nothing in her unsatisfactory life would ever change. Michael would never return, and Nona would live alone indefinitely, picking up enough free-lance assignments to support herself in a rootless, unanchored, defenseless existence. Her depression lasted all through the day and into the night.

The next morning she began writing her article, channeling all her panic and fear into endless hours at the typewriter.

On the nineteenth she dropped off her manuscript on her way to the Hill, arriving at the *Metro* office early enough so that Jay wouldn't yet have arrived. Jay telephoned her on Saturday morning, seemingly pleased with the article. He read her some changes he had made on the copy and said he'd let her know when the galleys came back.

That night, ironically, Michael telephoned, his

119

voice was colder almost apathetic. Nona strung out and over wrought accused him of being stoned, of having turned on right before calling her. He denied it, but even his denial sounded spacy and that provoked Nona into asking if he was with some woman . . . if perhaps he had found sanctuary with some old— or new—friend with whom he'd fallen in love. They quarreled bitterly, and in a flash of frustration Nona hung up the receiver.

Michael did not call back. Breathless with outrage at him and at herself Nona thrashed about on her bed, mentally resuming the telephone conversation, erasing the earlier call, reassuring Michael that she was still trying to help him, requesting that he phone again in several weeks in case she made a breakthrough with Sam Kinkaid and needed some advice. But the telephone didn't ring.

She stayed home in her apartment all day Sunday, puttering about with her plants, drinking endless cups of coffee, flipping through the newspapers, looking around the studio and thinking of how to improve it, considering scraping the paint off the narrow wooden trim around the front windowpanes or buying unbleached muslin to make into curtains or ordering some unfinished lumber to build into bookshelves or bargaining for an old velvet armchair that she'd seen in a Spanish secondhand furniture store on Eighteenth Street. But eventually despair and desolation would rise up in her, destroying any effort to distract herself with fantasies of disguising her apartment as a home, and then she would drift off on a wave of memories as fresh and as strong as when they were first minted.

Seven

On the twenty-fifth of June, the first day of John Dean's appearance before the Committee, Nona reached the Senate caucus room an hour earlier than usual, only to find most of her colleagues already there reading the morning papers. By the time she made her first coffee run down to the cafeteria, the room was vibrating with excitement. By 9 o'clock there was a cocktail party edginess to the exchanges in the corridor and aisles; even casual encounters were more sexy and sprightly than usual. Anticipation about Dean's testimony had reactivated a fresh swell of competition among the reporters and Nona settled down in her chair to watch the impromptu guerrilla theater in the press section.

It was at 9:30 that Anthony Lewellen appeared in the doorway for the second time since the start of the hearings, and his arrival punctured Nona's composure. He was darkly tanned and looked illicitly healthy. Nona lowered her eyes, afraid she might display some sign of emotion that would upset her precariously neutral position in the delicate ecology of the Watergate press corps. But Lewellen walked directly over to her table, bringing a bouquet of male smells—toothpaste and mentholated shaving cream, soap and early morning tobacco—back into her life. He set down his attaché case and took the chair beside Nona.

"Hello," she said twisting around to face him. "It's good to see you. How come you're here?"

121

"Oh, I wouldn't miss John-boy for the world," Lewellen said. "Besides, I'm going to be coming in every day from now on. I took the family up to the Vineyard—so I'm home alone now and have more time for daytime soap operas."

"It's going to be wild," Nona mumbled nervously. "They say he's going to sing like a canary."

Tony leaned closer to her. "I saw Sam up at the Vineyard. He's coming back Friday and wants us to come over to his place to have dinner and talk. He's got a pool so bring your bathing suit."

Nona didn't respond. She was searching for clues in Tony's eyes.

"I don't think he's come to any decision yet. He still hadn't talked with his lawyer," Tony said. "Will you let me take you out for lunch?"

"O.K.," Nona smiled.

He stood up and walked back to take a seat near the head of the second table.

Determined to act businesslike, Nona returned her attention to the new cast of characters assembling in neat rows behind the witness chair. Maureen Dean had just arrived to lend the first sexual interest to the proceedings. A perfect candidate to play herself in a Warner Brothers' rendition of the Watergate caper, she sat implacably calm, clean, kempt, Kewpie-doll pretty, wrapped in a blanket of imperturbability as she awaited her husband's appearance. Nona could hear a rustle of sexual speculation sweep through the press section as the men studied the preternaturally blond bun of hair gathered on her neck and the heavy voluptuousness that seemed more ponderous than seductive.

It took John Dean the entire morning to read his prepared statement. The newspaper men sitting around Nona followed the text of his statement as he spoke, clearly trusting the written word more than the human voice. Every few minutes a fluttering noise would ripple through the chamber as pages

122

were turned in unison. Occasionally the reporters would look up from their press releases to watch a fresh group of sightseers being ushered in or to check out their colleagues' faces for an instant reading of their reactions to Dean.

When the session adjourned for lunch, Tony was waiting for Nona at the top of the stairs. They walked across the street to the dark cloistered restaurant in the Carol Arms where they ordered drinks and sandwiches and talked about Dean's testimony. But the noisy crowd and crush of customers waiting to be served was too distracting and Nona felt herself withdrawing both from Lewellen and the tumult of the scene.

By 1:30 they were back in the hotel lobby, near the newsstand that stretched along the wall toward the registration desk. The proprietor, hemmed in behind the racks, watched as Tony began surveying the magazines, side-stepping slowly from section to section, studying covers or flipping through the pages of a new *Atlantic*. Edging along beside him, conscious of the old man's suspicious looks, Nona glanced at several paperbacks and then looked at her watch.

"Come on, we'd better get going," she urged.

"Hold it," Tony hissed. But he kept moving toward the registration desk, obviously using his magazine canvass as a cover to eavesdrop on a conversation between an elderly couple and the dour desk clerk.

Nona slid closer to him. "What's the matter?" she whispered.

"Go stand by the elevator," Tony ordered, kneeling down to inspect a pile of *Esquires* on the bottom rack.

Frightened, Nona crossed the narrow hallway just as the gray-haired couple hurried away. Tony leaned over the desk and muttered something to the clerk. Nodding at the response, he took a handful of free matchbooks from the enormous glass container on the counter and walked over to push the elevator call bell with the wooden handle of a room key. When the brass gate rattled open, Tony cupped Nona's elbow and pushed her inside the wrought-iron cage. Quickly, he pressed one of the floor selectors and waited until the gate clanged shut before he backed her up against the wall.

"What are you doing?" she whispered, as he began nuzzling her face into line with his lips.

"We're going to borrow the old folks' room for a little while," he said. "It's four oh eight—the honeymoon suite."

"Where'd you get the key?"

"They just turned it in at the desk. The clerk didn't even see it. The damn hotel is all filled up so I thought we'd use their room for a little bit."

"Oh, Tony," Nona moaned, "that's housebreaking or illegal entry or something. I'm not going to go into somebody else's room."

"Yes, you are."

The decrepit elevator grumbled unhappily as it leveled off on the fourth floor.

"My God," Nona groaned, horrified, "what if they come back up? What if the old lady forgot her purse or something?"

"Don't worry," Tony smiled. "They looked like uptight old geezers. They probably spent the whole morning getting ready to take a three-hour tour of the Smithsonian.

Nona let him lead her down a dim gray corridor underlined by a faded red runner. He unlocked 408 and pushed her inside.

"The police can say we came in here to steal their stuff," Nona said in a panicky whisper, watching Tony jog around the bed en route to the windows where he fumbled around behind the red brocade curtains until he released a cord that sent the venetian blinds tumbling down with the thunder of an avalanche of rocks. He was unbuttoning his shirt when he turned around.

"Oh, no," Nona said very firmly. "No way. I can't, I really *can't*, Tony. I'm scared shitless. I'm not kidding."

He bared his chest, first arching back to struggle free of the sleeves and then creasing his body down the center as he dipped his shoulders forward to shrug off the shirt.

"This is too much," Nona said.

He unzipped his trousers as if tearing a sheet of paper in half. The crotch of his shorts looked crowded and overstuffed.

"Do you want me to undress you?" he asked cheerfully. "I will or you can. But we goddamn well better hurry."

Nona walked over to the bed and sat down with her back to him. The small window air conditioner had begun shaking the slats of the venetian blinds. The sleeves of a frilly silk blouse, hung on a hanger over the closet doorknob, stirred like a scarecrow. Strange accessories, unfamiliar cosmetics, and various dark-green medicine bottles were lined up on the old-fashioned dresser. A too-sweet scent of dusting powder permeated the room, and Nona felt nauseated from the smell. When Lewellen crashed onto the bed, strong-arming her down with him, she went limp.

"It's been too long," he said in a choked voice. "I never stopped thinking about you."

His mouth drifted about her face, skimming across her cheeks, gliding along her nose, touching her eyes so her lashes grew wet and heavy as if weighted down by rain or tears.

"This is the worst goddamn thing I've ever gotten into," Tony complained, sculpting his hand over her breast. "Say something," he demanded. Nona lay perfectly still. Lowering his arm he liberated her shirt by unzipping her Levi's.

"You're going to be in big trouble if the hotel dicks bust in here," Nona said as he curled away to kiss her bare midriff. "I'm not going to take the rap

125

for this one." His lips were hurrying back and forth across the flat street of her stomach. "I'm going to give them a sex-crazed-syndicated-columnist story that will blow John Dean off the front page of the *Post* tomorrow. It'll be a kidnapping and rape charge —a double forced-entry."

He laughed and his breath slid inside the unzipped V of her blue jeans as he burrowed further down to rut about in the carpeting of hair that crept above her bikini pants.

"Besides that, the old man probably has a heart condition. Look at all those medicine bottles on the bureau. He's probably on his way back here right now to get his digitalis. It's too hot to run around sightseeing on a day like this."

Lewellen crouched on his knees and began to wrestle the Levi's out from beneath her.

"And by now the cops have probably heard rumors I'm having a rendezvous with one of their Ten Most Wanted, and they're going to come in here shooting."

"Not before I do," Tony said, lifting the lower half of her body to half slide, half roll the blue jeans and underpants down her legs. Then he lunged at her again, using his head as a crowbar to force her thighs apart.

"Don't," Nona said unconvincingly.

He ignored her while his mouth hunted for the slash between her legs.

Involuntarily Nona's hands cradled his head as her body fell silent, feeling him make love inside her.

O.K., she thought. It's O.K. He's just people like everyone else. . . . He's no better or worse. And she let her consciousness sink into a whirlpool of suspense as his mouth fondled her.

Slowly she began to squirm, losing clarity in a swirling sensation of pleasure. Her entire being was on alert, summoned to attention by the teasing of his tongue.

126

Feeling herself mount, Nona snarled her fingers through his hair and moaned softly.

Then he stopped and slid up along her belly to lay his wet slippery face against the empty pelvic pocket above her crotch.

"Don't come," he said. "Try not to come. Let's see how long we can fuck around without coming. Let's try to last all afternoon."

"Hmmmm," Nona said distantly, too distracted now to worry about any of his ploys, forgetful that they were trespassing and missing prime-time testimony over in the Senate caucus room. Shyly her hand began hunting through his hair, pressing his head down again until silently he obliged her, sliding over the hard rock of her pelvis.

Then her inner muscles began to clutch and clench seeking some focus, chasing satisfaction with the pouncing motion of a kitten trying to catch a ball of yarn that rolled away at the first touch of a curved paw.

Panting, Lewellen reached out and snared a pillow to cram beneath her hips, hunching above her as he adjusted her body.

"What we have to do is get right to the edge of coming and then just hang in there," he said. "You know what I mean? If you get too close you've got to quit. Cold-turkey it. Just stop yourself."

"Hmmmm," she consented again without any intention of compliance, drifting out of cerebral control and crossing the frontier into fleshiness as he nuzzled his head between her legs. On the crest of increasing pleasure, Nona felt her pelvis begin to punch back and forth, moving with a steady cadence.

"That's all," Lewellen said, suddenly straightening out to lie alongside her. "You're getting too hot. It hasn't been that long yet, lady. I can still remember how you come."

Then he lay still. Only his breath, battering his chest with harsh soundings, broke the silence. With

127

her face near his, she could smell her own sweet-sour odor on his skin. Apologetically her hand rose to wipe his cheek.

"Don't" he said, twisting his head away from her fingertips. "I just want to rest a minute."

She flattened out away from him, feeling forlorn and sensing anxiety welling up again. Nervously she listened for sounds in the hall.

Tony folded his arms beneath his head. "I really can't believe this," he said.

"What do you mean?"

Nona rolled over onto her stomach, instantly feeling less naked, and built a frame for her face by folding one arm beneath her cheek. From this position she could see him clearly and watch the expressions racing across his face as he spoke.

"I mean I had everything going for me. Everything was coming up roses. For a change none of my kids were freaking out, my wife had finally started a little keep-herself-busy business. My columns were falling out of the typewriter, Richard Nixon was catching it in the ass, and my tennis game had taken off into outer space." He slid a low whistle out from between his squarish teeth. "And so what did I do? I got involved with you. Yessiree—no little stewardesses or waitresses for old Tony Lewellen. Oh, no! I even had a nice thing going with a little journalism intern up at the *Post*—a very sweet girl. . . ." He thought about her for a moment with an inconsolable expression. "But I must have been fucking up somewhere because they really socked it to me with this one. Out of the clear blue sky! Somebody up there must of said, let's blow this guy out of the water, he's been having it too good lately. Let's turn him on to this broad and really let him have it. Oh, sure, you've got big knockers and you're beautiful, but you're so fucking uptight I can't believe it." He reached out to take her hand. "For Chrissake, lady! You are big trouble politically, too. You've probably

128

got a half dozen FBI and CIA agents on your tail—
and your tail is the only thing I worry about anymore." He hit the palm of his hand against his forehead. "Who do you think I am? Jean Paul Sartre,
maybe? I needed a Marxist for a mistress like a hole
in the head. When I think . . . when I stop to think of
all the pussy walking around this town. . . . Shee-it!"

"What's with this Marxist bit?" Nona asked.

"Well? Aren't you a Marxist?"

"No. I'm a registered Democrat."

"Aw, come on."

"Well," she spoke slowly, "if you want a simple
yes or no answer, I guess we're . . . I guess . . . I'm
part of a sort of non-Communist Marxist left."

"Now, what does that mean?" Tony asked. He
turned on his side and propped his head in his hand
to look at her with enormous interest, as if she were
revealing intimate sexual details about herself.

"Jesus, Lewellen. It's really very complicated,"
Nona said evasively. "And this is hardly the time
or the place. We're going to get arrested if they
catch us here. And I've already got a record."

"Well, I'll speed things up a little if you say you'll
be my girl this summer. If you say you'll hang around
with me."

Nona burst into laughter. Despite her nervousness,
she enjoyed the nearness of him, his constant curiosity
and interest in her, and even his stubborn determination to nail her down.

"I mean . . . maybe I can help you," he said in a
soft, magnanimous whisper. "I could maybe help
you if you tell me what you need—or want."

Now he had adopted a businesslike tone taking
her practical needs into account, eager to offer whatever accommodations were necessary to secure the
pleasure of her unsanctioned company.

"I don't want anything," Nona said firmly, trying
to resist some of his Dutch-uncle protectorship.

"Oh, everybody wants something," he said confidently, running the tip of his forefinger over her profile.

I want my other life back, Nona thought. I want those goddamn files Michael stole back in their goddamn file cabinets in Media, Pennsylvania. I want Michael to come home so I can have a baby and a life of my own.

Tony remained silent out of respect for the complicated emotions she was emanating. Then, very gently, he reached out for her hand and began smoothing open the ball of her fist, stroking the fingers apart to draw out the tension.

"How are you fixed for money?" he asked.

Stunned, Nona looked up at him with a jeering expression.

"That was stupid of me," he apologized. "I was just trying to say that maybe I could make things a little easier for you if you'd let me." His voice trailed off as he hit up against the dead end of his own circumstances. "I want to be your friend, Nona," he said very slowly and deliberately. "I care a lot about you."

Nona tightened her fingers around the width of his hand.

He's a nice person, she thought. He means well.

"My parents lent me some money," she said suddenly in a conciliatory way. "It's enough to tide me over for a while." She tucked her cheek into the crook of her elbow.

Secretly she was smiling to herself for she knew what he really wanted. She knew he had no tolerance for ambiguity and that he needed to institutionalize their affair—confirm it verbally—so it would feel like a permanent arrangement to him. Some tenderness for him stirred her and she felt the loneliness that clung to her soul slip away.

He lay relaxed beside her. Suddenly she felt generous and loving toward him.

O.K., she thought, carefully severing her real self

from her present behavior. O.K. I'm going to take a dive. I need someone to lean on for a while. I know I can make it on my own so it's O.K. to rest for a while. People need a little help from their friends sometimes. . . . I'm not selling out. . . . I'm the one who got left behind. . . .

He leaned over to kiss her forehead.

So I'll make the scene with him this summer. So what? I don't have to play Dostoevsky every day of my life. It's O.K. to take a spin in sin city once in a while, cop a feel from the inside for a change. I'll see where these people are really coming from. For one lousy summer I'll be up instead of down, on instead of off, in instead of out, easy instead of hard on myself. I'll have a husband for the summer.

In the next room a radio smeared across several stations before settling on WLOL the station Nona left open in her car. A loud rock record began humping its rhythm behind the wall.

"O.K. I'll be your girl," she said.

"Really?"

"Sure. But I don't want to miss the whole Watergate investigation or the impeachment proceedings or his resignation if. . . ."

But she was suddenly cut off as he lurched above her and began pushing a pillow beneath her belly. Dazed, Nona felt the heavy mass of his chest grind against her spine as he slid on top of her and reached down to seek the opening of her body buried in the billowing pillow, his fingers finally finding and following the roadbed between her legs.

Nona lay motionless, trying to still the sound of her breath and the rustle of her lashes against the sheet so as not to disrupt the exquisite expectancy that flooded her body as he touched her.

"How's that feel?" he asked after a moment.

"Good," she consented.

"You like hand jobs, don't you?"

She didn't respond.

131

"Or do you want to get laid?" he asked as his hand strayed deeper inside her.

Nona turned her face away.

"Tell me. What do you want?"

Silence.

"Tell me what you want!"

"For you to stop talking," Nona said.

Instead, he stopped stroking her. "That's funny," he mused. "You mean . . . don't the younger guys talk while they fuck?"

"Oh, God," Nona grimaced. "What are you? An investigative reporter all of a sudden?"

"O.K., lady. You asked for it."

His words blew into her ear as he entered her.

"Say it," he insisted. "Say it or I won't do it."

Desire mixed with desperation. Beyond argument, animatedly suspended by anticipation, Nona surrendered.

"More," she whispered to the bedspread, summoning his solidness deeper inside her.

"You want more cock, love? You want some more? You want all of it? You have to ask." Partially withdrawing to open her wider, he began inching higher again.

"Oh, yes . . ." she gasped against the bedspread gulping her own hot breath as she felt the start of an internal acceleration. Urgency lay siege to her as she sensed the advent of the intolerable, unstoppable spasms that led to climax. Euphorically poised on the tip of perfect anticipation, balancing precisely on a prepeak of pleasure, she delicately evaded the explosion of her own orgasm.

"You're too hot," Tony said suddenly, jerking himself out of her, violently withdrawing the hard arching presence of his body.

Nona clutched with shock, stunned by her sudden emptiness. She felt her insides clutching vainly at the void where Tony had pumped pleasure into her system. Instantly the core of her body began to contract, dispersing the sensations it had been collating for climax.

"Noooo," Nona whimpered feeling her breath dampen the sheet beneath her mouth as her body shivered from the chill of dislocation. "Oh, Tony, don't."

He rolled away from her so that the loss of his weight and warmth sent her body temperature tumbling.

"You were too close," he panted against her cheek. "You weren't supposed to come yet."

Nona's breath was punching out of her as she turned to look into Lewellen's face, tangled and snarled by his effort to control himself as well as her.

"You son of a bitch," she said slowly, smiling as her organs contracted and retreated from the now empty battleground beneath her belly, unsuccessfully triyng to smother the spasmodic shivers that rippled through her.

"You O.K.?" he asked quietly.

Nona chuckled softly. "No," she said. "No, I'm not O.K., Lewellen. As a matter of fact I feel sort of . . . well, actually, now I know what they mean when they say prick tease."

Lewellen loved her with his eyes and reached out to brush his hand along her cheek. "We'll try it again," he said, closing his eyes. "Just as soon as I cool myself out."

She looked at his tight dissatisfied body.

"Doesn't that hurt?" she asked solicitously, fingering his raw red penis. "Don't you want to get rid of it?"

"No."

"You know grans and gramps are probably on their way back up here by now."

He reached over to hold one of her breasts. "What time is it?"

"I think it's time to come . . . and then go."

"You're too much," he said to the ceiling. "How

133

the hell in this crazy fucked-up world I ever got hooked up with you Ill never know."

"Look," she said. "I mean it. I don't want to miss the whole damn afternoon. I've been sitting in there for five weeks waiting for John Dean."

Tony got off the bed and began wrestling with his trousers finally extracting a box of Trojans from one of the pockets. "I brought my own this time," he said looking at her with a tough smile as he came back to the bed. "You or me?"

She unwrapped the rubber.

This time when he entered her he was finished with teasing and used the rhythm of her orgasm to trigger the spill of his own seed.

Eight

The day after her reconciliation with Tony Lewellen in their borrowed room at the Carol Arms, Nona began to follow a new routine. As soon as the hearings adjourned each day, she hurried home to transcribe her hasty fragmentary notes into typed double-spaced sentences that became convictions as soon as they appeared on paper. Since she seldom knew precisely what she thought before she wrote it down, she invariably fell in love with her first drafts and remained totally committed to them until the next day when she reread what she had written.

Always high when she finished working, Nona would instantly begin straightening up her apartment, trying to make it look neat since it was always so miserably hot and stuffy when she and Lewellen returned to it late at night. He had finally adjusted to her cramped bedroom and had learned how to make love to her without catapulting either of them off the edge of the narrow cot. Then she would shower, dress, and hurry outside to take a taxi to whatever restaurant Lewellen had chosen for dinner. Dining had become an elaborate part of Lewellen's sexual foreplay, a ritual way of erasing the day and easing them into the sensuality of their evenings.

It was always dark when she left her building but the heat still clung to the city, blurring any hard-edge sense of time so that the hours melted indiscriminately together. Some evenings Tony craved the incestuous embrace of other journalists and, in pursuit of the pack, he and Nona would glide from one chic air-conditioned hangout to another continually encountering the same crowd of newspaper and media personalities. Island-hopping by car or taxi across the humid sea of the city, Nona felt pursued by the heat. Other nights Tony seemed to require a quiet hideaway where he could talk to Nona uninterrupted —about possible topics or themes for his columns or the political consequences of impeaching the president. Then he would choose some commercial restaurant, crowded with tourists but assiduously avoided by Washington types.

By dark the Watergate crisis created a carnival atmosphere throughout Washington and wherever they went Nona sensed a weird mixture of sickness and revelry. A smell of corruption tainted everything like the faint odor of mildew on a tropical island. The city had been contaminated by a deadly cynicism that seemed to loosen inhibitions and unleash bizarre behavior. People were drinking heavily, talking loudly, carousing longer and later. One night during dinner with Senator Dempsey at the Rive Gauche, Nona recalled and retold the Edgar Alan Poe story about a royal court fleeing a plague-ridden capital to hide at the king's summer castle only to encounter Death there—disguised as a reveler at one of their costume balls.

Repeat broadcasts of the hearings filled the evening air, providing the background music for their nightly odyssey. Cars carried the story of Watergate along the avenues, and through the open windows of houses and apartment buildings TVs relayed reruns of the hearings fulfilling the function of bush drums repeating the same dire warnings over and over again. Small transistor radios ran the endless epic of corruption in parks and supermarkets as Washington's black natives listened to the droning narrative, relishing all the details of the criminality of their white government officials. From behind the heavy doors of restaurant kitchens or bottom shelves of whiskey-bottle-lined walls in usually quiet bars—in all the territory controlled by black workers—radios replayed the Senate investigation.

Sometimes, spinning along in Lewellen's car or laughing flirtatiously in some cocktail lounge, sunk conspiratorially close together in the horseshoe curve of a fake leather booth, Nona would be stung with guilt at her shameless behavior and pressed into a reconsideration of what she was doing. Thrashing through buffers of alcoholic immunity she would wonder why she was whipping around northwest Washington, from one air-cooled cave to another, playing out an illicit love affair while her real life hung in abeyance, suspended above some vague disaster. The constant movement in and out of bars and bistros exposed her to fast temperature changes that triggered or accelerated drunkenness and Nona eagerly embraced oblivion—wanting not to think, perversely trying to dim the thoughts that assaulted her when she was alone and sober.

It seemed to Nona, in her drunken haze, that they floated above the city—levitated by heat and alcohol, sustained by the political hysteria that filled the atmospheric air waves and egged on by strangers also celebrating celebration. Lewellen's endless supply of money and credit became the key that turned Washington into a high-powered windup toy and Nona was becoming addicted to the action.

During the last days of June, as John Dean continued his testimony, the Washington weather hit its summer stride. By 10 o'clock people were already rumpled and wrinkled. Temperatures hit the nineties and the humidity would continue to mount until an invisible geodesic dome hung over the city. Only the days remained discreetly separate—transparent chunks of time frozen solid by the heavy-duty air conditioning of the Senate caucus room.

The excitement of the press corps crescendoed with

137

the temperature and by the last Friday of June, when the hearings adjourned for the Fourth of July weekend, most of the national press corps were convinced that the country couldn't tolerate Dean's awesome accusations against the president and that Congress would have to impeach Nixon for desecrating the democratic system.

A wild sense of victory broke over the pack of political reporters as they streamed out of the Senate office building, and it took almost an hour for Nona to find a taxi she could share with three other people going to Georgetown. She was the first one to be dropped off and she felt embarrassed disembarking at the huge Kinkaid mansion set into the side of a lazy hill only a block off Wisconsin Avenue. Unexpectedly intimidated by the classiness of the place, she pressed the bell and listened to rich chimes echo her uneasiness through the unseen interior.

Sam opened the door immediately. He looked tanned and rested, beach scrubbed and boyishly eager.

"Hello. How've you been?" he grinned. But his initial enthusiasm wilted when he realized Nona was alone and his smile sank. "Where's Tony?" he asked, looking down toward the street with an apprehensiveness that erased any sincerity from his welcome.

"Isn't he here yet?"

"No. But Cindy's late, too. They'll probably show in a few minutes. Come on in."

Making a cavalier gesture that clashed with his tense expression, he led her down an icy hallway. Nona felt that they were crossing the lobby of a large hotel, traversing a stretch of public space in order to reach familiar territory. But even in the living room, Sam still moved tentatively, as if he were some timid summer subleasee, careful not to disturb the contents or position of any furniture. The Kinkaid mansion clearly belonged to its absent mistress whose

138

presence hung in the house like winter clothing left behind in a closet.

Jesus. He's really uptight, Nona thought, standing transfixed at the edge of the living room as she watched Sam's awkward arabesque around various obstacles toward the tavern-long bar. He's going to nix the whole thing.

"What would you like to drink?" Sam asked, absently inventorying his supply of jiggers and shakers, mixers and stirrers. Safely ensconced behind the wooden barricade, armored by an arsenal of glasses and silver cocktail equipment, he looked more self-confident.

"Just Scotch, please, on the rocks." Nona began walking toward a huge white sofa that floated atop the blue carpeting, riding at anchor in front of a glass wall that faced a sea of green land outside. Capsizing into the foamy cushions, she looked around the high-ceilinged room, noting the scars where arches and beams had been amputated to create a more open space for the modern glass-and-steel furniture.

"This is a very nice spread you have here," she quoted Sam in a teasing voice.

He looked over at her with a slim challenging smile. "I thought for sure you were going to deliver me a critique on the inequitable distribution of property in America."

Nona felt a fierce discomfort developing between them—he's going to tell me he doesn't want to do it, she thought. He's going to say no.

"Well, what'd you think about Dean spilling the Enemies List?" Sam asked, emerging from behind the bar to hand Nona her drink before skirting a large glass cocktail table to collapse on the twin sofa across from her.

"Oh, it's a trip!" she agreed with a warm beseeching smile. "Everyone freaked out this morning when he announced it."

Sam shook his head with incredulity as he sipped

his drink. "It's really weird that you and Daniels weren't on it," he said, watching her speculatively. "You might just get drummed out of the Movement for not being officially recognized as a presidential enemy."

Nona gulped down several mouthfuls of Scotch. "Well, every agency probably has it's own exclusive list and since Michael's on the FBI's Ten Most Wanted, the White House probably decided to drop him." Laughing, she met his eyes, pleading for him to come across.

"Listen," Sam said, succumbing to the pressure. "I did get in touch with my lawyer, and I asked what he thought about your . . . proposal. He vetoed it right off the bat—mostly because we haven't decided yet what we're going to do. You know, whether we'll bring a civil suit and sue—or what. . . . So, he felt very strongly that I shouldn't make any public statements in regard to my case at all."

Nona felt a sad smile float across her face.

"Actually, though, that was his only stipulation . . . nothing public."

He's embrarrassed, Nona thought, watching Sam. He's a poseur who only cares about his public image. He doesn't want people to know he turned down evidence against the FBI. He doesn't want people to know he was afraid to publish those files.

"Anyway," Sam said, his eyes bright with promise, "the more I thought about it, the more I felt that the best way to find out what they have—whether or not they actually have tapes of my telephone calls— is from someone inside the government. And I was thinking that maybe Eric Kessler would be willing to check it out for me and see if Daniels's call did get picked up and recorded."

"I don't understand," Nona said. "Why should he do that?"

"Well—he might want to get in on the action so he can publicly separate himself from the bad guys.

He's tired of being Kissinger's protégé. After all, Kissinger brought him down here and created a position for him. Kessler might want to score a few brownie points with the liberals. Anyway, if it would serve any of his interests, he'd come up with goods P.D.Q. He doesn't want to go back to practicing law. He wants to stay in government. As a matter of fact, he might just do it because I ask him. We've been pretty good friends for a long time."

Nona looked doubtful. "Gee, Sam. I don't see why he would. The D.C. Four case was the only political conspiracy the government won. Kessler wouldn't want to see that verdict overthrown. Since it was his staff that collected the goods, he's obviously got a vested interest in keeping those guys in jail. He's not going to want to see them get sprung because of any new evidence."

"I'm not so sure of that," Sam insisted. "I think there're a lot of good reasons why he might do it. Anyway. I'll be glad to talk to him if you want me to."

Nona drained her glass. "Well, I guess so." She was confused and upset. "I mean *you* know him, *I* don't."

The chimes rang, and Sam jumped up. When he returned he had Cindy positioned in front of him.

"Hi, Nona," Cindy said gaily.

Well turned out in a high-fashioned pants suit, Cindy floated forward reminding Nona of those TV commercials in which a model wafts across a sandy dune toward her lover with her hair flowing out behind her in slow-motion, soft-focus, hard-sell.

Sinking down into the sofa beside Nona, Cindy created the impression of a high school girl out on a double date and Nona felt overwhelmed by a sense of trespass. She and Cindy were obviously invading and occupying another woman's home, acting out the classic role of summer replacements for a set of vacationing wives. They were luxuries which men such as Tony and Sam felt as much entitled as to second cars.

"Sam, I need a drink," Cindy groaned, sinking back so the pillows billowed around her. "The office was wild today, and you have a hundred phone calls waiting for you. You guys can scamper around the Vineyard, but I have to run your office for you. You can't just pop your head in to kiss me hello." Sam brought her a drink. "Did Sam tell you about his big plan yet?" she asked Nona.

"No, I didn't get a chance to," Sam said quickly. "When I saw Cindy this afternoon we decided to give an enormous party for everyone on the Enemies List—a big bash to show those fuckers over in the White House that we're not afraid of them."

The chimes rang again.

"It should be really fabulous," Cindy said in a charged-up voice to cover her embarrasment as Sam left the room. "We're going to invite everyone on the list. At least everyone who we know," she qualified quickly.

They sat in silence until Tony came down the stairs and jogged over to the couch. Stopping in front of Nona, he paused for a second and then dropped straight down toward her, breaking his plunge only at the last second by extending his arms as a brace against the back of the sofa. High on affection and anticipation, he ducked his head down near her face.

"You O.K.?" he asked rubbing his nose against her cheek.

She could feel his excitement and knew it stemmed from pleasure at the four of them being there at Sam's together, each couple comfortably complementing and reinforcing the other.

With a strong thrust of his arms, Tony pushed himself back onto his feet, "Sam just told me about the party he's going to throw." Walking to the bar, he picked up a martini shaker, thought for a moment, and then rejected it to splash Scotch halfway to the top of a tall tumbler.

Sam came bounding back into the room. "You know something? This time I'm going to break my own embargo and invite some society reporters to cover the party so Nixon can read about it in the papers."

Nona sank back into the buxom pillows and looked at Tony, wondering if he had known about Sam's counteroffer.

"Of course, a lot of people are out of town," Cindy said. "But there's still plenty of enemies here and in New York who can probably make it." She looked over at Sam. "Anyway, we can pad it out with enemy sympathizers, can't we, Sam?"

"Sure. I wanted to anyway."

"All the Kennedy liberals," Nona said in a quiet but incendiary voice.

Tony stopped dropping ice cubes into his glass and turned to look at Nona with a warning frown.

She smiled back at him demurely.

"Get a paper and pencil, honey," Sam said to Cindy. "Let's make out the guest list right now. You got that page from the *Star*?" Then he looked at his wrist watch. "Another half-hour and they'll be starting the reruns of the hearings. We'd better hurry."

"You're not going to watch them again tonight, Sam, are you?" Cindy complained, poised to take dictation with a spiral notebook on her lap.

"I bet this Enemies List is only a cover for some other one that hasn't surfaced yet," Nona interrupted. "I mean, after all, there aren't any dangerous types on it—no Panthers or Weatherpeople. I bet Nixon probably has another list for the real heavies—the ones who were never in the running for White House dinner party invitations."

"What did you write your column on for tomorrow?" Sam asked Tony, ignoring Nona's speech.

"I did a takeoff on Nixon's Enemy List . . . a little

143

posthumous something I threw together for Adolf Hitler."

Sam and Cindy laughed.

"Nixon must really be a paranoid nutgoody to worry about that group of people," Nona insisted belligerently. "That list looks like the lineup for some TV marathon fund-raiser for the Democratic party." She was beginning to hear the mellow echo of alcohol behind her words. "In fact, most of those people would have gone to dinner with the Nixons if they'd been invited. That's probably the most dangerous thing about them, because they're certainly not any threat to the system."

"What about all those journalists on the list?" Sam asked, turning toward Nona with an angry expression. "They're the ones who've been getting all this Watergate stuff out into the open."

"Well, if they're doing anything right, it's only been for the last few months," Nona said, her voice beginning to rise. "Most of these journalists never had the balls to criticize Nixon before the *Post* took off after him."

"I think," Sam said slowly, "that Nona's upset because she didn't make the list." He spoke in a neutral voice so she could interrupt his words either as an attack or a teasing appeasement.

"Oh, I'm glad I didn't get listed with those finks," Nona persisted.

"Listen," Sam said more roughly. "A lot of those people are close friends of mine."

"Oh, I'm sure of that, Sam. That's clearly your zone . . . the central committee of the eastern liberal establishment."

"And who the hell do you think is the left wing in America?" Sam demanded.

His counterfeit tolerance was wearing thin, and his eyes were superimposing a stereotypical image on Nona that made her seem politically preposterous and personally offensive.

144

"Well, it's not Carol Channing," Nona started. "And it's not Jack Valenti or Sarg Shriver or any of those glamour pusses. . . ."

No one responded. Sam walked over to a table in a far corner of the room and began rummaging through a pile of newspapers. Tony emerged from behind the bar and after several seconds of indecision sat down between Nona and Cindy.

"I also want to get some source people over here," Sam said. "People from Sam Dash's and Weikert's staffs." He returned to perch on a chair across from the sofa, opening the *Washington Star* to its full-page reprint of the White House Enemy List. "Write down Woodward and Bernstein."

"They won't show," Cindy said. "They don't like to talk out of school."

"Why should they?" Nona asked. "Finders, keepers, losers, weepers."

Her glass was empty so she got up to fix a refill. Everyone watched as she inserted herself behind the bar. She could feel the sting of Scotch in the center of her body, heightening her anger. "I mean . . . wouldn't you call pumping investigative reporters a tertiary source?"

"That's enough, Nona," Tony said firmly.

Everyone remained silent until Nona returned to her seat. Tony removed his arm from the back of the couch as she sat down.

"I mean, everybody knows it's hard to do a hatchet job when you're up on water skis off Hyannisport, but I don't think it's kosher trying to get poop from other reporters."

"Come on, let's go take a swim," Tony suggested in a fraudulently friendly voice that offered a last chance for reconciliation.

"I'm not going to do anything until I get some food," Cindy interrupted. "I haven't had anything to eat since breakfast."

"O.K." Sam put down the newspaper with a petulant

gesture that implied his good times had been permanently spoiled.

Tony and Nona remained on the sofa, silently separating further apart as they waited for Sam and Cindy to disappear down the hallway.

Nona took another pull of Scotch and looked over the rim of her glass toward a patch of sunlight on the carpet.

"You knew he wasn't going to do it, didn't you?" she asked. "You knew it when you came back from the Cape. You just wanted me to think it was going to happen. You put me on so you could get laid."

"Now wait a minute!" Tony twisted around to confront her. "I think Sam's offering you something better than a goddamn press conference where he tells a bunch of people who can't do anything about it that Mike Daniels once called him up. I think there's a strong chance Kessler might help. He really is a good friend of Sam's."

"And of yours too, isn't he?"

"Believe it or not, Nona, Eric's a decent man."

"Are you kidding?" she squealed. "He lied to the press about police actions and crowd control from the beginning. He's the one who did the hatchet job on what those guys like to call dissidents. Well, now you guys are the dissidents and he fucked you. How can he be a good guy if he lies to you? And how come he lies to you if you're such a good friend?"

"Jesus, Nona," Tony groaned with disgust, "you sound like . . . one of my kids."

"Well, maybe they're right, too." she persisted, feeling the almost forgotten burn of parental contempt.

Tony set down his drink on the cocktail table. "Now, look," he said, "Sam's got plenty of troubles of his own. I think its damn decent of him to try to do something for you. In fact, he's already made arrangements to get us invited to a Justice Department boatride on the Fourth of July that Kessler's giving so you can meet and talk to him personally. Now what the fuck more you think Sam Kinkaid owes you, I don't know. But if you don't get off your high horse and mind your manners, he's got every right in the world to tell you to fuck off. And I sure as hell won't intervene, because I think you're acting like a punk kid."

Nona sat back waiting for her fury to subside.

Tenderly, Tony reached out and stroked her hair away from her face. "I know it's important to you," he said. "Things have been tough. But you've got to behave yourself. What's so terrible if we take a swim and kibbitz around for a while without you trashing everything in sight? As long as we're here why can't it be nice?"

"O.K.," Nona said, setting down her glass. "O.K. Tell him I want to talk to Kessler. Tell him we want to go on the boatride."

"It's all set." Tony tried to draw her toward him. "But it's five days away, and I want you to pull your shit together and act like a lady in the meantime."

"O.K.," Nona said, desperate to avoid his touch at that moment and trying to find enough leverage amid the billowing pillows to stand up. "But let's get something to eat. I feel dizzy."

Cindy was singing and dancing around the kitchen, flinging open the cabinet doors in a drunken pirouette around the room. "Let's eat everything we can find," she trilled. "I'm starving, really starving. Let's just eat the stuff right out of the cans with rusty ole spoons."

Sam was leaning against an enormous butcherblock island in the center of the room, watching Cindy ransack the cupboards with a heretical, encouraging smile on his lips.

He likes this, Nona thought, standing motionless and watching the scene with a queer, light-hearted

147

sensation. Cindy's sacking his wife's kitchen and it's turning him on.

"See if she's left any steaks in the freezer," Sam prompted. "She usually stashes a couple of cows away in there."

The contemptuous hiss of the word *she* singed Nona's ears.

Cindy went skating across the brick floor toward the double Frigidaire. She swung open the freezer door and began pulling out neat, tin-foil-wrapped packages. "Jesus," she squealed, "there's a ton of meat in here. God! She paid four seventy-nine a pound for this porterhouse. If she could boycott herself for a week, she'd bring down the price of beef single-handed. Nationwide! And look! She's labeled all of them, too. Every one of them's got a little label stuck on it." Cindy kept rummaging through the frozen steak, but her flamboyant inventory was beginning to verge on hysteria as she flung the frozen packages across the metallic shelves.

"If she'd use Saran Wrap she could just look inside and not have to write everything down. Look at this!" She read aloud. "Two porterhouse, two and a half pounds each. Does that grill on the sundeck work, Sam?" she asked, emerging from the freezer.

"Sure." He looked puzzled at the possibility of some appliance not being functional.

"O.K., then, let's grill tons of steaks out there," Cindy said. She began piling tin-foil packages on the counter near the sink, frowning slightly as she read the labels, rejecting some and enthusiastically claiming possession of others.

Nona walked through a glassed dining area flooded with pale late afternoon sunlight and out through French doors onto a wooden deck extended above the green landscape.

The Kinkaid's pool was a giant blue ceramic shell planted in a forest of bamboo trees. On one side was a tiled patio where clusters of pink and blue floral-padded furniture grew like wild flowers. Lush island shrubbery crept across the page of green lawn down to a half-hidden tennis court.

Cindy emerged from the kitchen to stand beside her.

"It's really pretty," Nona murmured, impressed by the lyrical quality of the garden despite her allergy to affluence. Huge primitive pots held miniature bamboo trees or tropical plants while other earthen jugs were upended and transformed into robust mushrooms so their rough-textured bottoms became plump tables set cozily among the luxurious clusters of garden furniture.

"Isn't it scrumptious?" Cindy bragged. "I just love it. Harrison Thrower designed it. He's done a lot of the Kennedys' houses and most of the best ones in Georgetown. The thing is—he really tries to integrate a pool into the environment. He doesn't just stamp it down like a postage mark in one corner of the place. I just love his style. And it's really wonderful eating outside here at night. Sam's going to make a fire. It's really going to be nice."

The four of them had dinner at a round glass table on the sundeck. They ate enormous quantities of charcoal-broiled steak and salad that Tony had made and finished off five bottles of red wine while watching the rerun of the Senate hearings over a portable television set Sam had brought outside. Dusk was falling like dust, dropping tiny particles of night upon them and only the weird white electronic light of the television spliced reality back into the romantic scene.

Nona sat in silence, refilling her wine glass as soon as it was empty and flicking her cigarette ashes onto her empty dinner plate as a lame show of social protest while she watched the bright eager face of John Dean and listened to the senators' slow circuitous questions followed by Dean's precisely phrased answers.

Senator Montoya asked, "Were these particular

149

conferences at San Clemente designed to just discuss the matter of Watergate?"

"They were designed to discuss how to deal with this committee so that the cover-up would not unravel up here before this committee," Dean responded.

Uneasy about an ambiance aimed at homogenizing her into the group, Nona tried to disassociate herself from the others without actually alienating them. She ignored their running commentary about the proceedings, dismissing their pat comments as the received opinions of their social classmates. Their talk was as chic and seductive as they were.

But as hard as she was on her companions, Nona was being even harder on herself. Her infatuation with Tony Lewellen mocked all her political convictions and experiences, and she couldn't reconcile her lust for him with her contempt for his lifestyle. Bitterly she admitted being there—accepting a second viewing of the hearings, allowing Sam's occasional sarcasms and tolerating Cindy's sickening shows of sycophancy because she was waiting for Tony to want her again, waiting for the animal in him to rise up once more and come to take her apart again. Painfully she conceded she had been flattered into her childlike compliance and acquiescence by Tony's well-staged seduction campaign and that she was mated to him despite the disappointing responses she was getting in her attempt to help Michael.

John Dean said, "On March thirteen we discussed both clemency and the fact that there was no money. . . . He asked me how, you know, how much it was going to cost. I gave him my best estimate which I said was one million dollars or more. He, in turn, said to me, 'Well, one million is certainly no problem to raise,' and turned to Mr. Haldeman and made a similar comment. . . ."

"This is incredible," Sam roared.

"Yeah, it's a whole new ball game now," Tony

150

nodded. "If Nixon doesn't resign, they'll have to impeach him. There's no way out."

Nona watched the camera shift to Maureen Dean, the buxom beach-bleached homecoming queen sitting loyally behind her husband. Nona got a few fast sadistic hits seeing the Deans sweat jail, for they seemed to even off the score for all the Movement people who had stood trial. But even as she tasted vengeance, self-contempt gripped her. Who was she to judge John Dean while she herself was power-tripping with Tony Lewellen. She mocked her own self-righteousness. A little lust was bad for politics.

For another hour they all remained stationary listening to the variations played on the theme of corruption at the White House. Eventually the Kinkaid mansion evaporated into darkness, and Sam pushed himself away from the table to lie down on a chaise.

"Come 'ere," he said to Cindy, patting the stingy margin of space he allotted for her.

"Do we have to watch the whole thing?" Cindy whined as she relocated herself beside Sam.

Tony staggered to his feet and came up behind Nona's chair to drop a strangle hold around her neck, crooking his elbow beneath her chin.

"You're my friend," he whispered against her cheek. "I don't want you to feel bad." He began to massage her neck, kneading the high-tension cables knotted beneath her hair. "Come on, let's go skinny-dipping. I'll wash some Watergate off you." His hands slid around to the front of her neck and then slipped inside her shirt to cup her breasts. Corralling all the movable flesh, he let their weight undulate in his hands.

"No," she said, "I won't swim naked here."

"Well then, go put on your swim suit, honey," he whispered more insistently. "Hurry up!"

Nona hesitated and then, more out of discontent than consent, she rose to return to the house. In the all-yellow powder room off the kitchen she changed

151

into her tank suit and tried to regain her composure for she felt perilously anxious and out of focus. When she returned to the sundeck Sam looked up and rutted his face into a speculative expression as he assessed her figure, obviously comparing it to Cindy's slim hard little body.

Humiliated at having exposed herself to him, Nona ran down toward the pool without waiting for Tony.

From the diving board she sliced through the air as if off the end of the earth. Unshackled and unharnessed for a few seconds from the weights and constraints of gravity, Nona knifed into a blue universe of such totally different forces that for a moment she felt free.

She swam relentlessly, punishing her body for its rebelliousness. But after several laps, winded and exhausted, she clutched the rim of the pool and looked up to see Tony coming across the patio, his knit trunks cupping the fistful of fruit at his crotch. He moved directly onto the diving board, his muscles jostling beneath the brown satin spread of his skin, and lifted up easily to dive into the water. Nona turned to watch him surface, but when he finally emerged he was beside her, his hands sliding up the sides of her body as he broke through the water.

He shook the hair from his eyes, spraying Nona's face. "You're so beautiful, it's not real," he said. His words were meaningless, like a distracted groan in the midst of lovemaking, a gratuitous sounding to relieve some intolerable swell of emotion and thus avert its inadvertent conclusion.

"Feels good, doesn't it?" he panted, catching hold of the pool ledge and bracing his arms on each side of her.

Nona smiled, secretly positioning her feet against the wall to escape beneath the bridge of his arms. But suddenly she felt his fist between her thighs. Quickly she bent her knees to push off and tunnel

152

into the water, but he forced her back up against the wall. His chin bit into her shoulder as he pulled aside the crotch of her swim suit and wedged his fingers inside the incision of her sex.

"Oh, Tony, don't," she whispered, trying to wiggle away from him. "Please don't."

But his chest and shoulders riveted her against the slippery tile and his hard fingers, curved like a fish hook, expertly separated the rubbery flesh around the plump clitoral partition.

"Oh, don't, Tony, please don't," Nona begged, her whisper crescendoing into a moan. "Please don't." Her head bobbed below the surface and water flooded into her mouth. She could feel Tony's nail snagging the invisible lining of her vagina, hooking her ignobly like a piece of fabric caught inside a zipper as he pressed his fingers deeper inside her body. "Let me go," she moaned, spraying water from her mouth into his face. With one hand she clung to his shoulder to keep her head above water while she thrashed about trying to disengage the hand sunk inside her.

"Be still," Tony said, his lips sliding against her wet cheek.

"I don't want you to do this," she pleaded. "I mean it, Tony."

But now she began to feel drugged, weighted down by the pronged anchor of his hand. His fingers kept snailing higher inside, coiling and flexing rhythmically. Nona felt herself helplessly gripped by an internal current of pressure and pleasure.

She quickened.

"You've got to stop," she gasped. "They can see us. They're watching. Please, Tony." She was still squirming about, trying to escape, as she felt the acceleration of sexual tension.

The movement of his fingers, plugging and unplugging the locks of her body, was tightening and

153

tensing and collating her reflexes—staging her for climax.

"Is it nice?" he whispered with anxious affection.

"Oh, Tony." Her breath bubbled the water between their faces. Her legs were clamped together now, netting and trapping his hand between her clenched thighs, and as she felt herself begin to rock and grind against him she surrendered herself to the violent convulsive contractions. The involuntary muscular spasm began to mount, and her mind, rushing like white water toward a rocky precipice, plunged off a high, high cliff into a chasm.

Her center moved.

After a moment, her head sank down against Tony's shoulder as she felt herself dissolving into the water. Then she put both arms around his neck and clung weightlessly from him like a child who didn't know how to swim.

When they returned to the house, wrapped in huge beach towels, Nona realized that Sam assumed they would stay the weekend and she let it happen.

At the top of the Hollywood spiral staircase Sam opened a door to the guest room, indicated an enormous antique fourposter bed, said good night, and disappeared.

"I'm pretty tired," Tony announced as Nona headed toward the doorway of an adjoining bath. When she flicked on the light she was assaulted by an infinite number of sleepy wet-haired women in the mirror-tiled walls. Above the silver-plated sink, glass shelves climbed to the ceiling carrying heavy cargoes of deluxe cosmetics—Pantene, Le Galion. Rochas, and Scandia bath products were multiplied endlessly by the mirrors so it seemed that all the world's beauty resources were stashed away in the Kinkaid's bathroom. Nona kicked the door shut behind her as an involuntary redistribution-of-wealth reflex possessed her. Drunk on wine and resentment, Nona felt driven to attack the elegant packages, to smash jars of oils and creams, moisturizers and facial masques, shampoos and hair lotions, to break the boxes of perfumed soaps, bath crystals, and imported colognes.

You fucking rich bastards, she swore silently, imagining herself undoing tops and beheading bottles, raiding and ravishing the conspicuous cosmetics, spilling the abundant expensive ointments down the toilet.

This isn't a bathroom, it's a goddamn department store, Nona thought. But all the perfume in the world can't cover up the stench from this scene, Sam baby. Someday you'll have to pay for all this. . . .

Her anger mounted and for one insane moment she considered flushing all the perfumes and colognes down the toilet. But finally worn out and weary, she went back into the bedroom.

Tony was sound asleep, lying face down on the bed. Nona covered him with the blanket he had thrown aside and then lay down beside him, falling quickly into a wine-heavy sleep.

Nine

Throughout the weekend a tempestuous tropical heat bloated the days and impregnated the nights with a decadent restlessness. A never-ending parade of Sam's friends kept dropping by his house to swim or play tennis. Nona and Tony kept their distance from each other and the crowd that sunned themselves around the pool accepted Nona easily as just another unknown Watergate reporter. Most of the time Nona kept to herself, lying a bit apart from the others on a chlorine-scented chaise beneath the palmlike trees at the edge of the patio. Sipping white wine, she would watch the people in their beach apparel or tennis togs wandering in and out of the Kinkaid mansion, towing small or teen-aged children in their wake.

Gradually the house took on the aspect of an elite resort and the poolside scene became a posed photo for some Newsmakers or Personalities section of a weekly magazine. The group that drifted in and out, uninvited and unannounced, was composed mostly of journalists and their families who lived in Georgetown, but also seated around the sundeck were politically famous faces whose names Nona momentarily forgot from the surprise of seeing them up close—as if the identifying captions had been torn from beneath newspaper pictures of them so that a reader assumed, rather than knew, their importance.

All during the long weekend, Democratic congressmen, pre-Nixon administration officials, network producers and newscasters, syndicated columnists and foreign journalists, leftish diplomats, liberal law-firm partners, art curators, local politicians, and national campaign organizers—accompanied by fashionably trim, determinedly beautiful wives and long-haired children—turned up at Sam Kinkaid's. The men would shake hands, as if congratulating rather than greeting each other, while the women embraced and kissed the air beside a friendly face. But gradually mutual esteem, with the ease of a runner-thread releasing a hem, would relax everyone and awkwardness would unravel into affability.

Cindy, who apparently had put in enough time with Sam to be considered a legitimate summer stand-in, helped distribute towels and pull chairs into conversation circles. Since many of the visiting women were second rather than original wives, they were relatively tolerant of Cindy's hostessy ministrations and straddled the difficult line between disapproval and forgiveness, never forgetting that Cindy could become Sam's next wife.

Nona moved about with the air of an accidental guest, careful not to intrude upon the caste party. Occasionally Tony would make a teasing remark to her when he passed by so as not to seem suspiciously uninterested in such an attractive stranger, but Nona avoided any lengthy conversations until Sunday afternoon when Barry Stein appeared.

He emerged through the French door leading from the kitchen and chatted with people on the sundeck before walking down to the pool where he spied Nona sitting off to one side. Their eyes met, mutually surprised by each other's presence, and Nona felt a flush of embarrassment at being caught fraternizing with the enemy after years of criticizing the Georgetown liberal establishment.

"What are *you* doing here?" he asked as he advanced toward her, visually acknowledging the fact that she now outranked him among the clique of press elite after whom he lusted. He squatted down beside her chaise and shot her a hot high-school smile of silent applause— So? You're making it with old boy, huh? How is it?

Nona looked back unable to explain that her incriminating collusion with Tony Lewellen didn't reflect any real infidelity to Michael.

But Barry wasn't buying it. "You're laying on quite a tan," he commented. "Veeery heavy."

Nona sighed, ashamed and despairing.

"Personally I'm here on business," he announced. "Big business. . . ."

Glad to be left off the hook, Nona asked what was happening.

"I am hot on the trail of a very big story," Barry said, rocking back and forth on the balls of his feet. "I think I'm on to who signed the order to tap Sam and the other reporters."

"Really! Did you tell Sam yet?"

"No. That's what I came over for." Barry's eyes clouded briefly at having to explain his presence at a social event where he didn't rightfully belong. "He's going to flip out. I just got my tip yesterday, so it's pretty premature, you know . . . but. . . ."

Nona experienced an unusual feeling of warmth toward Barry because his pleasure was so genuine and his commitment to getting his story almost physically manifest.

"Need any help?" Nona asked.

"Not at the moment." He stood up. "Do you know where Sam is?"

"Playing tennis, I think."

"Take care." Barry touched the top of Nona's head and walked away.

Uncomfortably warm and charged up by Barry's excitement, Nona walked back to the house. Cindy was standing at the butcher block counter in the middle of the kitchen emptying bags of potato chips and pretzels into huge plastic bowls. Nona parked

158

her empty wine glass on the countertop and began to help.

"Well, how do you like this scene?" Cindy asked in an angry provocative voice.

Uncertain how to reply, Nona simply shrugged her shoulders.

Cindy began to scoop stuffed olives out of a tall skinny jar with a crooked forefinger. "God, some of these broads piss me off with all their airs. They think I don't know about them."

Nona lit a cigarette, deciding that Cindy's position as Sam's mistress had begun to elevate her political consciousness.

"Do you know Joan Kinkaid?" she asked delicately.

"Oh, sure," Cindy answered, rolling her eyes heavenward and moving along more quickly about her chores. "I know Joan. She just doesn't know me. As a matter of fact, I know everything about her. And not from Sam either," she added virtuously since a philandering husband was not a legitimate news source for any liberated woman. "Joan's a real classic. She does the whole bit—from being a trustee of the Smithsonian to flying to Paris every spring to buy her clothes. She collects Cardins—they're all upstairs if you want to see them—and she gets her hair done three times a week at Roberto Fucigna's and she buys all her little accessories at Dorcas Hardin's and she works out at the Watergate Health Club and takes tennis lessons from Aly Ritzenberg over at St. Alban's—that's where their boy goes to school—I think their little girl's at Beauvoir." Cindy tore open another bag of potato chips with her teeth. "But she gets her brownie points working for all the 'in' charities like Cancer or Leukemia and she helps do the National Symphony Ball and makes nice little luncheons for all the other ladies on the benefit planning committees."

Cindy reached out for Nona's cigarette to light

159

one of her own. "And of course she's always re-decorating this house so she has to go antiquing around Maryland and Virginia all the time. Joan only likes the finest things." Cindy sucked in some smoke with a disgusted grunt and expression. "And she's always trying to get some of her friends' husbands to take her out to lunch at the Jockey Club so it looks like maybe she's got something going on the side. But I don't think she wants a lover—all she wants is to make perfect little dinner parties, you know? She wants to make the ultimate dinner party outside on the patio with six round tables seating eight and flowered cloths and matching centerpieces and matching candles and those bony bamboo chairs she rents from Ridgewells and a crew of invisible servants and a combo playing down on the tennis court and the perfect guests, so there'll be a couple government Mercs parked outside with those goose-necked reading lamps sticking up in the back seat like a hard-on and a chauffeur shining the fucking fenders all night long—and a couple of network anchormen and some faggoty bachelors and some socialites and a couple of Kennedys, of course. And do you know what the pissing end of the whole thing is?" Cindy paused to ask Nona. "The whole frigging time she's carrying on like that she keeps getting richer and richer. I think she owns half of IBM or ITT or one of those companies. She even has a little foundation so she can fund artsy-craftsy little projects like other rich ladies—some safe little culture things. Oh, I know Joan all right. I know everything about her except whether or not she knows Sam's in love with me."

Suddenly embarrassed, Cindy became supremely efficient. "Let's get this stuff outside," she said lifting several bowls.

Nona followed her out to the sundeck.

When it grew dark Sam made a fire in the barbe-cue pit and roasted hot dogs and hamburgers while his guests sat around drinking and talking. Nona retreated to the edge of the sundeck at the farthest end of the house and perched on the railing where she could watch a breeze ruffling the water of the swimming pool and see the people lounging on the patio below where Tony was talking to several women.

Feeling intensely excluded from the comfortable clusters of friends, Nona remembered the feeling she had grown up with—the sense of being a perpetual outsider. Pretty enough to almost fit, but too exotic. Smart enough, but too judgmental, too opinionated. This sense had always been her best guide. It had made her a journalist. It had lead her to investigate radical politics, and it had led her correctly to Mike Daniels. Its flip side was pain—the same dazzling pain produced by seeing the camaraderie of a close-knit crowd from the railing of the Kinkaid sundeck. Sometimes the powers of these people seemed almost supernatural to her—as if they were in possession of some extraordinary capability to make all their own wishes come true, and Nona could not ascertain whether their bewitching styles were the cause or the result of their enchanted existences.

Early on the morning of the Fourth of July, Nona and Tony left Sam's house, climbed into the Mercedes, and drove down to the marina.

"It's sort of nice to be alone for a change," Tony said, studying the heavy traffic bottlenecked on Wisconsin Avenue and waiting for a chance to break into line. "You look great in that T-shirt; you'll be the best-looking woman on the boat."

Flustered by the flush of pleasure she felt from his approval, Nona became businesslike. "Do you think Kessler's going to show?" she asked.

"Why shouldn't he?" Lewellen swung the Mercedes in a wide U to avoid the cars in the curb lane. "He likes a party as much as the next guy."

161

"Well, maybe there was some big security crisis during the night or something." She was desperate to have the meeting so she could retrospectively justify her days of mindless self-indulgence.

"Don't worry, tiger. He'll be there," Lewellen promised.

Nona sat happily and quietly beside him until they were slicing through the center of the city along Rockcreek Parkway. "They said on the radio this morning that there was an eighty percent chance it might rain today," Nona worried.

"Eighty percent of what?"

She tried to figure it out.

"You mean eighty percent of the weathermen think it's going to rain?" Tony asked. "Four out of five of them?"

She watched his smile unravel. Seduced by his indulgent affection, Nona felt like a refugee being offered sanctuary. A great greedy yearning rose up within her and she caressed Lewellen's profile with her eyes, aching to touch him.

And somehow he sensed her rush of feeling because he turned toward her then, as if she had called out his name, and they faced each other for a bewildering second.

Then, instinctively, Tony began to withdraw, edging away from the abyss of the awful intensity that endangered him. He turned on the radio, and started to hunt around on the car seat for his cigarettes, canceling out their closeness, silently denying that anything had happened—that they could possibly have shared each other in such a way for that quick moment. Fixing his eyes on the road, he accelerated the car, speeding past the high-rise ghosttown of Foggy Bottom and the Watergate complex that grimaced over the banks of the Potomac.

Nona fell silent as she registered Lewellen's evasion and felt the moment fizzle into a nonevent.

"You're a tease, Tony," she said in a quarrelsome

voice, looking out the window. Shocked by the intensity of hurt she had felt, she turned her anger at him. "You're an emotional tease."

He paused only briefly before denying it. "No, I'm not. You just forget that I'm a married man with three kids."

"It's not because you're married," she insisted. "It's because you're afraid to come across . . . you can't deliver . . . you have to hold back."

"I don't know what the hell you're talking about," he half shouted.

"You're right," she agreed in a voice designed to inflict a pain equivalent to his evasiveness. "So, let's drop it."

"You know something?" he said, suddenly impassioned. "I'm getting God damn sick and tired of this shit. Here I am trying to put the screws on a government heavy for you, and you have the fucking nerve to tell me that I can't relate, that I'm afraid to get involved."

The car was skulking beneath the white marble terrace of the Kennedy Center.

Nona straightened up in the seat to reprimand herself for being reckless. Totally surprised by the unexpected quarrel she'd initiated, she felt her heart pant with panic. At the very moment she needed Tony the most, she had let some antique emotion—some regressive possessiveness—endanger everything.

"I'm sorry," she said. "I think I'm upset because I'm scared about meeting Kessler."

Lewellen swung on to Memorial Bridge and Nona looked across the river toward the Lee Mansion, a white spot of tranquility dotting the hill of Arlington Cemetery. A little shudder of panic ran through her.

"Who else is going to be there?" she asked, her voice breaking.

Tony found his cigarettes and pressed in the lighter. "You sound like you're about to cry," he said coldly, gulping smoke into his throat.

163

Nona reached out and took the cigarette from between his fingers, but before she had finished taking a drag, he thrust his hand impatiently forward and she felt anger permeate the car.

"It's not about you or Kessler. I'm afraid of bridges."

"You've gotta be kidding. A tiger like you afraid of a little bridge? Look for a Columbia Island Marina sign," he said. "It'll take your mind off it."

"It's right over there." Nona pointed toward the next exit.

Her spotting the sign caused his aggravation to peak again and he braked the car with jarring overkill as he pulled into the parking lot along the river.

Turning off the ignition, he slammed out of the car and Nona had to scamper after him down the path toward the pier.

"I'm sorry," she said again.

He was silent for a few minutes waiting for his anger to subside and then he took her hand in his as they walked out onto the long wooden dock double-breasted with pleasure boats on both sides.

"Tony . . . can this get you . . . in trouble? Bringing me?" The weather-warped planks bounced beneath Nona's sandals. "I mean . . . some of your friends might. . . ."

"It's all fixed," he said in a clipped voice. "Look—there's the presidential yacht." He raised his arm to point toward the next dock and, with parental casualness, lifted her hand inside his own.

His thoughtless gesture of possession caused a whisper of love to pass through her, making her totally susceptible to him once again. But in that moment of vulnerability, Nona suddenly understood that her feeling for Lewellen paralleled some perilous childhood passion that she had transferred intact over to him—bequeathing Tony Oedipal powers he did not rightfully possess.

"We're lucky," Nona said, distracted by the realization that had washed through her. "There's a good wind, even if it is hot."

Tony stopped and, since he still held her hand, Nona was drawn up short beside him.

"We're not going out on a sailboat," he said putting both hands on her shoulders and pulling her close to him, erasing their estrangement.

And then, moved by his tenderness, Nona thought of one of his unseen daughters who probably ached, as Nona did, to regulate the uncertain supply of Tony Lewellen's love, yearning to control the amount and regularity of the affection he delivered.

The boat, tied in the last slip, was larger and longer than its neighbors. Nona looked down at the wide wedge of water between the deck and the dock.

"You go first," she said.

Lewellen jumped onto the hull and then turned around to catch her. But Nona jumped badly, hitting against him so that they both slid backward, grappling for balance as her body slumped against his.

Tony groaned—a soft animal signal of desire—and pushed her against the railing so for an instant he could staple himself against her.

But suddenly people began emerging from all directions and Tony spun around, looking down indiscreetly at himself before greeting anyone, his guilt and embarrassment attracting rather than deflecting attention from the rocky bulge of his erection. Nona stood mute in the blazing sunlight reflected off the water, heeding the motion of the river rocking the boat, hearing voices fading in and out like a car radio passing through a tunnel, and feeling totally compromised, desperately disadvantaged by the incriminating evidence of Tony's inopportune passion.

The boat was full of lawyers and lawyer's wives. They nodded to Tony whom they recognized. He nodded back.

She swayed on her feet and when the group began to move topdeck she followed them up the narrow stairs, hanging onto the rope railing while waves of dizziness passed through her.

She reemerged into the sunlight and hurried forward to sink into a deck chair, grappling to maintain self-control until her faintness receded. She dug out sunglasses from her beach bag and put them on. Someone handed her a Bloody Mary and she nodded her thanks before turning at an angle to avoid any conversation. From the corner of her eye she could see a cluster of half-nude, elegantly emaciated women pasted flat on the deck nearby, glowing and glittering in the sun, the gaunt bones beneath their skin glistening as they lay gossiping—a Greek chorus flattened out by fate. Their lazy voices floated past Nona's chair, circled the boat, and flew over the water.

"Oh!" Awe suddenly orchestrated choral excitement. "There's Eric."

"Who's that with him?"

"A movie star, Johanna Dupres. Boy, he's really putting on the dog for us today. That's an old Kissinger ploy."

Nona turned slightly to see the large stocky man posed at the top of the hatchway. Leering downward, he waited as the body of an iridescently luminous blond slowly surfaced—a voluptuous bosom exploding out of a scooped-necked dress and trailed by a slim mermaidish torso—until all of her emerged. Then, smiling proudly as if he himself had designed and produced the blond, Kessler grasped her elbow, extending her arm shotgun style in front of them, and waited until his Secret Service agent scampered up on deck.

The Greek chorus began to chant again.

"What's he doing with a Secret Service agent?"

"There was a threat on his life—anyway, that's the story."

Johanna Dupres was smiling into the emptiness before her. Blinded by the glare reflected off the water, she strained to see the enthusiastic response of her audience, but automatically sprayed near-sighted smiles at random along her route. As she and Eric Kessler advanced across the deck, the coalition of their power and glamour created a force that combed and parted the crowd like wind rushing through a field of wheat. The admiring audience swayed forward.

The boat engines churned. Nona flattened out in her chair as the boat blundered away from the dock and moved out of the marina into the river, sliding imperviously past the national monuments. She could feel the nervous union of vodka and vibrations in her stomach, as she reviewed the scenario Tony had helped her work out.

The Washington Monument shoved itself at the sky. Off to the left, beyond the blue sheet of Tidal Basin, the Jefferson Memorial rose upon a sweet round hill of land.

Nona's chair pitched violently to the left as Tony perched beside her.

"Are you almost ready?"

"Where is he?" Nona asked. Her tongue batted against the dehydrated roof of her mouth.

"Get up. We'll take a walk around the deck."

Nona untangled herself and rose to her feet. The ladies lying on the deck turned their heads as slowly as flowers following the sun—to watch her pass. Instantly paranoia beset her, for Nona knew the women were whispering about her to each other behind their smiles, winking into each other's silver-framed sunglasses. She quickened her pace as they passed the gaunt chorus line, but she still felt the intense exclusivity they exuded—the cliquishness that both provoked and pained Nona. She was totally disoriented by the time they reached Kessler's group.

Tony introduced her to him.

"How do you do?" He spoke with the clipped precision of a Rhodes scholar, taking her hand into his with extravagent elegance. His big squat body seemed anchored by a kind of arrogance and he assessed her carefully, determined to detect any fanaticism that would push her beyond social proprieties. Then, seemingly reassured by her uneasiness, he nodded at the Secret Service agent standing beside him and the man moved back a few steps so Kessler could introduce Johanna Dupres.

The movie star produced a glossy-print fan-club smile and shook Nona's hand so vehemently that her head bobbed up and down scattering sunlight over the long yellow shafts of her hair.

"Have you begun making your movie yet?" Nona asked desperate to affiliate herself with someone.

"Oh, no. They never start on schedule." Johanna Dupres's words were soft husky little breaths that blew off her lips like little baby kisses. "And the longer they postpone it the more nervous I get because this is my first big role." Her enunciation of "big role" made it sound like an obscene act. "But I really love being in Washington. I think it's just like Hollywood except in the east everybody's always much more on—*really* on! I just love it here." She suddenly turned to Tony. "Oh, we've met before," she panted clinging to his hand with silky lassitude. "We met at that McGovern fund-raiser in Los Angeles. Remember? You spoke on the beach—it was down at Malibu."

"Of course. I remember you," Tony nodded. "I just didn't think you'd remember me."

"How could I ever forget?"

Nona watched Johanna with curiosity, trying to locate the source of her glamour, eventually deciding that it was her own excitement about being beautiful that made Johanna seem extraordinary. Admira-

168

tion simply corroborated her own certainty about the fact, and it was their mutual agreement that translated her beauty into glamour.

"And how do you like Washington?" Tony asked.

"Oh, it's ab-so-lute-ly in-cred-i-ble. Power *is* sexy, and you can just smell it all over the place. I loveit. I loveit. I loveit." Johanna laughed, leaning forward, filled with conviction that any reasonable man would want to possess her, burrow inside her perfection to send seed into the marvel of her body.

Nona stepped back, feeling unsatisfactorily prosaic. As jealousy began to grow, Nona felt disfigured, bent out of shape by intrusive competitive itchings.

Then Kessler sidled back into the circle. "Will you excuse me for a few minutes?" he asked Johanna. "I'm going to have a talk with Tony." He touched Johanna's hand encouragingly, as though she were an underdeveloped child with a separation anxiety, and then turned to shepherd Tony and Nona into motion, first dispatching a nod of dismissal toward the agent. "Now, let's see where to sit. At least in the middle of the Potomac there is little danger of being overheard."

He chuckled as he moved forward, and Nona retrieved his little joke to ponder its meaning since it hinted at Kessler's view of himself. His suggestion that he too was vulnerable to spying intimated he was different from the men he worked for, that he was uncontaminated by the corruption around him and thus suspect in their eyes.

They sat on the deck at the prow of the boat, separating themselves sufficiently from the crowd to show their isolation was intentional. Kessler held a Bloody Mary in his hand, and he sipped it occasionally as he looked toward the shoreline. When he finally turned toward Nona he had donned a bright benevolent expression.

"Your friend Tony here has told me something

169

about you." He looked above Nona at Lewellen, displaying a fraternal understanding of the irrationality that could link a good man to an inappropriate woman, but he clearly considered odd sexual liaisons as important as political ones.

"Now, then, I hear that you are interested in some hypothetical transcripts of some alleged recordings of some theoretical phone conversation that the *Washington Post* claims the White House supposedly has." He paused, awaiting a show of appreciation.

Nona laughed, flipping her hair back from her face with a seductive silky motion. Tony and Kessler exchanged looks of collective enjoyment, sharing the profits of her laughter and understanding the rewards of servicing her.

"Of course everything which we say here is both off the record as well as completely personal and confidential."

"Of course," Tony agreed with an effortless smile, consenting for both himself and Nona with reassuring speed.

"I am trusting you on the basis of Tony's word to me," Kessler said solemnly to Nona. "I know he wouldn't put himself out on a limb for someone who wasn't trustworthy . . . not that I am confirming *in any way that* any such wiretap was conducted or that any tapes were acquired or that any transcripts of such tapes exist or that anything I say assumes the validity of any such alleged materials."

"Yes," Nona said, "I understand that." Then she looked at Kessler sympathetically as if accepting the myth of his innocence, pretending she faced a man who had been held hostage by the enemy for the past six years, a helpless prisoner of the discredited administration. She smiled, smothering her contempt, as the unforgiving sun beat down upon her head and body.

"I'm a very old friend of Michael Daniels," she

began, synchronizing the lighting of one of Tony's Salems with the start of her story. "We lived in the same commune for almost five years, so when I read the story about Sam Kinkaid in the newspaper, it occurred to me that if the dates were correct—about the alleged wiretap on his phone—I'm pretty sure that there was a conversation between Sam Kinkaid and Michael Daniels during that period of time."

"He is the one who went underground?" Kessler asked.

"Yes. The other three are in jail. What I was thinking, Mr. Kessler, was that if Michael Daniels was overheard, even accidentally, on the Kinkaid tap, that would be new evidence for his defense because the government testified he was never electronically monitored. On the basis of that . . ." she began to say "perjury" and stopped herself, "the court might order a new trial."

Kessler's face had gone slack. The flesh that framed his pudgy smile flattened out.

Tony had turned away and was watching a small motorboat scooting past them, whipping a white foam as it crisscrossed down the river.

"Well, what do you want?" Kessler asked abruptly.

"I guess I'm just asking if there's some way you might find out if there actually is any record of a phone conversation between Michael Daniels and Sam Kinkaid."

Kessler's face became stony, twisted into a tight knot. "So that his lawyer could subpoena the tape?"

Now Nona's heart was lurching and bucking about in the cage of her chest. "Well, I don't know if he'd have to do that," she waffled, shrugging her shoulders. "I mean, if it doesn't exist there wouldn't be any proof of a conversation. But if it was recorded, well, I guess then his lawyer could just claim Michael had been overheard. I don't know if he'd have to try to get it as evidence, I mean, well, I don't know."

171

"Well, dear child, we are of course still dealing in the realm of probabilities. I strongly doubt that any of the journalists were ever wiretapped and, if they were, I doubt that whoever is responsible is going to want to admit it by producing a tape or transcript of any particular conversation. But," he shrugged philosophically, "I'll ask around. That's all I can do to help you." He leveled a look at Nona that deplored the audacity that had led her to make such a seditious request. Then, with a simple postural shift, he dissociated himself from her and reaffirmed his exclusive allegiance to Tony Lewellen.

"So, Tony," he began, indicating that for him Nona had ceased to exist. "What is your feeling about how the hearings are developing?"

"Excuse me," Nona said, struggling to her feet. "I left my cigarettes. . . ." She stumbled across the boat back to her deck chair and collapsed into the canvas sling. Then she reached up and unsnapped her barrette, letting the warm blanket of her hair block out the sun and hide her from spying eyes.

Woozy from emotion, she looked at the wall of trees that held the river in place. The incredibility of her conversation with Eric Kessler struck her full force. The episode seemed as unreal as a foreign movie about political intrigue set in some revolution-ravished country. The fact that she was bargaining with power was unbelievable to her, and she was angered by the involuntary sense of intimidation she had felt. Tears of frustration rose to her eyes as bitterness bent her heart.

She looked toward the prow where Tony and Kessler were still sprawled on the deck, surrounded now by a cluster of long, lean ladies who were swaying elegantly above them, their carefully frosted hair billowing out, giving them the silhouettes of palm trees leaning into the wind. Kessler was talking. His mouth moved with tight jerky motions and there was an explosion of admiring laughter when he finished.

"Get ready, gang," someone shouted through a bullhorn. "We're putting down anchor."

The boat stopped near a heavily wooded island and eventually two crewmen lowered a rowboat to ferry over the picnic luncheon. The guests could swim to the island to eat or stay on board. Nona waited for the others to descend to the lower deck and when she heard them begin diving off, she stripped down to her bikini, climbed up on the prow, and dove into the water.

But Tony was waiting for her only a few yards away from where she surfaced. He laughed as he swam toward her to slip his hands around her waist.

"Come around here," he said.

She swam beside him to the far side of the boat, away from the splashing and noise that filled the water near the island and they clung together.

"Are you O.K., tiger?" he asked, panting from the exertion of treading water.

"Yes." She kissed him lightly on the lips. "It was awful, but thank you."

"He said he'd phone me."

"When?"

"He didn't say." Tony's face was close to hers. "He's going out of town for a couple of days so it'll probably be the beginning of next week. He's freaking out over the Watergate stuff. He can't stand being implicated. He's really uptight about it."

They swam side by side around the boat toward the narrow white beach.

Lunch was served with white wine and afterward, while people rested on the slim strand of sand before swimming back to the boat, there was an atmosphere of sexual headiness and authentic excitement. Back on board, there was music and more wine until the sun set, and when they anchored again in a wider part of the river, the crew grilled filet mignons over a large hibachi set up on the deck. Huge foam-rubber mats were spread out, making a rail-to-rail mattress, and Tony and Nona sat together while they ate, too drunk to worry about appearances, savoring the smooth sensuality of the scene, growing mellow together during the ride back to the marina.

Ten

At night when Watergate fatigue downed them, Nona and Tony would often retreat to the Kinkaid mansion after work rather than suffer the intolerable heat of Nona's apartment. Exhaustion melted her reluctance, and slowly she drifted into a rhythmic routine of meeting Tony at Sam's house around six or seven o'clock each night. By the time they finished their first round of drinks and took a swim in the icy pool, they were all too tired to dress to go out to a restaurant. Then the four of them would make dinner together, and while they had coffee or brandy on the sundeck, someone would usually drop by to take a swim. By nightfall anywhere from five to ten people were sprawled around the patio getting plastered on Sam's Scotch and laughing at the rerun testimony on the portable TV in the corner.

As the days passed they began eating dinner a little later each night, drinking more before and after, staying up longer after midnight to watch the reruns of the hearings, too tired to know the depths of their own exhaustion. It was often two or three in the morning before the last guests finally disappeared so Nona and Tony could stagger up to the guest room to make drunken love on the fourposter bed.

On the day John Ehrlichman began his testimony, Tony ran over to Nona's table the moment after the hearings were adjourned for lunch.

"Come on," he said, taking her arms with unchallengeable authority. "Kessler wants to see us and Sam. He's made reserevations at the Sans Souci for quarter to one."

When she slid inside the taxi Tony hailed, her skirt hiked up beneath her and her bare thighs stuck to the plastic upholstery cover. Resting her head against the back of the damp seat, she looked out the window at the flat surreal spread of Capitol Hill until the drone of sunlight on the oppressive imperial-white buildings undulating in the heat produced a giddiness in her.

The driver spun past the east wing of the White House, and Nona saw a long line of sightseers waiting for the next guided tour. Fathers, oppressed by heat and impatience, wore large sweat splotches of honor on the fronts of their short-sleeved sport shirts, and mothers, their hair pasted by humidity into damp skullcaps, tried to corral kids who strayed away.

When the cab reached the Sans Souci, Tony hustled Nona out of the taxi and hurried her beneath the awning as if rushing out of a rainstorm. Inside the chic restaurant, Nona surveyed the blurry approximation of Edwardian opulence and waited while the maître d' greeted Tony with the half-subservient, half-condescending manner that had turned the Sans Souci into an elitist encampment. He led them down the carpeted staircase, turned at an obsequious angle that simultaneously summoned and announced them.

The maître d' moved between his tables, critical as a mother among her children, quickly spying faults or virtues and silently signaling his waiters to correct any oversights. Without interrupting his Secret Service-showbiz shuffle, he led them forward.

As they neared the rear of the room Tony summoned Nona back to where four men, whom she recognized as McGovern campaign officials, sat at a table.

Looking down at her with the pride of an overly

indulgent father displaying an adorable toddler, Tony introduced her to the group.

One of the men complimented Nona on her July *Metro* article, causing Tony to become even more proprietary, motionlessly gathering Nona in toward him and spacially repossessing her without any contact. He was beaming at her as if from some enormous height. And suddenly Nona realized that Tony was using their sizes as a sexual metaphor, evoking a parent-child simile to indicate their sexual intimacy.

The four men watching Lewellen were hip to his silent sexual advertisement and responded with appropriately congratulatory or complimentary smiles. Tony happily absorbed the envious acknowledgments.

You fucker, Nona swore silently. You had to let them know you were balling me, didn't you?

She felt the fragile pride inside her chest crack. Then a great subversive sensation swelled up, and she felt a violent urge to start smashing dishes or to lunge at Tony's face with her nails.

I'll pay you back, she promised. Later.

But with the practiced hypocrisy of a call girl, she smiled a shy sly smile up at her lover, publicly notorizing the adultery he had announced, reconfirmed it with a dreamy glance at the group around the table and then moved on to the chair the maître d' had waiting. He seated her up against the wall with the air of a florist arranging a spray of flowers for some connoisseur and then disappeared.

"Well, did you get your rocks off?" Nona asked when Tony finally joined her.

"What do you mean?"

A semiaudible swish of awe suddenly swept through the room. Nona looked up to see the maître d' leading Eric Kessler to a table, instantly activating the tremor ambitious people feel when power passes in their presence.

177

Kessler seemed to flow forward and sideways simultaneously, extending himself toward certain people seated along his route and retracting to ignore others, granting and withholding recognition as he walked. Occasionally he would bend over one of the tables, imitating a grade-school teacher peering over a student to inspect his penmanship.

He greeted Nona politely before sitting down, and then, warming up his pudgy smile, he turned toward Tony to discuss the morning testimony as if he were an uninvolved spectator. A few minutes later Sam hurried across the room unescorted, nodding with businesslike efficiency to the gallery of his acquaintances before sitting down.

They ordered cocktails, but Kessler began to talk before their drinks arrived.

"I don't know whether or not you're aware of this yet," he said, looking first at Sam and then at Tony. "But of the million reporters running around town trying to win themselves a Pulitzer Prize on that damn wiretap story, your guy—Barry Stein—has been questioning some ex-employees of mine trying to put the blame on me." His distress was authentic, and his rage only barely concealed.

"Apart from the fact that the charges are groundless, it is particularly difficult for me since most of the reporters they claim were tapped happen to be close personal friends of mine—people I care about. I'm not going to bother defending myself to you against such absurd accusations. You know me, Sam, and you also know how unfounded, unsubstantiated charges based on revelations by undisclosed sources get blown up to the point that it doesn't matter whether or not they're true. The press has been using some pretty shabby practices that do nothing but cause personal and political havoc, and I certainly don't look forward to becoming tomorrow's scapegoat, victim of the day—accused of God knows what by some unnamed, undisclosed source who may or may not even exist. But the fact that *your* own reporter is trying to implicate *me,* accuse *me* of participating in an act against friends of mine is intolerable. It has to stop. You must stop him, because . . . apart from my personal embarrassment——"

He stopped speaking while the waiter circled the table, theatrically depositing cocktails as if they were little May baskets in front of each of them.

"You and I know that there are some precautions that are necessary to protect our national security. You've both been in Washington long enough to understand that. There is absolutely no avoiding the fact," here he lifted his drink and glanced briefly toward Nona, "that there are people who believe in peace and justice at the expense of freedom and liberty, who believe in passive resistance rather than self-defense—masochistic types who insist on some higher truth than reality and who would go so far as to jeopardize the entire nation for some idealistic commitment to something they call political self-determination, which they would grant to every nation in the world except this country. You also know that occasionally it is necessary to find out how and what these people are up to—never doubting the 'good intentions' of the plans they concoct in the name of justice and equality. Protective measures against this sort of thing are essential, and I believe that's why the president hasn't buckled under during this incredible witch hunt. That he has made horrendous mistakes in judgment is perfectly obvious, but I also believe he has behaved rather gallantly and judiciously throughout this entire Watergate affair—at least insofar as defending our national security during a period of upheaval and stress."

The waiter returned to take their orders. Nona selected the most expensive steak on the menu and then looked around the room. Now many of the recognizable faces were turned toward her, and she realized with a start that she had become part of the lunchtime floor show.

"But to continue . . . what I'm trying to say is that if some security taps were undertaken, it was not done lightly or arbitrarily. Our security agencies do know which people and groups work actively to undermine our security. If you remember," he said turning graciously toward Nona, "during that pleasant boatride on the Potomac, you asked me to ascertain whether a certain telephone conversation was overheard. It took a rather long time—for obvious reasons—rightful reluctance to talk about such sensitive matters, and so forth, but. . . ." He paused melodramatically, carefully seeking language that would reconcile the paradox of his being able to obtain proof of things he refused to admit existed. "It appears that *at some point*—and I am in no way suggesting that it occurred over Sam's phone—Michael Daniels was overheard by a military intelligence office of which the government prosecutor had no knowledge and which was in no way related to any regular police or FBI checks."

Nona lifted her glass and finished the remainder of her drink, letting the ice cubes bump up against her lip. The audacity of Kessler's remarks was so stupendous that she couldn't believe Tony and Sam were letting them pass unchallenged.

"Thus, I am able to tell you, Miss Landau, that your friend Mr. Daniels was overheard—probably inadvertently—perhaps because he phoned a known security risk covered by a legal wiretap. Regardless . . . some such record could be excavated if it were in everyone's interest to do so. Ahh," he paused to inspect the duck à l'orange, crisply broiled and elegantly garnished, which was being set before him. "Let's eat. This looks too good to let grow cold."

He attacked his food with compulsive zeal. Tony and Sam gratefully concentrated on eating, afraid to raise their eyes, knowing what was to come and trying to postpone the inevitable offer.

"Well, so," Kessler said, after devouring his entire entrée in a surprisingly short time. "Let me make my suggestion. Sam, we all know how much leadership you exert among the Washington press corps, how influential you are both personally and professionally."

Sam looked up with a blank expression having snuffed out his sensibilities in order to survive the bribe. But Kessler knew better than to down-play his offer. A preemptive act could serve both as an attack and a defense.

"Sam, I am asking you, as someone whom I've known for a long time and someone who knows me, not to allow my name to be sullied in this careless destructive manner. The Washington press corps has become vociferous in hounding individuals. They act like a pack of hounds trying to snare a rabbit, destroying and discrediting a man before he can rally his forces. I'm not asking for any special treatment simply because we're old friends, Sam. I'm simply asking you to tell Barry Stein loud and clear, that I'm in *no way* involved in any wiretap activity and that you won't allow him to start such an insane witch hunt. I would also appreciate it if you'd talk to some of the other editors and warn them against implicating me without any substantive proof of their charges."

He polished off his salad in four huge gulps. "Apart from the personal injury that I would suffer, they are also endangering national security by undermining and undercutting my work. I want to remind all of you that a threat to national security does not necessarily come from *outside* the government. The threat can come also from within. . . . The power elite, too, can plan a coup. A frightened president is as likely to try blackmail as any man who feels cornered and persecuted. Any intelligent person knows

I'm the only one left in the administration now who has any sympathy or understanding of the liberal position. You know we share the same basic beliefs, Sam. We've spoken together hundreds of times about all the major issues. Believe me when I tell you this— I'm holding the fascists at bay, Sam." Here he lowered his head and dropped his voice perceptibly. "It's me and only me. I've been the only one for the last six years to encourage some restraint, to maintain some semblance of support for basic civil liberties and freedoms. They would have butchered every individual and political freedom by now if it hadn't been for me. And the president's running scared now, you both know that. I'm the only one on the inside who could possibly prevent a disaster—a real military-type disaster."

He refilled his wine glass. "So, what I'm asking is that you tell your man that he's off base—that he's crazy trying to drum up evidence against me. Ninety percent of the people from this administration would like to implicate me in this Watergate mess. But I was never involved—I was never part of that rogues' gallery. Still, as soon as all the sheep hear Stein is checking me out, they'll all move in to nail me.

"And of course what will happen in the rush for a scoop, one of them will print a pack of lies that will get picked up and blown into a scandal and I'm not sure I'll be able to weather it and still keep going about my business—which is keeping Nixon honest . . . if you know what I mean. Because when that pack of bloodhounds smells blood they all join together. It's insane, you both know it, but I know you aren't so committed to a scoop or a flashy headline that you'd forget either human decency or the basic code of journalism, which is not to accuse a man without proof of his crime. And, I do not want you to forget the basic political necessity of keeping at least one enlightened mind *inside* the administration. I'm the only one in there now, Sam, the only one. So I'm not appealing to you on personal grounds only, but on professional and political ones. All I'm asking is that you attempt to restrain your own staff and a few of your influential friends."

He elevated his arm, gently motioning heaven to deliver him a waiter. "I don't even want you to attempt to respond now—not today. I have an important appointment at two. Please, just stay where you are. Have some dessert. Have a brandy. Miss Laudau, please have a chocolate mousse. They're quite up to the mark here. Drink a cup of coffee and think about what I've said. Please don't make the mistake of jumping to any conclusions. Discuss my . . . position . . . shall we call it? Think how the victim of a mob attack—a political mugging even—feels. I know that no one has any proof of my committing any illegal acts. Barry Stein is running around in circles trying to manufacture this thing, so there's plenty of time to put a lid on him and stop this wild-goose chase before it blows up. That's all I'm asking you, Sam, Tony. Make sure your friends don't publish anything without solid proof. Make a few phone calls. Warn them I know what's brewing. and I'm ready to sue for libel ten minutes after they print any false charges. But if I'm driven out of the Justice Department, believe me there will be much more serious consequences. There will be no one left, not one soul, to hold back the president from using the military to maintain what he considers law and order. He's not above a military takeover, believe me, gentlemen."

Then he shrugged and stood up. A variety of crumbs that had collected in the creases of his shirt and jacket fluttered to the floor. "My dear," he said, reaching out and lifting Nona's hand from the table, "if . . . I am not totally distracted by an all-out attack from the Washington press corps, if I can avert any unnecessary trouble by holding the press to some standards of ethical procedure, I will certainly pursue your request and attempt to retrieve some actual recording or transcript that might be of help to you."

Although he spoke directly toward her he was watching Lewellen with the devilish accommodating leer of a professional pimp. Then, without another word, he turned and hurried out of the restaurant.

"I'll be a goddamn son of a bitch," Sam said very softly.

Tony sat silent, with a stunned look on his face. For the first time Nona saw his hard rugged features frightened into a soft boyish expression.

"Well," she said with a reckless toss of her head, "I think we've just been made an offer we can't refuse."

Both men looked at her incredulously, and Tony focused a stern frown in her direction to warn against any horseplay at such a serious moment. Then he signaled the waiter. "Look, we don't want any dessert," he said when the man arrived, "but will you see what you can do about getting us a round of double Scotches?" Then he assumed an expression of cynicism and determination. "We've got to get a handle on this," he said to Sam. "That son of a bitch just offered us an out-and-out bribe—Daniels's tape for our sitting on that story."

"Can you believe it?" Sam sucked on the cigarette dangling unattended from his mouth. "Barry didn't even tell me he was that close. I knew he was stalking Kessler, but I didn't know he had him running scared. Stein's really got balls."

"Yeah. But I wonder if he's got anything else," Tony said, "whether he can come up with anything hard that can really stick. Eric's smart enough to cover his tracks."

Sam whistled between his teeth. "That fucker. If he's the one who did it—if he ordered that tap put on me. . . ." Sam's hand clenched into a fist on the table, and his arm jerked from the force of his rage. "How could he? I can't believe he'd do it to me. . . . That—I can't believe."

Nona jabbed out her cigarette and began drawing designs in the ashtray, pushing the dead butt around in circles amid the ashes. Sam's shock was comparable to that of a man discovering incest in his family—a betrayal beyond any other treachery.

"For Chrissake, he knows I'm no . . . crazy, that I'd never risk national security even for the biggest scoop of the century." He looked at Nona with an uncomfortable expression. "We were friends," he explained rather plaintively. "Kessler and my wife, Joan, are really very good friends. He always did things for my kids. He likes my daughter a lot—had her up to his office for lunch one day and even went out to her school to talk to her civics class, or whatever they call it now."

Nona began gnawing at her lip. Sam was still reacting to the wiretap as a personal insult. Unable to fathom the dangers of fraternization between government officials and the press, he couldn't comprehend being treated as a natural enemy by a consummate politician. His personal and professional lives were so intertwined he couldn't distinguish between the private betrayal of a friend and the illegal infringement of his constitutional rights.

"That son of a bitch," Sam groaned. "After all we've done for him."

Nona swallowed her moral and professional outrage. "Listen," she said, intending to sound helpful. "There might have been some big security scare of some kind or other. If he did it, it might have been because he had to."

"But I've been tapped for a couple of years," Sam objected.

"Well, maybe he didn't think of it like that. Maybe he was trying to protect you. Maybe some of the other White House people thought he was leaking Watergate stuff to you, and he was trying to prove neither of you were involved. Maybe Haldeman was on his back, and he thought a tap would prove you were innocent. After all, people knew he had leaked other stories to you."

It sounded all wrong, as if she were accusing Sam of complicity, if not conspiracy, with a corrupt administration, and he looked at her reproachfully.

"I didn't mean it like *that*, Sam," Nona said in the same persuasive voice. "I'm not trying to do you, but look—if he leaked stuff to you before, maybe this time he felt he had the right to, you know, make sure you were on the level with him. I mean, maybe a news source thinks he has the right to check out his own conduits or something."

But her innate disapproval kept inflecting her voice with a critical tone.

"Nona," Sam said in the deep formal voice liberals used for explaining politics to women and children, "a journalist operates in the best way he can. If a guy publishes a national news magazine once a week he needs some inside government contacts to find out what's really happening and for you to get all moralistic about that is asinine and distracting. You know damn well if you got hold of a blabbermouth who wanted to spill the beans on some CIA operation you'd use his information in a minute. Well, that's what Tony and I do. We've used Eric for what we could get off him because he was the only accessible guy in the Nixon administration. You might not like it, but that's how things work in this town."

"Look," Nona said quickly to avert any tangential quarrel. "Kessler's days are numbered. If Barry doesn't have the goods on him right now, someone else will eventually. So why can't we just go along with the gag? By the time the hearings are over, Nixon will have to resign anyway. They're all living on borrowed time. Why can't you just cool it—say you'll call Barry off and see what you can do about holding back the others for a little while? Let Kessler think he's bought you off. Just give me enough time to get Michael's tape off him. I'll go see him alone and tell him you've decided to do what he asked—not because of me, but for the political reasons he laid on you. Then, after he gives me the tape, you can do your number."

"Are you crazy?" Tony groaned. "Do you understand what he asked us to do? He asked us to censor a story in exchange for doing you a personal favor."

"It's not *quite* a personal favor," Nona said sarcastically, lunging for the Scotch that appeared in front of her. "It's not for *me*. It's to get three innocent men out of the Harrisburg pen and to let another guy come out of hiding. That's an old newspaper tradition, isn't it? Trying to spring innocent inmates? Well—three guys are doing time because the government framed them or used illegal means of obtaining evidence. They're entitled to a new trial at least, aren't they?"

"I can't believe you're saying what you're saying," Tony interrupted. "You're asking us to do the same thing Kessler asked us to do—to censor a story because it serves your interests." He paused pompously. "It doesn't matter whose interests are at stake, Nona. Sam Kinkaid would never censor a story."

"Oh, fuck off," Nona said, voicing over him. "Please save me from that crock of shit. One thing I don't need is any lessons on ethics from. . . ." But then she stopped, and the unspoken "you" hung in the air between them. Tony's face was chalk white.

"Now let's cool down," Sam said. "That SOB laid a lot of crap on us, and we're all upset. Look. Nona is being honest, Tony. She wants to help her friends, and there's no reason to get sore about it. On the other hand," he turned directly toward her, "I won't take a dive no matter how many good reasons there are for doing it. But if we keep cool and use our heads,

187

we might still be able to get what you want off Kessler without buckling under."

With a cigarette-dry cough-quilted laugh Sam reached over to grab Nona's hand. It was a last desperate effort to avert an irreconcilable split. "Anyway, where's the old sense of humor, Miss Landau? You've just been proved dead wrong. After all your bitching about our hanging around with government officials, you were right there when one of the biggies dumped a great big fat story in my lap."

Nona tugged her hand away and turned back to Tony. "I'm not asking you to kill the story," she persisted. "All I'm asking for is a little bit of time—for you guys to horse him around for a while. You can stay on top of the story, but you don't have to make a big rustle about it. You can just pretend you're letting it slide."

"Now you listen to me," Tony said, leaning forward so his breath slapped against her face. "I'm dead serious about this. I won't let Sam be put in a space where it looks like he took a bribe. How the hell you could either expect or want him to. . . ."

"Oh, for Chrissake . . . this isn't the first time Kessler's put the make on you." Nona grimaced with contempt. "It isn't as if you've spent the last four years busting your ass trying to get the goods on him. How come none of you ever found out about the Huston plan before it came up at the hearings? Why weren't you out investigating him instead of giving each other blow jobs at cocktail parties? You let Kessler bullshit you ever since he got to Washington. You believed everything he told you . . . that they weren't bombing in Cambodia . . . that they weren't killing people in My Lai . . . that they weren't murdering black militants or jailing white radicals or running illegal mailcovers and telephone taps and IRS audits and all the other shit they've pulled. You let Kessler get away with murder for *six fucking years*, and now all I'm asking you to do is lay off him for a couple weeks or at least act like you are. And then you get all moralistic and self-righteous and come on like this is the first time he's ever put his hand on your thigh—when everybody knows you've let other stories slide. So? So he asked you again? So what? So go along with him once more . . . at least something good might come from it this time."

"Hey," Sam interrupted, straining toward some judicial height. "Listen, Nona. How does this sound? I can tell Kessler that we're willing to go along with him—since we can't make any moves until Barry comes up with the goods anyway. I'll just tell him to be supercool so no one knows what he's after. Then— if and when he comes up with the story—we'll put the screws on Kessler." Sam paused, seemingly surprised by his own wisdom. "Right before we're ready to publish we'll go to Kessler and try to strong-arm him into turning the tape over to us. How's that?" he asked.

Convinced that with a little time she could work her will, Nona reached out and lifted Sam's hand off the table to her lips offering him a kiss of absolution.

Then, weak with gratitude, she sank back in her chair.

Eleven

For Nona, the days and nights of that week ran together like the colors of an abstract painting. Tuesday's soft yellow evening of dinner and drinking with Tony and Senator Dempsey at the Jockey Club drifted onto a hot pink Wednesday night when she and Tony wandered along M Street in Georgetown stopping for drinks at any appealing bar they saw until they ended up, drunk out of their minds, at the Cellar Door howling at a comedian whose name they never knew. On a damp green rainy Thursday they joined Barry and a crowd of already rowdy wire-service correspondents to crash a deadly boring party at the British embassy and then tumbled out, shortly after their successful infiltration, to escape through the garden as surreptitiously as they had arrived. Piling into cars they drove off to drink in the dark cloistered bar at the Watergate, getting smashed on champagne before running across Virginia Avenue to the infamous Howard Johnson's where they made a meal out of malted milks and hot-fudge sundaes. Later Nona and Tony took a drunken walk through Montrose Park, behind Dumbarton Oaks where they kissed beneath a tree before returning to a side street near Nona's building where they parked and necked, watching the darkness thinning out to show the beginning of early morning light at the farthest edge of the sky.

Each night dripped onto the following day, blurring the edges of the mornings, discoloring and spoiling any sense of freshness or renewal. Nona awoke, tired and hungover each morning to rush about fixing Tony's breakfast before returning to Capitol Hill, disheveled and disorganized as the power high she felt at night dissolved in the light of day. Discrete events became difficult to distinguish, while enormous exhaustion and an anxious expectation began to grow inside her as she waited to see what Barry would find, and what move Kessler might make.

Claiming he needed some help preparing for his Honor Thy Enemies Party, Sam insisted Nona and Tony come over to his house on Friday evening. After a long sex-flavored night around the swimming pool, seasoned by several joints and a bottle of Havana rum, Nona and Tony retired to the guest room and fell into the fourposter bed where they made drunken, stoned love all night, falling asleep and then awakening to pursue some romantic theme they'd lost among their variations. But Sam knocked on their door early Saturday morning, and by nine o'clock Nona was making omelettes in the kitchen while Cindy and Sam discussed final party arrangements.

Although worried about the preparations, Sam still insisted there was time for a quick set of tennis, and he cajoled Nona into coming down to referee a match between Tony and himself. Tired and testy, Nona followed them resentfully down the flagstone path through an old-fashioned English-flower garden to the tennis court. The sun was busily drying up the remnants of cool night air. Sullenly, she climbed onto the overgrown linesman stool near the gate and opened the box of Winstons she was unconsciously clutching in her hand.

The two men sauntered up to the net as if a million cameras followed their swaggering arrival. Sam sported a pregame nonchalance that was as affected as the warm-up sweater knotted by its empty arms around his neck. Tony, gripping a can of tennis balls in the pit of one arm, swung his racquet back and forth with mock-epic strokes. In his usual macho manner, he was making himself into some mythic hero descending from an olympic height to partake in human fun and games.

Where the fuck does he get off acting like that? Nona thought, enraged by his arrogant style.

Up at the net the two men laid hands on each other in a moment of laughter about choosing courts. Sam accused Tony of risking the sun to improve his tan, and Tony, with a long deep laugh, claimed it was the only handicap that could possibly even up their games.

Nona tugged at the soft flesh of her bottom lip with her front teeth, aggravated by their showy sportsmanship and courtly charm.

They're teases, she decided, enunciating her judgment very formally to herself as she lit the cigarette she'd been holding in her hand. They're all style with no content. All their priorities are personal ones. Their superstar shtik is just a come-on, a front because they know they're full of shit.

She swallowed a deep gulp of smoke and watched Tony cross to the far side of the court with easy affluent strides, wearing his superiority as a substitute for the old Jantzen-diver emblem missing from his white T-shirt.

"Go ahead and take a couple," Sam invited. Wired for action, he stood center court, crouched over in cocky, expectant jock position.

"I'm ready. Will you call them on your side, Nona?" Tony asked, squinting into the sunlight. He moved toward the baseline, his loose stance belying his determination and doubling the threat of his power by diplomatically ignoring it.

"Ready?" he called. Positioning himself for service, he initiated the ritual motions as if it were an act of sexual foreplay, an ardent mixture of craft and expectation. But he climaxed his approach by slamming a stunningly hard ball into the opposite court.

Nona watched the first few games fascinated by

192

the psychodrama of two men playing tennis in perfect harmony, and suddenly she saw the game as their way of relieving the intensity of their mutual affection, by turning it into a contest between narcissistic and platonic love.

But as the sun became more aggressive about warming up the day, Nona began to feel restive and oppressed by their performance.

"Howya doing?" Tony asked as he moved past her to change courts after the third game. Sweat matted his T-shirt to his chest and a strand of wet hair fell across his forehead.

She didn't respond.

It was when Tony pulled into a 4–2 lead that Nona heard a clatter on the sundeck and looked up to see Cindy running out of the house, dashing around the swimming pool, and calling out to Sam as she circled the ivy-braided fence that hid the tennis court. Her voice, strung tight and tense by the message she carried, vibrated through the heavy air.

Both men looked up. Tony, toeing the baseline as he aligned himself for service, paused, with his left arm reaching for the sky, to measure the time and space between Cindy and the gate. Then, with champion concentration, he shifted back, rose upward, and smashed into the ball.

Sam never came close to it. The serve skimmed over the net, dipped quickly, and then spun off toward the rear right court.

But Tony never had the pleasure of winning the set because Cindy assaulted them even before she stepped inside the fence.

"Barry's up at the house," she called, breathless from exercise and excitement. "Come on! He saw a copy of the FBI wiretap order, and Kessler signed it! He's got the goods on Kessler."

Nona's heart accelerated, filling her ears with drumming intensity.

Sam stopped, stricken in the center of the court, the

tennis racquet dangling spent from his hand. Shock blanched his face. "I don't believe it," he said.

Tony came running around the net to put an arm around Sam's shoulder, but Sam shrugged him off and stooping to snag his canvas racquet cover and towel, he started back to the house with the others stumbling along beside him on the path, crowding close in school chum fashion.

Barry was standing on the sundeck waiting for them and they all went inside to sit around the kitchen table. Cindy unplugged the coffee pot and brought it over.

"The cleaning people and the caterers are coming in a few minutes," she said, pouring out five cups of coffee. "But the gardeners were supposed to be here already, Sam."

Sam patted his hand against the air to silence her trivia and turned to Barry. "O.K., shoot," he ordered.

Barry wrapped his hands around a coffee mug. "Well, originally, my source at the FBI told me she thought one of Kessler's top staff people had signed the order, but when she actually got to see the file, it was Kessler's signature. There's a helluvagood chance that we'll have a Photostat of the thing within the next week."

"Jesus Christ," Sam groaned, suspended between excitement over the scoop and pain about the truth. "I can't believe the whole thing. Why would he do it to me?" he asked, turning beseechingly toward Tony.

Tony shrugged. "He must have been scared. No one knew where the leaks were coming from."

"But he *knows* me," Sam protested. "He must have known it wasn't me. Jesus, we've been skunked on every story, including Watergate, for the past three years. I obviously had no sources at all."

"He signed the order on December thirteen, nineteen seventy," Barry said. "All eight names were on it, and there wasn't any cutoff date or need to renew after six months." Barry's speech became more syncopated as he spoke. He ejected each word forcibly from between tight lips.

Nona sat frozen between Sam and Barry.

"I can't believe it," Sam mumbled again, lifting the coffee cup Cindy had set in front of him and then returning it untasted to the saucer. "So? How long will it take you to tie it all up?"

"Maybe a week or ten days. It should be GO for the August tenth issue. I've got some more facts to firm up and another lead I want to check out too."

The front door chimes rang, and Cindy, who had been sitting primly in her chair, shredding petals off a marigold she'd taken from the centerpiece, got up and disappeared. A few seconds later she reappeared with two black women dressed in white uniforms. With a nod of his head, Sam indicated that he and Barry should go outside to the sundeck.

Tony sat still, studying the blueprint of veins on the back of his hand, reluctant to get caught up in the curlicues of intrigue about to be initiated.

Cindy began to show the women where the cooking equipment was kept.

Nona said softly, "Does Barry know anything about our talks with Kessler?"

Tony shook his head, avoiding her eyes.

"Should we go out there and tell him?" she asked.

"I don't know. Maybe Sam's explaining about it," Tony said, looking beyond the French doors. "Look. I have to go out to my place and pick up a suit to wear tonight. Come on. Take a ride out there with me."

"But Barry might be gone when we get back," Nona protested.

Tony looked at her intently. Disheveled from his tennis game and disturbed by Barry's announcement, he seemed tired. "O.K., tiger," he said wearily. "Come on."

They walked out onto the sundeck, and Nona felt

herself become invisible as the three men exchanged glances.

Sam had clearly been waiting for her to show. "Come on, sit over here," he said, moving toward a three-seat glider and patting the section beside him. He looked intent and earnest.

Nona sat down.

"Well, I've told Barry about things," Sam said quietly.

Nona looked at Barry who returned a noncommittal smile.

"And as you have heard, it's going to be ten days or so until he gets everything firmed up and double-checks his facts. But then, of course, we have no choice but to run it right away. With luck we'll have it for the August tenth issue." Sam spoke with a clear tone of inevitability.

Nona swallowed to relieve the tension in her throat. Tony had walked over to the bamboo bar and was fixing himself a drink, excluding himself from the conversation.

"Apparently both the *Post* and the *Times* are on to it now too. Of course, they don't know Barry's source, but. . . ."

Nona's eyes patrolled Sam's face, determined to pick up any sign of ambiguity, any ambivalence that offered an option. His T-shirt was opened wide at the neck. His hair was rumpled, and his face strained from the effort of trying to convince her he was being straight.

"So," he said, "we better figure out what to do. We don't have too many cards in our hand."

Tony returned to sit down near the glider.

"We could approach Kessler now and say we've got the story and that we'll sit on it if he comes up with the tape," Sam said in a war-gaming strategy voice, "but then he'll ask what guarantee he has that we won't publish the story after he turns over the tape. And since I can't give him any kind of guarantee, I don't know quite where to go from there." A bookie-weighing-the-odds expression developed on his face.

"What guarantee does Kessler have that I won't take the story somewhere else?" Barry asked.

"I could say you're willing to forget it in exchange for a bigger job," Sam spoke speculatively.

"Look—right now Kessler is running a waiting game on us," Tony said thoughtfully, "and it's to his advantage to hold onto the tape indefinitely because that supposedly ties Sam's hands, right? But if we can get a real confrontation set up, an immediate-threat situation with a definite time limit attached—like an August tenth deadline—then we've got some leverage. We're going to have to put some pressure on to make anything happen."

Nona looked at Tony. Despite his weary appearance, he seemed tougher and stronger to her than ever before. His sudden decision to assert leadership hit Nona hard, and she felt familiar lust and new gratitude combine to create something akin to love for him. Despite the dangers inherent in the situation—for Sam and Tony and their professional and personal reputations—Tony was formally announcing that he cared enough for Nona to get involved.

"It's clear we're going to have to stage this thing," he continued. "I mean, arrange a time and place to put the make on him. Play a hard cop, soft cop routine on him."

"Whaddya mean?" Sam asked.

Tony spoke slowly, "Well, we're going to have to pull in someone to muscle him. Because right now we've got nothing to give Kessler but our word, and he knows once we have the tape there's no way he can make us stick to it. There's no reason for him to trust us—especially now that Sam knows he was the guy who did him in."

"It won't work," Barry said. "You don't have anything solid to offer."

"Shit!" Sam cursed. "My head's all bent out of shape, and I've got to get cracking on this party. Let's table this until later."

Disappointed, Nona followed Tony into the house where she reclaimed her purse before walking outside with him to his car. They drove up Wisconsin Avenue to River Road. Nona sat silently beside her window watching the unfamiliar scenery unroll. Here the expensive houses set back from the road had a semiauthentic rural charm that seduced her even though she knew she was riding through a swanky suburb. She looked out at the quiet affluence, trying to put her thoughts in order, regimenting her arguments, trying to figure out a strategy. She wanted to understand the men's tactics completely, so she could design an action independent of theirs—a fall-back position—in case their strategy failed.

Fifteen minutes outside Washington, Tony turned onto a dirt lane that led through a long stretch of wooded land. In a clearing beyond the trees was a large renovated farm house. He parked in front of the rustic-stone entrance and came around to help her out. Obviously suffering some remorse about having brought her there, he turned around twice to see if anyone was coming up the road before he opened the front door. Inside the house he beckoned Nona to follow him into the living room, but there he moved quickly to an antique library table covered with a pile of mail and began flipping through the letters while Nona looked around. The empty house had a comfortable country quality. The chairs were upholstered in intentionally gay prints, and the couch, covered in an Appalachian patchwork quilt, was dotted with soft chubby pillows. Convenient side tables held ashtrays, fat round-bellied lamps, and amusing trinkets. The books on the shelves were punctuated with perfectly placed plants and silver-framed photographs. Nona moved forward, wanting to examine the pictures, but stopped when Tony spoke.

"Do you want a drink or something?" he asked.

He was still pawing through the third-class mail trying to hide his discomfort at having brought her home with him.

Nona smiled cheerfully, touched rather than hurt by his remorse. "No thanks. Just get your stuff and let's go. I'll wait here."

"O.K." He sounded relieved, as if he had half-expected her to further violate his home by requesting some sexual encounter upstairs in the master bedroom. "Here're some magazines to look at. It'll just take me a few minutes." He handed her a new *Newsweek* and the July *MS*. "Do you want some coffee or anything to eat?"

"You just asked me that," Nona smiled. "No. Just hurry so we can go."

She heard him hammering up the stairs above her head as she looked down and saw Ms. Elizabeth Lewellen on the *MS* mailing label.

That hurt. It hurt so much that she tossed the magazines down on the couch and walked through the archway into the den.

But there she clutched again, this time ripped apart by the casual incongruous clutter of things strewn around the room. All around her were a million little clues to the family's clannishness, individual contributions to a common cache that became a testimonial to their closeness. Magazines, games, toys, records, and tapes for diversified ages and interests were mixed together in confident chaos, knotting and tying their owners together into a single unit.

Jealousy scratched inside Nona's body, clawed at her skin to get out.

The pain came not because Tony had a wife, but because he was part of a family.

Oh, God, she thought, feeling barren and bereaved. They all live in this house together. They all go

199

tearing through their private lives, taking each other for granted, bonded together by love. There's a whole slew of them, and they all have each other, and they hang together and keep the world at bay. They're a family, and each of them is part of the other.

A silent pain, not for the present but for the past, caught her. And suddenly she remembered her own childhood, and a rush of yearning to belong somewhere again swept through her. She moved to the window and as she looked out into the yard at a row of bikes tilted against the utility shed, Nona thought that perhaps she'd like to be one of Anthony Lewellen's children, too.

She was waiting in the front hall when he came downstairs carrying a small leather suitcase. Without speaking he led her out to the car, surveying the road again to see if anyone was approaching. Nona felt like a prowler who had smashed through a security system of love to invade and vandalize the Lewellen home, trespassing into the family sanctuary to threaten and terrorize them briefly before fleeing back into oblivion.

Looking out the window at the smug houses snubbing River Road, Nona regretted not having looked at the photographs of Tony's wife and children. She felt almost perversely alien and alone, a solitary misfit in a culture composed of families.

Neither of them spoke until they had reentered the city.

When he turned onto Wisconsin Avenue again, Tony reached out to grip Nona's hand. "It'll work out," he said. "It's complicated and it feels sticky, but we'll think of something."

Filled with emotion, Nona withdrew her hand to curtail her vulnerability.

"I don't think I want to go back to Sam's right now," she said. "Just drop me off around P Street."

"What are you going to do?"

"Oh, I don't know. Maybe I'll buy a new dress to wear to the party tonight or something."

"How will you get home?"

Nona stiffened at his concern. "I'll take a taxi. I have to water my plants and stuff anyway."

"Do you have any money?" he asked, wrestling for his wallet.

"Yes," she lied, looking away and seeing the fancy boutiques sweep past the car window.

Tony tossed two fifty-dollar bills on her lap. "You're lying," he said. "I looked in your wallet last night. You had three dollars. And not a credit card in there."

She didn't answer.

I'm losing touch with myself, she thought. He's turning me around so fast I don't know who I am.

She experienced a quick surge of acquisitiveness and in the next instant felt the inevitable sense of glut that always followed a rush of greed.

"I don't need this," she said handing it back.

"But I want you to take it. Please."

On P Street, he stopped for a red light and reached across to open her door, pushing the bills into the outside pocket of her shoulder-bag purse.

Nona got out of the car.

She walked along Wisconsin Avenue looking into the shop windows and studying the denim rears of the lean couples walking in front of her.

She knew that soon enough she would have to toughen up and kick her growing addiction to the fringe benefits of exclusivity and elitism. She had taken herself too lightly and allowed herself too much leeway. There could be no more vacations from her own conscience. The holiday was over, but that hundred dollars was the ticket for her last ego trip. In the window of Trapeze, she saw a simple white gown, an elegant shell cut like a T-shirt.

This is it, she said, feeling the old eternal urge toward glamour. O.K. Lewellen, you're the last guy I'll ever do this for. Nona dashed into the shop, tried on the dress, bought it, and took a taxi to use up the meager remainder of Tony's largess.

Nona leaned back against the seat feeling both corrupt and pleased while the taxi carried her away from the quiet of Georgetown back to the frantic frenzy of Columbia Road where dark-eyed beige-colored little girls, whose cotton blouses hung loose outside their skirts, jumped rope on the sidewalk in front of Nona's building, filling the street with splashes of Spanish. Careful not to disturb their play, Nona walked cautiously around them and let herself into the foul-smelling hallway.

The heat had settled in thick layers around her apartment. It seemed she had to swat her way through the humidity to reach her bedroom. She lay down for a while, but the heat pressed heavily against her stifling her breathing, forcing her up again to putter around the room, rehang clothes in the closet, and straighten out her drawers.

When her bedroom was tidy she returned to the studio to tend her plants, feeling suddenly and unexpectedly forlorn as she thought of Tony and Sam and Cindy—lying on the flowered chaises beside the swimming pool discussing Kessler's betrayal while all around them professional caterers and gardeners were mounting the scenery for their party. For them, even trouble was attractive, a delicious dramatic crisis suddenly inflating their lives with excitement. Despite Sam's responsibility for his huge party, Nona knew he and Tony would amble off to play tennis sometime during the afternoon and then return for a swim, sharing the cool camaraderie of the water while the day evaporated gently around them, and they waited for the right hour to dress.

Nona went back to her bedroom and lay down on the bed again. It had begun to smell swampy, and the sheet was damp from sweat beneath her body. She thought it would be nice to take a nap, but instead she lay awake and planned the speech she would give to Barry at Sam's Honor Thy Enemies Party.

She was going to lay a guilt trip on him—an appeal for his assistance on the basis of his respect and affection for Michael. She wanted to lasso Barry as an ally and make him promise not to press ahead before she was in position to put the screws on Kessler. Having harbored the hope that Michael would be telephoning her soon, she wanted to be able to tell him that Barry was firmily on their side.

Twelve

Late that afternoon, Nona put on her new dress and studied herself in the full-length mirror nailed on her bathroom door. Startled by her own elegance, she considered changing into the loose caftan she often wore to restaurants, but gradually her resentment about the party reasserted itself, and emboldened by hostility she wore the dress as an act of protest.

Precisely at 7:30 she rang the bell of the Kinkaid mansion. A hired butler opened the door, and Nona walked down into the living room where she surreptitiously stashed her evening bag behind a chair in classic, but inappropriate, Movement tradition. Then, clutching only a package of cigarettes, she walked toward the French doors and looked out into the garden where a bouquet of women in pastel-tinted evening gowns and tall tailored men in pale colored summer suits fanned out across the grass.

They look very pretty, Nona thought, amiably.

And why shouldn't they? another part of her mind queried. What else have they got to do?

Celebrities were drifting aimlessly around the pool, pausing to greet anyone whose path intersected theirs. The guests gliding about the patio seemed more pretentious and were surveying the star-studded landscape to select special targets, assiduously avoiding lesser luminaries who were only friends of named enemies. The people layered about the bars were poised in store-mannequin poses, their hands curved around glasses that they held aloft as offerings to some invisible goddess of social success.

Nona walked down the stairs into the crowd, instantly absorbing the excitement they emanated. The women were sparkling with expectation—empty sockets avidly awaiting the prongs of male attention to turn them on. The men, juiced up by their new political notoriety, were prepared to play their customary charade of seduction, which satisfied their sexually hungry but dieting female counterparts.

Sam Kinkaid was standing at a long bar beneath the tropical trees at the far end of the patio with a woman in a haremesque halter-top print gown whom Nona recognized as Margo Dempsey. Nona walked over to them.

"You know, it's been years since I've gone to a party where we didn't pay admission," Mrs. Dempsey said, ignoring Nona's arrival. "You're sure there's not going to be any pitch at the end to turn this into a fundraiser? Something for the protection of National Enemies Facing Extinction or extermination?"

"Margot, you've paid," Sam protested enthusiastically. His forehead was strung with beads of sweat, and his eyes protruded with pleasure over the early signs of a successful party. "You've paid, I've paid, we've all paid plenty. We deserve this bash." Then, turning to include Nona with a nervous smile, he said, "As a matter of fact, here we have a leading underground enemy—one of the sexiest enemies in town." He reached out to take her hand. "What'll you have, honey, Scotch?"

Nona nodded, and Sam transmitted the order to his bartender. "Do you know each other?" he asked.

Nona shook her head. But Mrs. Dempsey's attention was suddenly diverted by the arrival of another cluster of celebrities.

"I want to talk to you later," Sam whispered as he handed Nona the drink. "Something's come up."

Margot Dempsey positioned herself so she spoke

exclusively to Sam, and Nona, feeling excluded but not excused, sipped her drink and watched the guests arriving through the gate on the westside of the mansion. She recognized two *New York Times* reporters coming down the moss-carpeted path with their wives who in lifting the hems of their flowered gowns created the illusion of floating slightly above the earth. Members-of-the-press-by-marriage, these wives floated along with vicarious confidence, smiling populist smiles at the people they passed while preserving their secret selves for the circle of *New York Times* people standing near the pool with whom they clearly shared a special sense of superiority. Their arrival created a complicated social square dance as they do-se-doed to and fro greeting their peers. Enmeshed in the embrace of their colleagues, pride holding their sleek heads high with invisible strings of self-assurance, they settled in for the evening.

Nona took several fast swallows from her glass.

"Oh, oh," Sam said, looking toward the gate. "There's someone I better welcome officially. Excuse me." He disappeared.

"Excuse me," Margot Dempsey said with intentional rudeness, and, turning quickly, walked away from the bar.

"Excuse *me,*" Nona said to the empty space in front of her.

"Would you like a fresh drink, miss?" the bartender asked.

Nona whirled around, jolted at having been overheard. "Well, yes, thank you." She handed him her glass and then stood alone, disarmed and disoriented, until she saw Barry approaching the bar with a young brunette whom he introduced to Nona as Buffie Donleavy, a summer intern in a senator's office. The three of them ordered fresh drinks and then watched the party developing around them. Buffie Donleavy was totally unintimidated, almost unaffected, by the epic scene into which Barry had brought her. She seemed infinitely at ease with the languorous women swishing about seeking flirtatious distractions and the men who could only offer them sour deceptions.

Barry seemed inordinately pleased with himself and Buffie. Having found an appropriate date apparently fortified his resolve to infiltrate Sam's crowd in which he was only a provisional member. The young woman seemed to reinforce his fragile social claim on the clique that he had courted for so long. Nona knew she had to act fast to establish an independent claim on him. She had to pitch her appeal to his memory of old times and old commitments, evoking Michael as a symbol of that separate and special segment of their lives.

"Barry," she began, using his name as an invocation. "Will you promise me something?"

He looked startled at the serious tone she'd adopted.

"I don't want to blow this chance for helping Michael," she said. "And I've been trying to get my act together, but I'm having trouble figuring out a strategy for staging this thing. Would you promise me you won't move up the publication date without warning me first? I mean, this may be Mike's last chance. If I can't put the screws on what'shisname before you break your story, Mike will never be able to surface." She glanced at Buffie who seemed totally oblivious to the conversation. "Will you warn me if there's any change in your plans?"

Barry looked beyond her. "Here comes Tony," he said.

Nona turned. Lewellen was wearing a new, light-colored suit with a floral patterned shirt and matching tie that gave him a dandyish look. He moved in close to Nona, then moved back and blinked.

"Wow," he said.

"Did you think I was going to wear blue jeans?"

"No, but I didn't know you were a closet flasher," he laughed.

Barry introduced Buffie to Tony, surreptitiously watching his hero with hot eager eyes, studying Lewellen's special effects as if trying to memorize the magical combination of intimacy and arrogance that produced his extraordinary affect.

Then with an impulsive surge of political opportunism, Nona reached out to touch Lewellen's arm with a possessive hand that announced her claim on him. Before that moment she had never assumed any of the public privileges available to her. She had never interrupted Tony during conversations that excluded her or summoned his attention by any physical allusion to their sexual secrets. But now she wanted to flash her power and flex her muscle in front of Barry to firm him up.

It was with unexpected suddenness that Tony jerked his arm away from Nona's hand. An expression of constraint crossed his face, constricting his smile, and he turned to face the bar when he spoke to her.

"We're going to have to cool it tonight, lady. It's getting a little sticky for me because a lot of Liz's friends who I thought were out of town aren't."

Quickly Nona turned around wanting to recoup her losses and reestablish the status she had lost before Tony pushed her hand away. But Barry and Buffie were melting back into the party, evaporating easily and aimlessly into the crowd of media people and liberal politicians.

"I'm going to have to keep circulating," he went on. "Why don't you come over and talk to Bob Dempsey for a while? He's kind of out of sorts tonight. I think he and Margot are having a thing."

Nona turned and followed Tony's gaze down toward the pool where Senator Dempsey was standing near a trio of long-necked flamingolike women who were alternately admiring their reflections in the water and raising their heads to scan the horizon.

Nona picked up her glass and walked obediently beside Tony across the slick surface of tiles.

The relief on the senator's face when he saw them was sincere and he turned his back on the women abruptly. "Thank God, you're here," he smiled, "this is a real ballbuster. God, you look gorgeous. How you two doing?"

"Things are a little tough for me at the moment," Tony answered grimly.

Instantly understanding the problem, the senator turned to Nona and scooped her up in the steam shovel of his charm as he assumed responsibility for her. "I bet you haven't seen too many scenes like this one, have you?" he asked with a gentle baby-sitter smile of encouragement, trying to distract her attention as Tony slid silently away. "Do you know who these folks are?"

"Some of them," Nona shrugged, bruised by the obviousness with which Tony had arranged her transfer.

"Well, I'll fill you in on who's who," Bob offered. "It's interesting."

They treat me like a child, Nona thought. Like the little daughter of some old friend.

"Because tonight we are fortunate enough to have every social lion and cub from the Georgetown cat-pack here. . . ." The senator snorted a sound somewhere between rage and resignation. "All the chic Georgetown . . . sheiks and their sheiksas." He laughed softly, pleased by his pun.

Nona smiled and looked off toward a long white banquet table set in a gentle slope of the garden where the guests congregated briefly to flutter about the food.

"Yessiree . . . they're really coming out of the woodwork for this one," Bob said in an imitation sportscaster voice. "They are in rare form tonight—coming on like gangbusters because they've been saved by Nixon's Impotent-Democrat Reclamation

Program. Look how happy they are since their recognition factors have been restored to them. . . ."

The senator's eye began to twitch, and he rubbed it roughly with the back of his hand.

Nona looked over to where Tony was talking with an attractive red-haired woman. An associate host by virtue of his friendship with Sam, Tony was working the hors d'oeuvre crowd, stroking people with his warm social style. Nona felt a swelling of rage in her chest.

So this is how it is, she thought. This is how it feels to be one of the invisible women people pretend not to see. This is how Cindy has lived for years—a glamorous underground creature, the star of a big extravaganza never released for public distribution.

A spasm shattered the senator's face, and immediately he began to shake his head as if trying to ward off some insect. "Let me get us some fresh drinks. Sit down right here on this thing and don't move until I come back."

Nona handed him her glass and sat down on the edge of a chaise. Several yards away, Cindy, elegant-looking in a 1920-ish chiffon gown, was introducing a small group of people, and Nona listened, struck by the easy amiability with which the strangers met each other. They seemed to know just from looking at each other that they shared the same histories and futures, so, assuming acceptance and approval, they came together as easily as kids, as guileless in their snobbery as children in their innocence.

The effortless exchange of pleasantries made Nona remember the weird encounters that occurred between Movement people who could never dare be nonchalant. At parties or meetings—gatherings that were hard to distinguish—everyone was careful, rather than casual, with strangers. Often a newcomer was so coolly received that he would begin to pour out his guts to establish his legitimacy and prove he wasn't a narc or a plant or a summertime rebel.

Strangers—too shy to call themselves revolutionaries —would go through frenzied maneuvers to prove their radical credentials, dropping the names of Movement heavies who could vouch for them, alluding to political actions in which they'd participated, mentioning radical communities in major cities where they'd crashed. But here in the Kinkaid garden there was no need to explain oneself beyond offering a conversational job description or educational résumé and all of the questions were of a what-do-you-do-ish nature.

Bob Dempsey returned and handed Nona both glasses to hold. Then he upended another chaise and rolled it, wheelbarrow-fashion, alongside hers.

"Now," he said, sprawling out and reclaiming his drink, "let me point out to you some of the splendid specimens of threats to our national security who are here with us tonight—in case you give a flying fuck. Over there, near Teddy, you can see the Camelot contingent."

Nona looked at the cluster of Kennedys who stood together like refinished photos of themselves, blown-up frozen-in-time-and-motion wall-size posters.

"As in most mythology, it is the citizens who must deal with the descendants of heroes. It is the people who must forgive them their personal eccentricities so as to maintain . . . the memory . . . of the image . . ." He sighed heavily. "As a matter of fact we've got just about the entire Hickory Hill touch-football team out tonight. Plus a couple of live Redskins and our very own favorite ball club owner. Rather sporty sporting event, wouldn't you say?"

Nona returned her eyes to the senator's tortured face. His cynicism was scribbled in indelible lines around his eyes. Self-consciously, he turned away as if to stop her from prying into his private pain.

"I assume," he continued, switching into a Rona Barret from Hollywood voice, "that you can recognize the Kennedy ladies-in-waiting—the McLean bluebloods who live white-knuckled lives with good rings on their fingers. The frosted blonds are all Wisconsin Avenue shopkeepers who get adopted by political wives just like cab drivers used to get shlepped to formal dinner parties by drunk Manhattan socialities. . . ."

One of the uniformed waiters weaving in and out of the crowd suddenly presented them a heavy tray with a surprisingly graceful swoop of his stiffened arm. Nona clutched an impolite number of hors d'oeuvres and began eating them greedily.

"It's interesting to see how many new combos we're sprouting here tonight. This can be attributed to the fact that many of the wives the senators married in their youth—as the expression goes— are out of town sunning their fannies by the sea, so my esteemed colleagues are trotting out their favorite pussy tonight. To your right you can see a crew of skinny little secretaries who are scared shitless about being here. Ooh, oh," Dempsey drained his glass, "here's real trouble! That little lady heading toward us is really a very dangerous number. In fact, I might have to move if she zeros in on us. It just so happens that she's one of Washington's leading star-fuckers and has actually been diagnosed as having what's known as a presidential-candidate fetish that causes a terrific itch in the twat that can only be relieved every four years or so. That, of course, makes her a bit testy during the intervals, so she tries to make do with leading contenders or past also-rans."

Dempsey reached down to exchange glasses with Nona. He kept his head lowered until the lady in question passed by. Then he straightened up again.

"The media types are, of course, all too familiar . . . they're the ones you see between your toes every night . . . even the less famous ones have those tony Colortran tans. The *Washington Post* people are idenfiable by their unearned airs of self-righteousness. You can tell a *Post* editor by the fact that he walks around acting like an owner instead of a hired hand. Invariably they develop a form of amnesia that makes them forget that the managerial class is only one salary check away from bankruptcy." Dempsey finished Nona's Scotch. "The guys who look like lobbyists are really lawyers and the ones walking around with those shit-eating grins on their faces are ex-LBJ advisers. They're always sucking around trying to find out what people think of them."

The senator's hand, wrapped around Nona's glass, shook slightly. Finally he set the glass down on the ground.

"I know these people very well," he continued more sternly. "For instance, that weather-beaten man talking to Sam sleeps with that Diet-Rite redhead in the backyard tan. Her husband is one of our local merchant princes and he makes it—when he can—with the wife of that right-wing columnist garbaging up on the shrimp next to Senator Fulbright. . . . And coming toward us right now, stopping off first to chat with the senator from Boeing, is a very lousy Washington writer who once did a horrendous Broadway play but now only writes bad checks and worse novels. Over the years," Dempsey sighed philosophically, "these people have come to . . . disgust me."

He crossed his legs. Instantly the wooden heels of his shoes started clicking together like a pair of castanets and he looked down half-surprised, half-interested in the uncontrollable drumming. Finally he uncrossed his ankles and lifted his arm to summon another waiter.

There was a long silence while they waited for fresh drinks to arrive.

"I am slowly getting smashed," Bob Dempsey said gravely. "Otherwise I wouldn't dare tell you that I am acutely jealous of Tony for having found you for his . . . friend. It makes me wish I had found you first."

Why not? Nona thought, resenting him for the first

213

time. It's cheap enough—an extra body to keep around like a backup six-pack of cold beer. No married man should be without one.

"However, in an effort to stifle my envy, I will continue with my guided tour, if you don't mind. See that bag of bones over there? She's what we call a Washington hostess—a carnivorous member of the social-lion family. Although not native to this area, these creatures flourish here and develop an incredible skill for social climbing, so that they can only achieve what is colloquially known as a "Peak experience" at or under a dinner table. Indeed the true Washington hostess goes into heat at the first scent of a powerful politician and instantly begins producing aphrodisiacal aromas of haute cuisine—in a manner similar to a skunk—in order to snare him.

"As a matter of zoological interest, these lionesses have been mated most successfully with another breed of pack animals called journalists, who are the only half-parasite, half-host species yet identified in the annals of animal history. . . . Imagine a beast who can both hump and pump his prey at the same time—a feat unknown among any other phylum. The pack-journalists are great cross-country runners and are also known for their sheeplike qualities and incestuous instincts. Some observers think them nasty and brutish because they practice ass-licking with sources and ass-kissing with politicians, but their brown-nosing habits are quite appropriate—ecologically speaking. As you know, there are different strokes for different folks."

They sat side by side for over an hour, growing more dependent upon each other as they became drunker, chatting idly as they watched the parade of personalities pass by and commenting softly on the attributes of the most attractive women and interesting men. Sometimes Tony would flit by to make a quick furtive connection before disappearing again and occasionally Margot Dempsey would float past, pretending not to notice her husband hiding in the darkness. Cindy scurried back and forth, turning on when she wanted to charm a guest and dimming down when she gave quiet orders to the staff about replenishing the icy mountain of shrimp or lighting the Chinese lanterns. Sam staggered around completely intoxicated by his own hospitality.

Around midnight Bob Dempsey struggled reluctantly to his feet. "Well, if I stay here with you one minute longer, Margot will file divorce papers in the morning naming you corespondent. *If* she hasn't made herself a widow first. She's dying to be a widow, has been for years—the widow of the late Senator Dempsey was quietly married late this afternoon to a Greek shipping magnate."

"I want to talk to you," Nona said suddenly as a rush of anxiety passed through her.

He stood high above her weaving gently with the wind. "I'm flattered."

"Monday," she said breathlessly. "At your office."

He nodded and smiled before walking away.

Nona blew him a kiss, but she felt abandoned as he joined the crowd standing beside the pool, and she flattened out on the thick cushioned chaise, holding her drink in one hand and a cigarette in the other. A wind was sweeping the heat off the patio, jiggling the Chinese lanterns in the trees. Tired now, Nona watched the people passing by with the same mesmerized disinterest with which she read cast credits at the end of a long movie, too emotionally drained to absorb the names of bit players and technicians but immobilized by emotion. Vaguely she watched a magazine model wobbling, fully clothed, at the end of the diving board in a Statue of Liberty pose while an audience of sleazy one-dimensional Alan Drury characters applauded her antics.

Lying on the sidelines of the luxurious party, Nona fell asleep and didn't awake until several

215

hours later when she felt Tony move into her kinetic orbit, stirring the soft animal curled up inside her body. He sat down on the edge of her chaise, close to her loins, and his nearness evoked a warm pleasant sensation that made her feel totally physical—material and greedy.

I'm hooked, she thought sadly.

He cupped his hand over her knee, spreading his fingers so she saw the action of the blue strings along the back of his hand—hammers plying the keys of his fingers until she felt dizzy with desire.

"Where's everybody?" she asked.

"The party's over. It's after three. I found your nap very convenient so I didn't wake you until everyone was gone."

Up on the sundeck Nona saw Sam stationed behind the bamboo bar making drinks again. Barry and his date stood nearby while Cindy slumped in a white wicker chair—a pale shadow in the lantern and moonlight.

Eventually the four of them, carrying fresh drinks, came down to the pool, and Sam knelt over to sink his hand into the water. "I think we should fill it up with Scotch so that maybe the girls would want to skinny-dip with us."

Nona cringed at the way he said "girls"—the word suddenly took on the meaning of some subspecies of guppies or tadpoles. Vindictively she dropped her cigarette butt on to one of the immaculate tiles beside her chaise and squashed it beneath her sandal, spreading a sunburst of tobacco over the Caribbean design.

"Oh come on, Sam," Cindy complained. "Don't start in now. You drank too much."

Sam tossed her a look of irritation. "You know, the longer we're together the more puritanical you get. You think you can take the sin out of adultery by coming on like a prude."

Cindy looked up defensively, but then decided to laugh it off. "Listen, Sam. Whatever I'm doing, I'm

216

not committing adultery. You're married, but I'm not, remember?"

"Right, baby." Sam marshaled a pseudoconciliatory smile around the cigarette clenched in his mouth. "You're as innocent as the fresh driven snow. That's what I love about you." He leered at Cindy in a way that threatened either social or sexual reprisals for any further trouble.

Although a late-night heat still hung over the patio, Nona felt a sudden, violent chill. The whole scene seemed kinky and confusing to her. Even though the bickering sounded familiar, the elegantly appointed setting made it feel foreign to her, an extravagantly frivolous, drawing-room comedy.

"Nobody wears bathing suits anymore," Barry's date said flatly. "At least not in swimming pools." Very matter-of-factly she began to unbutton her silk blouse. Instantly her small red-eyed breasts sprang forward and began to swing crazily from side to side as she hunched over to unzip her white skirt. When she straightened up a second later she was naked except for two white bikini scars and the long sash of dark hair hanging over her shoulders.

The men stood in silence, studying her nudity, watching the white globes of her buttocks alternate rhythmically as she glided into the shadows before diving into the pool.

"Oh, shit," Cindy cursed. Her face was pinched with fear as the night began speeding out of control, hurtling forward at a reckless speed that crumpled customary constraints.

"Maybe we all should take a little swim," Sam suggested. "A skinny-dip in honor of the occasion."

"What's the occasion?" Cindy snarled. Tense and defensive, she stood a few feet away from Sam, defying him to promote a group sex scene that would cheapen or undermine her.

"Jesus Christ, Cindy. Don't start bitching," Sam groaned. "It's too hot. Besides, flat chests are *in* this

season. Little tits are *big* this year. Don't be so fucking uptight!"

"Somebody better make sure Buffie doesn't drown,"
Tony suggested dryly as he flattened out discreetly
beside Nona on her chaise.

Obligingly Barry trotted off toward the pool to protect his interests, clearly proud that his date had taken
an initiative that seemed to please Sam.

Nona felt the tension whipping around her and
experienced a grim sort of satisfaction at seeing the
opposition beginning to crumble.

"For God's sake, Cindy! What are you? A princess
or something?" Sam yelled. Challenged, he felt compelled to show that his mistress had not deteriorated
into a second wife.

"Maybe I should run upstairs and get all your little porn books, Sam," Cindy mocked, moving closer to
confront him. Now that Barry and his girl friend were
splashing around in the pool Cindy could counter the
threat to her respectability by attacking Sam's virility.

"Come on, Cindy," Sam said in a lordly manner.
"Take off your goddamn clothes and jump in. You're
acting like an old maid, for God's sake. What's your
problem, anyway?" He was flaying himself with aggravation, outraged at Cindy's resistance to his sexual
will, writhing with a determination to prevail.

"Should I go get the movie projector, Sam? Do you
want to run some of your skinflicks too? Or should I
go inside and make some popcorn to eat while we
watch our new little groupie perform?" Cindy raged.

They were standing face to face now, two recipro-
cal images locked in combat, caught up by a hitch
in their mutual fantasies, but fighting to maintain
the life-support system of their fairy tale.

Suddenly Cindy capitulated and began to undress,
tearing off her chiffon gown and throwing it angrily
on the ground to stand naked in front of them, as
uncomplicated and sexually noncommunicative as a
child.

218

"O.K.?" She was sobbing savagely. "Are you satisfied now, Sam? Is this what you wanted?"

Still crying, she ran across the tiles and jumped into the water.

Sam turned toward Tony and Nona with a sheepish but stubborn smile. "Well, let's get with it, kids." He began to undress, his hands stammering over his clothes. "This will be good for her. She's got to unwind."

And despite the tawdry scene they had just witnessed, Nona felt Tony start to harden against the side of her hip.

"What do you think?" Tony whispered against her face. "Are you up for it?"

Sam was waiting impatiently, demanding their participation. "I wouldn't have thought . . . *you* . . . would mind swimming nude," he said to Nona.

But his pauses of silence before and after the pronoun turned Nona into an ethnic object, part of a bulk quantity of stereotypes.

Nona looked up at the roof of the dark sky that billowed inward above them weighted down by the summer heat. Beside her Tony was guiding the lower part of his body against her leg, using his erection to prove the urgency of his condition.

Staring at Sam and feeling Tony, Nona experienced the same dizzying sensuality produced by making love in front of a mirror. Then, flooded by a revulsion that obliterated reason, she flung herself off the chaise. Laughing sportingly, she scuttled her dress before curling the nylon underpants down her legs. Then she ran off to dive into the deep end of the pool and swam several lengths letting the water cool her limbs and lighten her spirits. Finally tired, she stopped near the eight-foot-depth marker and looked back toward the shallow end where Barry and Buffie lounged on the semicircular stairs, the upper halves of their bodies glistening above the water. Cindy was clinging to the ladder near the diving board, hidden in the shadows. Nona tucked her knees up against her stomach and listened to her breathing as she bobbed up and down in the water.

"How is it?" Sam asked crouching down on the pool ledge near Nona. The spotlights lit up a devilish expression on his face.

"It's nice," she said drawing away as he slid into the water. "It's warm."

And then suddenly there was an explosion of shouts and splashes as people began swimming and splashing toward Cindy. In an instant she was surrounded by thrashing legs and bodies that churned the water and sent whooping noises into the night air. Nona swam in the shallow end, surfaced, and unexpectedly came up face to face with Barry Stein. In that instant the two of them looked at each, mutually shocked by their situation—what the fuck are we doing here, they silently asked each other and they both turned away.

Suddenly Cindy, clinging to the pool ledge, began to scream. Quickly Nona swam toward her.

"What's the matter?" she panted. "What's wrong, Cindy?"

"I can't," Cindy cried, her face sliding in and out of the water. "If everybody starts to . . . I can't . . . You don't know." Her eyes squeezed shut. "Some people can . . ." she sobbed, "but I can't. I just can't take it. Nona. Please . . ."

Nona pushed the long wet yarn of Cindy's hair away from her face. "Climb out," she ordered pushing her upward. "Get out."

Tony was beside them.

"Help her," Nona cried, grabbing his shoulder. "Help her get out."

They both boosted Cindy up and over the side.

"You've got to stop all this," Nona said. "Cindy's in a bad way."

"O.K." Tony said. "I'll tell Sam."

The men stayed in the water while Nona walked Cindy up to the house and Buffie went to retrieve their clothes. Once inside the kitchen, Cindy ran to the bathroom and they could hear her being sick as they dressed. When she came back out again the towel they'd wrapped around her was gone and she stood naked in the center of the kitchen, totally transformed by her panic. Her glorious hair clung to her skull and she had lost any resemblance to the glamorous creature who had danced about the party all night. Sniffling but speechless, she waited while Buffie ran upstairs and returned with a terrycloth bathrobe. When she finally spoke it was in a quiet but controlled voice.

"I think I'd better go to bed," she said. "This is Joan's robe. Sam would kill me."

She trotted away only seconds before the three men filed in through the French doors. They were dressed and subdued. Although Sam offered to make another round of drinks, Barry and Buffie declined and left a few minutes later.

"We'd better go now too, Tony," Nona said, trying to recall where she'd left her purse. She realized that she was still drunk.

"Oh, Christ! Sack out here," Sam growled. "It won't kill you."

Tony looked apologetically at Nona, and she shrugged indifferently. A few moments later they went upstairs and collapsed into the fourposter bed.

When the first sunlight began to call its alarm through the unshaded window, Nona forced herself awake, feeling an aching twinge in her loins and a damp sense of loss and spillage. Looking down she saw huge strawberry birthmarks staining the sheets. A great longing for her own apartment overcame her.

"I want to go home, Tony" she said loudly.

"What's the matter?" Tony mumbled. His eyes were dusty from sleep and he rolled over, flinging back the covers, to expose an indiscriminate early morning erection jutting away from the white untanned part of his torso.

"I want to go home," Nona repeated. "I'm wiped out. I just got my period and I want to get out of here."

"Oh, come on baby," Tony moaned. "Relax. This is it. The absolute, ultimate, optimum time. No rubbers, no booties, no nothing. You can't deprive me of my skinny-dip."

Nona evaded his hands. "Knock it off, Lewellen. Don't mess around. I've got to get out of here. I'm freaking out."

"Aw, come on. Relax. Don't go into one of your song-and-dance routines."

"We have to do something about these sheets. Look at this bed," Nona squeaked.

"Who's 'we,' white man?"

"Get up." Nona insisted. "Right now."

Tony got up, helped Nona to strip the bed, flipped over the mattress, and then disappeared into the bathroom. Nona wadded the sheets into a pillowcase and then went out into the hall to find the linen closet. She grabbed an armload of professionally laundered sheets and made the bed before Tony came out of the bathroom glistening from his shower and wearing a handsome set of tennis whites.

"Hey. It looks good," he smiled apolgetically. "What'd you do with the other ones?"

"I've got 'em," Nona answered, more composed now that her crime was covered up. "I'll just take them home and wash them."

"But how will you get them back in here?"

"I won't. I'm going to start redistributing Sam's movable property a little. He's got too much stuff, anyway. I'm going to liberate these sheets."

Wearing a short cotton dress she had left in the guest room, her sandles and a washcloth tucked inside her panties, Nona followed Tony ouside to his car. Automatically she sat with her weight on one haunch to protect the car upholstery from direct con-

222

tact with her crotch. When they drove past a drug-store on Wisconsin Avenue Tony pulled into an adjacent parking lot.

"O.K., tiger," he smiled, rubbing his knuckles across the crown of her head. "What do you want? Regular or super?"

Nona felt a spasm of shyness silence her.

"Well?" He waited.

She ducked her head out from beneath his hand and edged toward the door.

"Never mind," he laughed, enjoying her embarasment. "I think your pussy's super, but I'll just get regular."

When he returned he tossed a bag at her and then drove the car over to O Street.

Nona slouched down in her seat. Her body was having a civil war with her head. Tony Lewellen had put her insides into motion causing a daily dialectic between her body and her soul. She liked him. She liked what was funky about him. He turned her on. He called himself a nationally syndicated aphrodisiac and he was right. She was intoxicated with his militant affection.

When they reached her apartment building, Tony pulled over to the curb but didn't park.

"O.K., tiger, I'm turning you loose," he said. "I have the feeling you need some time. Go write your article. I'll leave you alone for a while. As a matter of fact, I'm three columns behind myself. You sure know how to ruin a guy's career." He leaned over and kissed the tip of her nose. "Leave the sheets, I'll do them at my house. There's no reason for you to go to that raggedy-assed laundry across the street. You're on the fast track now, baby. There *are* servants."

Nona collected her possessions and gave Lewellen the finger as she climbed out of his car.

Thirteen

On Monday morning Nona left her apartment early. She drove to the Hill and went directly up to Senator Dempsey's office. He was meeting with someone, so Nona sat in the waiting room watching his staff people hustling around, the women opening constituents' mail and answering phone calls, the men checking the day's schedule and watching the opening of the hearings on a small TV crowded onto the window sill. After a twenty-minute wait, Nona was ushered into the senator's office. Dempsey closed the door behind them and self-mockingly led her toward the red leather swivel chair behind his enormous glass-covered desk.

Nona sat down and waited while he took the visitor's seat.

"I need to pick your brains, Senator," she said.

"O.K."

She looked around the large book-lined office with its rich red carpeting and quiet expensive furniture. All around her, sober accessories insisted upon the importance and power of the room's occupant. Above a bar filled with tall glass decanters were two large photographs of the senator, one with Jack Kennedy and the other with Bobby Kennedy.

"Look," Nona said briskly, lighting a cigarette, "here's the deal." Then she leaned forward, elbows on the desk, and, swearing him to secrecy, told Dempsey the sequence of events prior to Barry

Stein's discovering Kessler was the person who authorized the wiretap.

When Dempsey recovered his composure and asked enough questions to feel convinced of the legitimacy of the story, he asked when Sam was going to run it.

Nona said, "On August the tenth. That's why I have to figure out how to stage a confrontation with Kessler before then so I can trade him the tapes for the story. If the story runs before I can do that, those tapes will be filed directly in the burn bag."

Bob Dempsey leaned back in his chair and crossed his legs. Then, reversing his movements, he got up and walked around the desk. For a moment Nona thought he was going to make a pass at her and her heart lurched. But he only jerked his thumb over his shoulder to indicate she should move.

"I can't think sitting over there on the wrong side of the tracks," he grinned.

Nona laughed, relieved that he hadn't endangered their friendship with any indiscretion, and changed chairs. Then she watched as he began pondering the problem.

"You're right in thinking you might have to pull in someone else," he said. "You need to have a pincher play—two separate forces that can squeeze old Eric in the middle." The senator lit a cigarette and put his feet on the desk.

Then Dempsey fell silent, puzzling over the scenario, smoking and creasing his forehead while trying to think of a way to force Kessler's hand. The notion that Nona's troubles were not his concern had apparently not occurred to him.

"Let's try out this one for size," he said tentatively. "How well do you know Jay Lazar?"

Nona shrugged. "Why?"

"Well, if he's straight—and on the side of the angels like the rest of us—he could be our trump card. He could set Kessler up by calling him and saying you'd come up with the goods. Then, under

225

guise of wanting to protect Kessler, which for all I know he might really want to do, Lazar could say you were ready to make an exchange and that he was willing to kill the story—either for a price or for some hot news leak or something like that. See, the problem with using Barry Stein is that Kessler wouldn't ever trust him. And he wouldn't trust Sam to kill the story since Sam knows now that Kessler was his hitman. Anyway, he'd have no guarantee that Sam could control Stein after the deal was made, even if he really wanted to, because Barry could go somewhere else to publish a scoop like that one . . . that's the problem. But you could be really paid off."

Nona nodded.

"Look, I've only seen Lazar a couple times at parties and things, and he never really said anything 'wrong' to me, but he did seem awfully hungry, you know? . . . eager. And I'm not certain you can trust him. On the other hand, you need some questionable type Kessler *would* trust, not anyone on the Left like myself, or personally involved the way Sam is. How would you feel about having a chat with Lazar and sounding him out . . . carefully? Do you think you could handle that?"

"Oh, that's easy enough," Nona said. "I don't really know for sure just how eager Jay would be, but since Kessler's clearly on the way out, Jay might . . . oblige me, although I don't know quite what he'd have to gain from it."

"Well, we could hold out the wonderful pleasure of my friendship," Bob Dempsey smiled. "What about you talking to him first and then me moving in to muscle him a little by waving a few post-Nixon dinner parties in front of him. That might turn him on."

"Yes, it might," Nona agreed.

Bob Dempsey stood up to indicate the interview was over, and Nona rose to her feet as if tied to him by an invisible cord that tugged her aloft. It was a conditioned Washington reflex.

"Should I have him call you if he's amenable to helping?" she asked hastily, suddenly feeling small and, unlike her usual self, intimated by the huge office.

"Yes, and then I'll talk to him privately."

"Thank you," she said following him to the door. Her back was to him as he opened it, and she felt him pause close behind her. Then the telephone on his desk rang, and he gave her a friendly pat on the shoulder.

"Better get on to it right away," he said, striding back across his office. "The hearings are supposed to end tomorrow or Wednesday."

Nona shut the door behind her, smiled as she walked past the senator's receptionist, and decided to skip the hearings so she could speak with Jay right away.

She drove downtown to the *Metro* office on Pennsylvania Avenue. It was almost eleven by the time she'd parked her car and got to the twelfth story of the new high-rise office building, but Jay still hadn't come in. Nona parked herself in the reception room to wait for him. She leafed through back copies of *Metro* stacked and filed around her chair and half-memorized five years of *Metro* covers, which were mounted, framed, and hung on the walls. When Jay finally slammed through the door he moved toward his red-haired receptionist before he saw Nona and then, startled, stopped and grinned.

"Don't tell me you're a week early on your deadline?" he said disbelievingly.

Nona shook her head and then got up and walked into Jay's office. He followed her, carrying a pile of mail that he began to open as soon as he sat down at his desk. The room was small and cluttered with high piles of manuscripts, magazines, newspapers, galleys, and clippings. There was only a small section of empty desk surface directly in front of where he sat.

"So what brings you up here off-schedule?" he asked, reading one letter while opening another.

"Senator Dempsey asked me to talk to you," Nona said.

Lazar put down the pack of mail and settled back in his chair. "Yeah?"

"He wants you to help us with something," Nona said averting her eyes as if to avoid any embarrassing questions about her relationship with the senator.

"No kidding? And what little problem do you two have?" Jay asked with a sneer.

Nona took her cigarettes out of her purse, stole an ashtray off the top of a pile of papers, and put it on her lap. As often as possible she avoided Jay's eyes while she told him the story. When she had finished, she tried to look as if she were summoning her last reserve of strength to look appealingly across the desk at him, meeting his eyes for the first time.

"Jesus," Jay grunted. "Now that's something else. When and where is all of this supposed to happen?"

Nona studied him intently. "I don't know. Bob . . . the senator, wanted to talk to you privately to set it up. If you're willing."

"Well, it sounds like it's right out of a James Bond movie. I wouldn't miss it for the world. Am I supposed to call him or's he gonna call me?"

"You'll do it?" Nona asked after a breathless hesitation.

"We'll see." Jay smiled sadistically. "I want to find out what's in it for me before I stick my neck out like that. I think bribing a federal official is a capital offense."

Nona stood up. "No, it's just a Capitol habit. Call Bob at his office. He's waiting to hear from you. And I really appreciate it, Jay. I really do."

He didn't stand up as she walked out, and she didn't say good-bye.

Senator Dempsey telephoned Nona's apartment that night. He had seen Jay for dinner and though he wasn't convinced of the man's integrity, Dempsey had called Kessler from the restaurant and set up a jaunt to Bobby Baker's Carousel Hotel in Ocean City on Thursday and Friday as an after-Watergate celebration. Kessler had accepted the invitation and asked if he could bring Johanna Dupres. Both Sam and Tony were ready to spend a few days at the beach as soon as the hearings ended.

Nona stood beside her bed, holding the receiver with both hands, weak from relief and anxiety.

"Are you there?" Dempsey asked.

A soft sob escaped from her lips. "Yes. I'm here. You're incredible," she whispered.

"Check back in with me tomorrow," Dempsey said before he hung up. "We'll work out the details."

On Wednesday morning, the last day of the Watergate hearings, Nona returned to Capitol Hill with a strong sense that the Senate office building was her real home. She hurried upstairs to the caucus room, eager to rejoin her tablemates or some other reporters with whom she shared a corridor comradeship. There was only a small crowd of early arrivals sitting at the press tables and many of them were already into the sports section of the *Post*—a sign of withdrawal and rejection.

Everyone looked unusually glum, and Nona began to feel some precommencement hostility in the room—the ambivalence of graduating seniors facing separation with a show of indifference. After the long summer of Watergate, the journalists had become so attuned to each other that any strong feeling swept quickly through the crowd kindling a collective reaction. Even the snobbish free-lance writers from

229

New York, having enjoyed the security of a group situation, looked a little forlorn on the eve of their return to competitive independence.

Nona took her seat and watched the press pack staggering in. After months of intimacy she could tell instantly that most were out of sorts as well as exhausted. They took their customary seats and began to read or write rather than talk—a sign they were troubled. Having memorized an infinite number of details—moles and pimples, hairlines and heat rashes, habits and tics, chipped teeth and wrinkles—Nona had no difficulty in interpreting expressions in her purview.

The cameraman whose belly folded over his belt, the man from *Le Monde* whose long front lock worried his eyes, the *Boston Globe* reporter who had worn the same diagonally striped tie for three months—all felt anxious this morning, and Nona experienced a proprietary empathy for her colleagues. Just as she could tell how many days had passed since the *Post* photographer shaved or when the attractive blond from CBS had last washed her hair, Nona knew instantly which reporters were up and which were down. Today was clearly a bummer for everyone. The hearings were ending without any sense of conclusion. Nothing had been resolved.

Nona turned to check out the last group of tourists being ushered inside, hoping the crowd of summertime sightseers might reveal some clue to the meaning of the Watergate hearings. Perhaps the visitors from the "Great Out There"—symbols of the mystery of middle-America that eluded and intimidated wary Washington reporters—knew some truths.

Nona returned her gaze to the press section and met the eyes of a woman reporter from the *New York Times* who, after a moment, mugged and mimed a message to Nona that the daily pantomime of the caucus room was too much for her. The tourists were blowing her mind and for all she cared they should get what they deserved: Nixon or nothing.

But even as the gallery filled up, the mood remained heavy, and there was an air of aimlessness as the session started. For reporters who had attended the hearings daily, truth had been so defiled that additional testimony was tortuous. Now the Committee was collecting evasions instead of evidence and impatience mixed with boredom pulled the press together like unhappy inmates in the dayroom of a prison or asylum. A storm of hysteria was beginning to gather.

Tony didn't show. Unconsciously Nona thought he would be waiting for her out in the corridor when the hearings recessed for lunch but he wasn't in the crowd, and she felt uneasy about his absense. By late afternoon she was drugged with despair and when Senator Ervin finally adjourned the Watergate Committee until some unspecified time in September, Nona walked out of the Senate building into the damp sticky heat of the street in a frantically nervous mood. Rain was rumbling around in the sky by the time she reached the parking lot. The humidity had reached the boiling point and was ready to spill over. She drove home slowly accelerating and braking her VW in rhythm with the heavy traffic. All around her Nona saw hot cars and cranky drivers, fuming and sputtering with despair and frustration.

The Watergate hearings were over. They had stopped rather than ended.

There was a sudden surge of traffic shifting forward. She cut over to Vermont Avenue and sped along Fifteenth Street, moving steadily for several blocks before stalling again. She felt a palpable emptiness, a sensation somewhere between rage and disappointment, a balloon of despair. The political purge had turned into a stand-off, cleansing the country's wounds only superficially, leaving the infection untouched.

231

She parked the car several blocks beyond her apartment building and then hurried back up the street past the antagonistic eyes of the black and brown men leaning against the storefronts.

It's like commuting between two continents, she thought. Capitol Hill and Columbia Road—two worlds. It's wild. It's crazy . . .

She stopped at the grocery store, and then went home to cook a hot dinner in her stale, airless kitchen because she felt herself losing touch with her own material world. But the sense of internal peril persisted even after she had eaten, and she hurried to her desk in the studio where she sat down to work while rain poured steadily past her windows. She began to write with an intensity that totally absorbed her, welcoming and embracing the relief of an oblivion that blotted out personal realities.

Furiously she spun out her Watergate impressions, hitting on the astonishment of liberals at what had been always taken for granted in the movement—illegal harassment, wire tapping, entrapment. She hit hard on the press corps' network of interrelationships with the government that induced self-censorship, laziness, stubborn blindness, and a kind of willful innocence.

Wringing her emotions through the typewriter, Nona began churning out one section after another, zipping pages out of the machine to maul with her pencil, crossing out platitudes and easy shots, discarding anything that didn't propel the facts forward, racking her brain for precise language and insight. The moment she stopped working, personal concerns slipped out of storage back into circulation again, and she returned to the typewriter to punch out another paragraph, sculpting meaning from raw experience, straining toward a stunning summation.

Finally exhausted, Nona decided to go to sleep, but insomnia waited for her in the hot narrow bedroom, and there was a long quarrel in the dank rumpled bed between consciousness and oblivion. Her apprehensions about the next day were heightened by her despair about the hearings. Somehow the country's crusading spirit had slackened and begun to fade. Perhaps in the fall, when Congress reconvened, impeachment proceedings would begin, but the sense of moral outrage had been dissipated into bureaucratic business. The moment in which the Movement might have offered moral leadership was gone, for the leaders were gone—some dead, some in exile, some in jail, some underground. . . .

It seemed to Nona that tomorrow was the last chance for freedom, and she felt afraid.

On Thursday morning Nona waited inside the entranceway of her building, a small space between storefronts. Most of the Columbia Road shops hadn't opened yet, and a crowd of displaced persons, locked out of their usual hangouts, moved aimlessly along the sidewalk eying the day distrustfully. Nona slouched against the wall with an impervious expression meant to ward off flirtatious aggressors, but most of the short, stubby Spanish men dutifully stopped to assess her and relieve themselves of some obscene comment as to her suitability.

She tried to ignore them, but their persistent intrusions interrupted her thoughts about the speech she would make to Eric Kessler and her scenario for the encounter. The Spanish obscenities disturbed her as she stood waiting.

"Fuck off," she hissed. "Fuck off!"

At exactly ten o'clock, Lewellen's Mercedes pulled up to the curb, parking between a Day-Glow painted Volkswagon van and an old Mercury displaying wax saints and furry monkeys on its dashboard. Tony climbed out of the car to put her suitcase and typewriter in the trunk.

"I need some cigarettes," he said, scanning the street aggressively. "You want a couple packs?"

Nona shook her head and watched him stroll away, casing the store windows, deciding where to strike. The sight of him on that street triggered her desire like the spring of a pinball machine releasing a hard silver ball that went ricocheting through her system scooting from one pressure point to another, lighting up one sensual sensation after another until he disappeared into a Spanish grocery, and her body tilted back against the seat to rest.

It didn't happen often—that big wet feeling of wanting—and it undermined her self-confidence. She knew she could deal with most of her other conflicts—her craving for inclusion and recognition, her nervous uncertainty about the origins of her politics and her ambivalence about what work to do. But this animal thing, this sassy prancing sexual beast inside her breast, that reared up and roared with longing at the sight of Tony Lewellen was disorienting. She never understood whether desire preceded love or derived from it, whether dependency evoked passion or resulted from it.

He was holding a grocery bag when he emerged from the store, pausing to survey the street in both directions with the speculative expression of some hokey TV detective on the lookout for mobster violence. It was the same sort of hype as when he clenched a wine bottle between his thighs to uncork it, or hitched his coat jacket over a crooked thumb, or rolled up his shirt sleeve in his slow, sensual way, or bent down to peer into a low set mirror bowing to his own handsome image, or when he caressively replaced his wallet in his trousers as if grabbing ass was such a pleasure he even enjoyed his own. They were corny put-ons, but they got to her, for they were the silent statements of a man who constantly suffered sexual stirrings.

"I got us some fruit," he said, handing Nona the brown paper bag through her open window, child-

234

ishly proud of his gift. Then he disappeared around the back of the car and got into the driver's seat.

"I get such a rush from you," Nona said sadly, holding the bag upright in her lap as if it were their child.

"Well, then tell me how to get to New York Avenue from here."

"Take Sixteenth up to Florida," she answered, hugging the groceries.

He reached over to open the glove compartment and extracted a map before he began to drive, twisting from lane to lane as he passed huge semis and delivery vans on the way out of the city. Then he began questioning her about what she'd been doing since Sunday, and, pleased by his jealous concern, Nona made him struggle for details. But when they reached U.S. 50, she insisted on repeating the scenario of their plans one more time, since they had only discussed it on the phone. Slowly and precisely she repeated how she and Jay were to meet with Kessler alone in one of the hotel rooms. If Kessler accepted the deal, Tony was going to produce a Xerox copy of the Photostat for Nona to give in exchange for the tape. If Kessler refused Nona's offer, Tony and Sam were going to repeat the same procedure saying they too had the story and that Sam planned to run it within the next two days although he would kill it in exchange for the Daniels tape. The rationale for this scenario was Tony's crazed infatuation with Nona who had threatened to stop seeing him unless he came up with Daniels's wiretap records. Sam, as Tony's best friend, was willing to compromise himself, despite the fact that Kessler had betrayed him, so as to save Tony's sanity.

Nona's mind began to feel cobwebby as she spoke. Each time they ran through the script she felt as if it was all too tenuous and too complicated to work. But Dempsey and Sam and Tony seemed willing to believe in it, and since she had no other options, she tried to sweep away her doubts. And when they reached the Annapolis by-pass, she almost forgot the pending ordeal as she began to sweat the prospect of crossing the Chesapeake Bay Bridge.

"How about some of that fruit?" Tony suggested.

She handed him the bag. "Have you ever driven across the Bay Bridge before?" she asked in a phony casual voice. "It seems sort of windy out there today."

He selected a peach and bit into it, flicking his tongue to catch the pendant-shaped drop of juice that began to slide over his bottom lip. "You know, that's the only thing I've ever heard you say you're afraid of."

"Well, how far is it to the bridge from here?"

He turned to smile at her. "I don't know. Why don't you come over here and I'll take your mind off it."

Nona felt anger climb up the overworked ladder of her nervous system. "Fuck off," she said irritably.

"Aw, come on," Tony wheedled.

She turned to look out at the flat blue bay backing up against the genteel sweep of Annapolis, a traditional southern set piece.

"Oh, come on tiger, you're not really serious about this bridge business. You must freak out on planes."

"No, because I always smoke a joint in the john before takeoff."

"You smoke grass in toilets on airplanes?" Tony groaned.

"I learned that from Michael," Nona said. "He always took a couple of hits to cool himself out and once I started doing that it really helped me a lot."

"I don't want to hear about Michael." Tony said gruffly.

"O.K." said Nona, feeling chastised.

"You know what I mean" he said softly. "You don't want to hear about my wife either."

The waters of Annapolis were filled with playcraft skittering about in the early morning tasting the water. Along the shore little white motorboats were tied up at private piers like little puppy dogs leashed to backdoors. It touched her that an allusion to Michael could hurt Tony.

To distract herself from the fear starting to grow inside her belly, she snuggled closer to Tony. They had begun the stretch of highway edged with last-chance-before-the-bridge gas stations and diners.

Nona took a peach out of the bag. The texture of the peeling skin against her lips gave her a queasy sensation, but the flesh of the peach was smooth and sweet.

Tony put his arm around her. "Hey tiger, you really are shook up. Why don't you just lie down here on my lap for a while?" He patted his thighs and separated his legs hospitably.

"Oh, Jesus," Nona protested. "It's only three more miles to the bridge."

The traffic was slowing down now as the cars bottlenecked at the tollgates. Her head had begun pounding, and she felt the early stages of vertigo stirring inside. Just as the year before, when she and Michael had driven to Rehoboth Beach, she considered getting out of the car and hitchhiking back to Washington.

Nona's heart was lurching wildly as they too were stalled in the line at the tollgate. Tony softly kissed the back of her neck and she felt electrocuted. She sank lower in the seat fighting for self-control, certain that any expression of panic would contribute to her danger. Silently she watched Tony hand a dollar and a quarter to the tollgate agent and then step on the gas.

Ahead and curving to the left was a double harpsichord of fragile suspension wires that some-how held the four-lane bridge up over the bay. A camper was spinning along in the right-hand lane and Nona vacillated between a vision of the van sideswiping them into another lane of traffic and a

237

picture of Tony failing to make the midway curve and driving straight off into the bright blue sky before plunging down—falling, falling, falling endlessly in an eternal spin into the sea.

Nona closed her eyes, sick with dread. Her entire body was knotted with expectation, waiting for the noise of the crash and then the free-falling plunge off the bridge through the sky and down into the ocean water.

"We're halfway," Tony said tenderly.

She was almost doubled over now, choking with panic, wild from waiting.

Panic held her and the dizzying weightless of vertigo pounded inside her head.

He pulled her closer. Cringing, she started to shake. He stroked her hair and murmured softly, as if soothing a child. By the time they reached the end of the bridge she was totally exhausted and her anxiety didn't diminish until almost an hour later. Then, at an intersection amid the flat dry landscape decorated with picturesque New Englandish outbuildings, Tony stopped for a red light. Nona knew they should continue south on the main highway to Ocean City, but she wanted to drive through Rehoboth to refurbish the fading memory of her last weekend with Michael, to recuperate and collect herself for the ordeal ahead.

"Which way?" Tony asked.

"To the left," she lied.

He crossed over onto the secondary highway and followed it into the town of Rehoboth, driving down the main street between two lines of tawdry storefronts. Nona looked out through her open window at the wide green island of grass studded with parked cars toed inward against the curb dividing the two boulevards and felt herself grow quiet inside. Sun-brightened vacationers were strolling along the sidewalk occasionally flinging out reprimands at the children who tore past them. The windows of flamboyant little beach shops fronting on the street were filled with pyramids of suntan lotions, piles of inverted straw hats, chains of Japanese sandals, and trapezoid mountains of Foster Grant sunglasses.

"I don't think we should have come into this town," Tony said. "There must have been a by-pass or a turnoff back when we came off fourteen." He continued along the boulevard until it ended in a horseshoe curve at the broadwalk.

"Oh, let's get out," Nona begged. "Please. I want to take a walk."

"No way," he protested in the parental tone that occasionally crept into his voice when he felt impatient with her. "There's no place to park, and it's getting late."

"Please! Park here, and if you get a ticket I'll pay for it. Let's just get out for ten minutes."

He reluctantly relented, showing his displeasure by making a big production of first locking both car doors and then rechecking them while Nona scrambled outside to gulp the salty ocean air.

She took Tony's hand to pull him to the edge of the boardwalk that hemmed the beach, stopping to look down at the sand, stretching wide and white in both directions, freckled only with little blankets of people.

"It's too much," she whispered, feeling the memory of her last days with Michael moving through her mind.

She clutched his hand and began to lead him along the garish wooden boardwalk. Counters of carmel corn and saltwater taffy flavored the air, and a wild confusion of sun-darkened children dashed between them.

For the first time Tony seemed neither like a father nor a lover to her. The fingers laced through Nona's were those of a friend.

She felt the wind touching her face and stirring her hair while the sun kissed the skin of her body.

239

"I hope it works out, Nona," Tony said simply. "It would make me happy to be able to help you."

She had to hurry to match the scissors of his long legs.

"It won't be easy for me," he said slowly. "I care a lot for you, Nona."

She blinked. Everything was happening too fast: her memory of Michael, her meeting with Kessler, the disorienting feeling of walking with Tony Lewellen where she had once walked with Michael Daniels. She looked up at Tony. He loves me, she thought.

They walked toward the miniature golf course with its tiny plotted landscape and beyond it to the row of machines that laminated driver's licenses, took photographs for a quarter, and engraved personal dog tags. Slowly Nona felt herself fusing with Tony as they strolled hand in hand alone and separate but sharing the day.

"I like it here," Nona said.

The seaside search for happiness was infectious. People were poised with delicious indecision, hanging between purpose and pleasure. Nudity was in the air, bodies were available, and the carnival atmosphere became an aphrodisiac, framing couples with immaculate clarity, elevating and exalting their intimacy.

But a few minutes later Tony made Nona turn back, and he steered her to the car, unlocked her door, and pushed her inside.

"I need some popcorn," she said. "I *need* it," and she watched him walk over to get in line at the open-air counter nearby, defending his front-line position against swarms of little kids who squirted past his legs in explosions of energy trying to get in front of him. Cool and reserved in his yellow linen slacks and the striped shirt that pulled against his chest with each press of ocean air, he lifted his head for a moment as if trying to swallow the salty flavor of the seashore town. Then he paid the salesgirl and came around to Nona's side of the car to hand her the box of popcorn.

"Listen," he complained. "We didn't have to come into this eyesore . . . we were supposed to stay on that highway."

"Well, I lied. I wanted a little time." Nona said.

He got behind the wheel again and drove past the newer boutiques on the opposite side of the street where mannequins in string bikinis and loud beach towels filled the windows. Eventually the commercial establishments dwindled away, and they reached the highway. Nona could feel the white heat of the day breathing against her as she ate her popcorn, absently watching the countryside unroll in a matinee travelogue.

"Jesus, Sam's going to think we crumped out or had an accident or something," Tony complained.

She turned her head so she could see his face, stained now from fatigue, and she thought he looked handsomer for being rumpled and upset.

"It's still another twenty-five miles," he said irritably, but then for some reason his aggravation subsided and when he reached over to net a handful of popcorn he squeezed her breast instead.

She sensed disaster as soon as they swung up the driveway of the Carousel Hotel. Built with money Bobby Baker had allegedly raked off in bribes while he was Senate majority counsel, the hotel stood as an awesome monument to Democratic party corruption. Arriving there at the tail end of the Watergate hearings gave Nona a cramp of political despair.

A plague on both their parties, she thought vengefully. The whole fucking system stinks. I want out.

"What's the matter?" Tony asked, turning off the ignition in front of the entranceway.

"Nothing," she shrugged. "Oh, maybe I'm nervous. I guess so. Look, I want to get down to the beach. I feel like I'm strangling. Please, hurry."

None of the others had registered yet although it

241

was exactly noon. A bellhop took the baggage up to their room, and Nona walked out onto a narrow balcony. Below was the beach, and her heart accelerated from the view and verged toward the sea. She came back inside and grabbed her suitcase.

"Not so fast." Lewellen was lying on the bed. "Comere first."

"Oh, no!" She darted into the bathroom, put on her bikini under the denim shirt that smelled from her long car ride, and reemerged into the bedroom.

"Look, Nona, I've got something for you."

"I'm not hungry," she said without turning around. She opened the closet, grabbed a blanket off the shelf, picked up her purse and escaped from the room before he could lunge at her. Then she went down the backstairs out of the hotel, skirted the congested swimming pool area, circled a shuffleboard court, climbed the stone breakfront, and finally reached the beach.

Fourteen

Nona walked down to the shoreline and then some fifty yards beyond the private beach belonging to the Carousel Hotel, stopping to look at various treasures dropped off by the tide. Eventually she spread out the blanket and lay down on her stomach. The sand smelled like sperm to her—the same marine and musky scent that flavored her fingers on the morning after a night of love. Lying very still she could feel the sand sifting beneath her, moving to accommodate her swellings and crowding in to find the shallows of her body. Her chin dented a sand cup to support her head so she could watch the waves swallowing the shore.

She felt an air of unreality about all her plans. Feeling drugged by despair, she got up and ran across the sand to the water, her breasts pounding against her body like waves upon the shore. For a long while she let the surf sweep her about, relinquishing her will to the sea and finding peace in surrender. But when she returned to the blanket and lay down again, she felt sand inside her bathing suit, collecting in the crease of her crotch like toast crumbs in the pocket of her bathrobe, and she squirmed about uncomfortably.

Finally sitting up to rid herself of the sand, she spied a huge horseshoe crab—a hideous prehistoric creature stranded on the beach a few yards away from her. Nona stared in horror at the armored but impotent thing, a nightmare monster of insufficiency doomed by its own destiny to be carried about or left behind by the tide. Deadly certain that the crab was a bad omen, a sign of her own powerless inability to control the circumstances of her existence, Nona began to gather up her possessions. It was then she saw Tony heading across the beach toward her, and embarrassed by her childishness, she simply pulled the blanket farther away from the horseshoe crab and sat down again, grateful for Tony's arrival and the gift of distraction he brought her.

He was wearing a terrycloth shirt over his trunks, and when he reached the blanket he towered above her.

"Want to take a swim?"

She stood up again and walked beside him down to the sea. But now she saw that the waves carried globs of jellyfish, thousands of translucent sacs that frightened her in the same way as the witless horseshoe crab. The formlessness of the jellyfish horrified her—substance without structure, matter without meaning—another marine symbol for her latent terror.

"I'm not going to go in with all those jellyfish around," she complained, hanging back.

"Oh, come on." Tony reached out and grabbed her arm, pulling her to him.

"Oh, no," she squealed. "I can't stand them. They're too grotesque." She pulled away. "They all look like little Eric Kesslers."

"Now that's not nice to say," Tony teased, standing braced against the waves, his body a resistant triangle rising out of the sea. "How would you like to have been born transparent so your varicose veins showed?"

She laughed but took advantage of his good humor to break away and run back to the beach while he dived beneath the next big wave. When he returned to the blanket later he was panting and rubbing an elbow he had scraped against the sand as he climbed out of the surf. He flung himself down beside her, one hand naturally settling upon her back.

"Did you see those horseshoe crabs?" Nona asked. "Aren't they awful?"

"They're not as bad as dinosaurs. Matthew. . . . ," he stopped.

Nona waited. It was the first time an allusion to one of his children had slipped through his lips. What a tight lead we've been on, she thought, for now his children were there between them.

"What?" she asked.

"Nothing," he said.

Nona braced herself on bent elbows. "Do you think Kessler would really bring the stuff with him?" She ran her finger through her hair, feeling the gritty sand beneath the salt-thickened tangles.

"I don't know," Tony grunted.

"If he gets mad at Sam, do you think he'd burn the tapes or the transcripts?"

"His boss didn't," Tony laughed, stroking her back to brush away some sand. "You know, I think I should probably get back to the hotel in case they're there. Do you want to come?"

"No," she said quietly. "I'll stay here."

A new idea had suddenly activated her mind. For the first time it occurred to her that she could run a search-and-seize mission in Kessler's hotel room while he was talking to Tony and Sam. Or, if Johanna was in there, Nona could wait until later when the whole group had a drink or meal somewhere. Then she could play sick and try to get Kessler's room key from the front desk.

Tony was looking at her suspiciously. "Hey! You're not thinking of breaking into Kessler's room, are you?" he asked. "That's probably a thirty-year federal rap."

"Ha!" Nona snarled. "You should talk! That's the name of the game you made up, isn't it? Breaking and entering? Think of those poor old people whose bed we violated."

Tony grinned and stood up. "Well, when I did it there was a good reason."

She watched him walk back across the beach, but before he reached the retaining wall behind the hotel he stopped and bent over. After a moment he straightened up, holding a horseshoe crab by its scaly tail, and winding up pitched it back into the sea.

Then a part inside Nona came open, and a warm splash of love spilled down through her, washing her insides so that everything came loose. A force tugged at her center, and a roaring need to enclose Anthony Lewellen inside her body shuddered through her.

Humbled she closed her eyes and gave herself over to the sun and the sand and the unfamiliar sound of the sea, hoping to be soothed into sleep. But a second later, shrieks shattered the day, and she sat up, her heart pumping furiously.

Down at the shoreline a young mother was holding a little boy who had come upon a crab and exploded into hysteria. The mother was carrying the child away, shaking him to distrupt his terror. But now Nona felt too unnerved to lie down again so she collected her things and walked back along the water's edge toward the Carousel.

On the private stretch of hotel beach, Cindy Reynolds and Bob Dempsey were sitting in canvas director chairs looking like actors on location.

"Hi." Nona quickened her pace to reach them. "I see you built a new civilization already." She looked down at the picnic cooler, piles of towels, bottles, suntan oil, hats, and lunch baskets spread in a semicircle around them, relieved that they had arrived, happy to reconnect with Dempsey's special brand of perspective.

"We just got here about twenty minutes ago," Cindy reported. "Bob drove out with Sam and me."

"I wonder why everyone else is so late," Nona worried, spreading out her blanket and lying down near Dempsey, hoping to absorb through osmosis a little of his wry vision.

The three of them lazed about in friendly silence, idly watching the people on the beach.

"You're getting a little sunburned," Bob said to Nona. "Your back's all red." The tips of his fingers touched her shoulder, trailing gently as if through water. "How would you like a gin and tonic to cool off?"

"You're kidding!" Nona squealed.

He took out a half-gallon Thermos, produced a plastic cup, and fixed her a drink. But when she looked back at him a few minutes later, he was staring off toward the skyline while his face shook and twitched uncontrollably, edging toward disaster.

"Hey," Nona chided.

He looked down at her and took a deep breath so his chest swelled beneath the thick quilt of curly gray hair.

Nona lifted her plastic cup toward him in a heartfelt toast but since the glass was almost empty he took it, thinking she wanted a refill from the thermos bottle, and Nona felt jinxed by the misunderstanding.

A few minutes later she looked up to see Patsy Bator slicing across the beach toward them. Wearing a string bikini that covered the small flourishes of flesh around her breasts and buttocks and using a loose chain to define a waist on her flat lean midriff, she seemed to be part of the setting from which she emerged. But when she reached them, her face showed devastating signs of trouble.

"Hi," she said.

"Hi, Patsy. You know Cindy Reynolds and Senator Dempsey."

Patsy smiled quickly at each of them and then collapsed on a towel alongside Nona. "What a trip," she said, shaking her head slowly and looking out at the sea. "In both ways."

Her unconscious beauty shone from beneath the cover of her unhappiness, and both Cindy and Bob were staring at her.

"But this is nice," she said, surveying the scene while clearly winding up to launch a marathon monologue. "Very nice."

For a moment Nona thought the pleasures of the beach would comfort and silence Patsy. The senator filled a cup of gin and tonic, passed it to her, and settled down for a nap. Surprised, Patsy smiled shyly as she took it and then began to talk.

"We drove out with Kessler and Johanna Dupres," she announced. "And a chauffeur. And a special agent." Her voice turned sour. "It was terrific."

No one responded.

"Anyway it was a great finale," she said to Nona. "We needed that because it's really all over between Jay and me. I think we're going to split. I can't deal with his shit anymore. He's no damn good. . . .'" Patsy's voice rose at each word. "He's a fink—I mean *really* bad."

"Stop *kvetching*," Nona said with a smile. "I've heard this a hundred times. It's like a top-forty song—your weekly I-hate-Jay number."

"I'm serious this time. He's just about ruined my career. I can't write anything anymore," Patsy persisted, glancing over at the senator who seemed to be asleep. "He's such an uptight constipated shmuck that he's got me blocking, and I've never had a writing block ever before—not once in my whole entire life."

Apparently afraid of being found guilty by association, Cindy was determined to silence Patsy's indiscreet aria. "Maybe we should all go back," she suggested, demanding compliance. "It's getting awfully hot. We're going to burn."

"I'm not going to take any more of his crap," Patsy continued, anger inflating her words so they exploded around her. "You just don't know what he's like."

Patsy rolled on to her stomach, propped her elbows in the sand, and rested her chin in her hand. "Oh, he's really done me." she said. "In every way possible —including physically. You know—well, probably you wouldn't, but—he's very big on . . . whadycallit? anal sex? You know? And after he does that he likes to . . . he wants to do it the regular way and that gave me a terrible vaginal infection. My gynecologist told me you're never supposed to do both at the same time— I mean right in a row—unless the guy takes a shower first because there's germs and viruses back there that can give you vaginitis."

Patsy's face had gone loose and slack. All of her classically elegant features were in disarray as if rumpled by a wild party.

"And when I told Jay what the doctor said, he looked at me like I was crazy, and said I should tell my stupid doctor that *he* should get up and take a shower in the middle of fucking his wife or his nurse or whoever he's banging."

Nona had a flash of Jay Lazar making that particular suggestion.

"And that son of a bitch gave me the clap the first time I slept with him. And I know he knew he had it. He still won't admit it, but after I moved into his apartment I found two bottles of pills in his medicine chest with dates from before I even met him. So I'm sure he knew he was still infectious when he did me. And, of course, I'm allergic to pencillin, right? So I almost died in the doctor's office because the nurse gave me such a strong shot, I mean, it was like for a horse. But at least Jay did leave work and drive over to pick me up when the doctor called him to come and get me."

Cindy and Nona exchanged helpless glances.

"But that wasn't even the worst of it because my gynecologist told me I should notify every single man I'd slept with—ha, ha!— every single *or* married man I'd slept with since my original contact. Well, right along I thought it was Jay, even though he swore it wasn't. And if he had just told me the truth, that would have made it easy because I only did two other guys *after* I started seeing Jay. But since he lied and said it *couldn't* have been him because he didn't have it, I didn't know *where* I got it. So I had to try to remember all the men I'd slept with during the past six months." Patsy stared at the waves breaking on the shore.

"Can you imagine? Six months? That's half a year! And I didn't want to leave anybody out because, after all, I wouldn't want some guy to drop dead ten years from now just because I forgot to let him know. Do you have any cigarettes? Oh, Winstons! Great! And I certainly didn't want some nice young girl who married one of those guys to have a blind baby just because of me. I mean, it's bad enough I probably won't ever have any kids, but at least I shouldn't go around blinding other ladies' children."

Patsy lit her cigarette and paused to taste her drink.

It was clear that Cindy was eavesdropping intensely. Indeed, like a wino spreading a newspaper over another drunk on a park bench, Cindy, motivated by self-preservation, was ready to help—for Patsy was one of her own class, an unmarried career woman struggling to survive in the dangerous jungle of Washington, and when one of them faltered or broke down in public, weakened by drink or dope or despair, the others would circle around to hide the sight of the disintegration for the sake of the victim as well as the rest of them. Nona nudged Patsy—a signal to lower her voice. But Patsy continued.

"Well, you can't imagine how hard it was to remember them all," she said. "I just had to start at the beginning of the alphabet, like when you forget somebody's last name and try to break it out by running through all the letters. You know, Joe A? Joe B? Joe C? until you hit a bell at the right letter. So I started with *A* and worked the alphabet and, it's funny, but there were twenty-seven of them. Just one extra. That might sound a little promiscuous, but it was during a time when I was in love with this married guy so I was sort of . . . uptight. You know?"

Listening to the naked narrative of Patsy's life, Nona stared at her flamboyant red-headed friend and over to the stylish jetset blond and thought of how much misery was covered by so much glamour.

"I don't mean I had one man who started with each letter of the alphabet." Patsy's voice trailed off as if the alcohol in her system was running low and failing to refuel her. "So I sat down and wrote to my first A—Arthur. Actually, I had three A's—Adam, Allen, and Arthur—and I said, 'You'll never believe this, it's really quite embarrassing, but someone (perhaps you?) gave me gonorrhea and my physician suggests you have yourself checked by a doctor immediately.' I wrote it in a way that sounded like I was too much of a lady to accuse him directly, but implying it had to be him because he'd been the only one I'd slept with. It was really a terrific letter, so I typed copies for Adam and Allen, but I was in the middle of doing that article on political divorces in Washington, and I couldn't very well spend my time typing twenty-four more letters, and I wasn't about to give them to my typist to do. So finally I thought what the hell, and I just Xeroxed a bunch of them over at the *Metro* office and wrote in the proper names up at the top.

"But when I finished filling in all their names, I thought, Now what kind of an asshole am I, anyway? There I was about to send twenty-seven Xeroxed announcements all over town announcing that Patricia Bator had the clap. So guess what I did? I didn't sign my name. I mean, I thought, what the hell's the difference who sent it, they'll either go to the doctor or they won't, right? And if they don't go just because it's anonymous, that's their tough luck. What did any of them ever do for me? All I ever got off any of them was a couple abortions, a case of hemorrhoids, and a fluctuating weight problem. Have you ever had hemorrhoids?"

"Stop, Patsy. You've got to stop." Nona said firmly.

This is panicking me, Nona thought, and Cindy is freaking, because Patsy's life is Cindy's life. But not mine; I'm just a tourist here.

Fifteen

It was after three when Cindy and Patsy decided they had enough sun. They woke Dempsey who offered to buy them all a drink, and the three of them went back to the hotel, but Nona stayed behind confiscating Cindy's chair. Then she watched the white-capped waves, whipped by the wind, leap on the shore. A few minutes later Sam and Tony came walking across the beach toward her. Tony was hunched over, listening to Sam talk, and their shoulders bumped occasionally in their preoccupation.

When they reached her, Tony walked a few steps beyond the blanket toward the shore and then stopped, jamming his hands into his pants pockets and curling his shoulders forward as he stared out toward the vast horizon. Sam sat down next to Nona, and then he too turned to look out at the sea.

The tide was coming in, sticking out its tongue at Nona's blanket. Young mothers and their children scampering along the water's edge had pulled shirts on over their bathing suits and unconsciously clustered close together for shelter when they stopped to inspect some treasure on the sand. An elderly woman, wearing a full cotton skirt over her one-piece suit, blossomed out like an umbrella when she stopped to pick a shell off the beach.

"Well, it's all over," Sam said to no one in particular.

"You've seen him?" Nona said sharply. "Why did you talk to him before Jay and me?"

"It wasn't our idea, Nona. He sent his man to say he wanted to see us up in his room right away."

"Well, what did he want?" Nona asked. The wind lifted her words off her lips and blew them skyward before tossing them into the sea.

"He wanted our balls," Tony said, striking a pose reminiscent of young Jack Kennedy straining poetically against the elements near the sea in Hyannisport.

"Well, what did he say?" Nona demanded.

Tony spoke with the voice of an interpreter doing a simultaneous translation. "Nona," he said, "Kessler has tapes of Sam and Cindy talking on the telephone. He's got lots of them. He knows that Barry has the photostat and he says either Sam kills the story or he'll have the tapes delivered to Sam's wife up at the Vineyard tomorrow morning."

Nona sank deeper in the chair, instinctively pulling her knees into the cup of her body, curling into a rigid fetal position. "Does he have a tape of Michael too?" she asked after a long silence.

Both men turned to look at her.

"I mean, does he have all the stuff here with him now?"

The wind swept through Sam Kinkaid's hair, blowing it back from the corduroy creases of concern digging into his forehead. Then he began to laugh.

"Jesus. You're really a fucking warrior," he said. Slowly he rotated toward Tony, shaking his head in wonderment. "This is no lightweight. There she sits, looking like a dream, and already she's doing a little reconnaisance to see if she can knock over Kessler's room to get the goods."

"Look, this isn't funny," Tony said firmly. "I think Kessler's freaked out. He's wound up tighter than a top. I think he might really be on the edge—not just because of what he said to us, but because of the way he's acting. He's out of sync with his body. He's really acting deranged. And poor old Johanna looks

254

like she wants to take off for California—yesterday."

"Oh, no doubt about it," Sam agreed grimly, hiding from the wind to light a cigarette. "We've got a real situation on our hands."

"Well, what's the problem?" Nona asked. "You made the big decision last week, remember? When it was the D.C. Four up for sale you weren't buying. You were going to run your story in the August tenth issue whether I had Michael's tape or not. Remember? You said you would never censor any story for any reason. So what's the problem now? What'd you do? Forget all your journalistic principles, Sam? Don't you remember the big peptalk you gave me?"

"I can't believe this is happening," Tony said between clenched teeth, his body rigid with desperation.

But that only provoked Nona more. She felt everything that had been soft and weak inside her system start to firm up. The irony of Sam's phony distress and Tony's theatrical conflict both sickened and strengthened her. Their fear had finally erased any vestige of glamour from them. Whatever romance they offered had only been a front for their cowardice. They were self-centered, self-protective, and morally crippled. Tony's only commitment was to promoting some hyped-up self-image he enjoyed peddling, playing his professional role without ever endangering himself, eschewing any risks, avoiding any self-discovery, evading any ethical commitments.

Nona felt a hard irreversible resistance to them build inside her.

"You mean now that it's your own little neck at stake, Sam, you're ready to censor the story and sell out all your principles? You mean you're going to end up protecting the man who ordered an illegal wiretap on your phone—just so he won't tell your wife you've got a girl friend?"

Sam looked away.

"It's such an obvious ploy," Nona said, suddenly

255

changing tactics, deciding to question the existence of any evidence so as to reassure Sam. "Anybody— even your wife—could see through a thing like that. Since Kessler knows Cindy's your girl, all he has to do is *say* he has tapes of you talking and you'd believe him."

"So would Joan," Tony intervened.

"So you're going to knuckle under just to save yourself from some heat in the kitchen?" Nona asked. "Believe me, your wife could hear much more damaging stories about the midnight skinny-dips from your neighbors." She manufactured a threatening look that Sam missed.

"It's not that," Sam said miserably.

"But how do you know Kessler really has any tapes? Did you see them? What if it's just typed transcripts? Then all you'd have to do is deny it— tell your wife it's a put-up job, a phony blackmail attempt to stop you from publishing the story. How do you know he really has any tapes?"

"Nona," Tony said, "if a guy's got enough power to order a wiretap he can get the goddamn tapes. We're dealing with a different problem here. Kessler can't stand personal criticism. He doesn't mind being involved in politically controversial situations, but when people say he's a bad guy, it freaks him out. And that's what's happening. He's falling apart. Wait till you see him."

"Look," Sam interrupted, "Kessler came at us— right off the top—said he knew we were going to double-cross him, that we were going to take the Daniels tape and then run Barry's story on the tenth. He even knew the right date. He knew everything. Somebody told him."

Nona reeled. "How? . . . How could he know?"

"I don't know. But there was no chance for you to get what you wanted, Nona, and so there was no reason for me to chuck everything . . . lose everything now . . . when the whole kit 'n caboodle of Nixon's

256

gang will be gone down the memory hole a few months from now. Kessler's all washed up anyway."

Nona looked back and forth between Tony and Sam.

One of them had betrayed her.

"Look, I might just be a little fish, Sam," she said. "But you're a real cocksucker. You set me up . . ."

"Nona, I swear I didn't," Sam yelled.

"Goddamnit, shut up," Tony shouted, lunging at Nona with one arm raised as if to strike her.

Sam moved forward to intervene and then turned, his head close to Nona's. "Nona, listen to me," he said, his eyes racing across her face. "Joan owns *The Week*. It's her magazine. It's her money, it's her house, it's her everything. I'm just the lap dog."

Pushing Sam aside Tony grabbed Nona's arms. He pulled her off the chair and began shaking her back and forth like a stuffed doll.

She could hear Sam yelling as if from a great distance as he struggled with Tony to free her.

"Christ, Tony, cut it out. Here they come. All of them." Sam groaned.

Tony released Nona's wrists and flung her back on the chair.

A Conga line of six people was winding its way down from the hotel, clumsily negotiating the wooden stairs of the breakfront. They resembled a column of ants winding across the beach burdened with booty —varied-colored beach bags, baskets, and bathing equipment. Shaken and confused, Nona watched the parade approaching. Eric Kessler was in the lead, flanked by Cindy and Dempsey. Patsy Bator tagged along slightly detached from the others. Two men, one black and one white, brought up the rear of the group, carrying beach umbrellas, inflatable rafts, and folded deck chairs.

Kessler stopped a few feet short of Nona's blanket. He was wrapped in a striped terrycloth beach robe, snug as a pillow stuffed inside a tight cover, but he looked ill. His face was a pale pasty color, and there was an unnaturally bright glaze over his eyes.

"Good afternoon," he said with a prissy smile as his eyes swept from Sam to Tony to Nona—trying to determine if the men had informed her of his threat. Assured they had, he turned to survey the Atlantic Ocean. "It's wonderful to get out of the city," he said. "This is pleasant. Set up the things over there," he said, pointing arbitrarily to a spot a few feet behind him.

The Secret Service agent who had been with him on the Fourth of July boatride set down some equipment and nodded to the tall black man who then dropped two beach chairs and umbrellas on the sand.

"My chauffeur," Kessler said, "has many talents."

The chauffeur had rid himself of his jacket, but he looked ludicrous in his white shirt and black uniform pants beside Patsy who was almost nude but for the two strings tied modestly around her tiny protuberances. The man began to poke the sand with the spike of one umbrella, attempting to plant Kessler's flag over his chosen territory. Everyone watched as he jabbed in the pole and ran forward to raise the umbrella, but the wind lashed it back at him.

No one moved.

His second attempt ended when the pole slammed heavily back against his shoulder. Then the Secret Service agent moved toward Kessler and nudged him a few feet back from the dangerous half-opened umbrella being whipped about by the wind. Finally, Bob Dempsey stepped forward to hold the spiked pole while the black man raised the red canvas umbrella.

"They look like the marines at Iwo Jima," Kessler chuckled. "Now with everyone's permission I would like to have a private word with these two ladies," he said indicating Cindy and Nona. He was having difficulty forming his words and his usual precision

258

was blurred. "We have some unfinished business to close."

Totally surprised, Cindy looked first toward Sam, who shrugged his shoulders in response, and then inquiringly at Nona.

"Come along. We will test the waters—in more ways than one."

Nona bent over to retrieve her denim shirt from the clutter that had collected on her blanket. Then she followed Kessler and Cindy down toward the shore where he finally stopped to pose in a dramatic, but basically bedraggled, posture, gazing out to sea.

"Please correct me if I am wrong," he said pompously. "I gather that Sam and Tony informed you of our discussion?" He directed the query at Nona who nodded consent without considering the politics of it. "But, and correct me if I'm wrong, Cindy here knows nothing of what has transpired?"

Nona nodded again, but this time more slowly with a protective feeling for Cindy.

"Well, then," he said, inclining slightly in Cindy's direction, "I feel that there is much you should know. I have, unfortunately, had to speak to Sam about something that involves you, so I think it's only fair to advise you of what has happened."

Cindy's eyes, blued by the sea, were fastened on Kessler with surprise and alarm.

"Apparently someone has brainwashed Sam into believing that it was I who ordered the FBI to wiretap those eight sensitive journalists who are now so outraged by the violation. Needless to say, this rumor has been very upsetting to me. Indeed, because of it, I have had to put myself in the hands of the president's physician who prescribed a steady diet of sedation for me. Since I am unaccustomed to drugs, this regimen has had a serious and quite unpleasant effect upon my system. However, I certainly don't need any more stress or trauma. I do not need *The Week* stirring up a new hornet's nest of accusations right on top of

259

the Watergate scandal. As I explained to you earlier," he said in a contemptuous aside to Nona, "it is not pleasant, for a man such as myself, to discover that his associates are a tribe of thieves . . ." His mouth began to quiver.

"So during a recent discussion with Sam I asked him to postpone his pursuit of this rumor—this last super scandal—in exchange for a small favor. I went to a great deal of trouble performing this favor," he flashed a teasing smile at Nona, "but then to my horror I discovered that Sam intended to double-cross me. Consequently, I was forced to make another deal with him. For, in the course of performing my first favor for Sam, I came across a number of tapes that included telephone conversations between you and Sam, Cindy, and they are compromising—to say the least. Once again, at lunch today, I asked Sam to postpone his story in exchange for which I promised not to send any of the tapes, of you two talking, to my dear friend, Joan Kinkaid, with whom I have had a close relationship for years and for whom I feel a great sense of responsibility. I would not want her to hear some of those nasty conversations. Such language you let him use to you! Why?"

Cindy was watching the sick grimaces that contorted Kessler's face and absorbing his words with absolute concentration. Then she blinked and wet her lips with the tip of her tongue before speaking.

"What did Sam say?" she asked. Her thin face was drawn tight with intensity but flushed with a slight glimmer of hope. Certain that Sam would never censor a story, for a moment Cindy saw the possibility of her own ascendance to legitimacy through the breakup of Sam's marriage.

"Well, of course, he seemed somewhat unhappy being presented with a choice," Kessler said. "It is not his style to have to choose between things. But he's a sensible man, and he finally said that he wouldn't publish anything harmful to me, and that he would forsake this wild-goose chase rather than endanger his marriage, which I know is important to him. So . . . it is my feeling that this subject should be dropped now and forever." Kessler smiled, turned, and walked slowly back to his encampment up the beach.

"God!" Cindy said in a distant voice that went beyond criticism.

Nona turned around so as not to look at Cindy and then saw Patsy running across the sand toward them, swerving slightly as she passed Kessler and then speeding up again, her long lean legs biting into the sand and the banner of her red-gold hair rising and falling behind her. When she reached them the wind slapped her hair violently across her face, and she pulled it behind her neck, leaving only one thin auburn strand that caught upon the corner of her dry lips.

"I have to tell you something," she whispered to Nona. She was stiff with fury as she spoke. "Jay told Kessler everything you'd told him, Nona. He just told me at the hotel. He told Kessler that you were going to screw him."

"Oh," Nona responded. "I was wondering who did it." The spray from the surf tickled the backs of her knees so she moved a step further up the beach. Her carelessness in evaluating Jay had lost Michael's chance for freedom.

Cindy neither understood nor cared what Patsy was saying. She had withdrawn into herself, shriveled up so that her skin pulled even more tautly around her miniature body. Inexplicably she knelt down on the sand, assuming an almost prayerful position on her knees, and stared out at the sea.

"I'm leaving him. For real." Patsy said. The single strand of hair tugged as she spoke. "I'm going to go back to Washington and get my stuff out of his apart-

261

ment. He's even worse than I thought. He's devious and dangerous and now—now he's even hitting on Johanna Dupres. He's monkeying around with her, trying to turn her on. Please," she said with pleading eyes, "come back to the hotel with me and help me find a bus to town."

"Sure," Nona said quickly. She looked down at Cindy who was filtering sand through her fingers. "Come on, Cindy. Let's go have a drink at the bar."

Cindy stood up. Barefoot she was a head shorter than Nona and barely reached Patsy's shoulder. She walked between them like a little sister, taking small uncertain steps.

"Where is Jay?" Nona asked Patsy.

"Oh, I suppose he's someplace with Johanna." Suddenly aware of the hair caught on her lips, Patsy tugged it away. "He said he had some work to do, and she said she was tired . . . very convenient. I'm sure they're off fucking somewhere."

The wind was pressing them from behind.

"He asked her if she would do a story for *Metro* about what it's like making a movie in Washington, and she got so excited I thought she was going to come."

Now they could see the men lounging on the chairs and blanket, drinking out of plastic cups. Sam, Tony, and Dempsey were arguing with Kessler, who sat like a Buddha on a canvas sling chair, flanked by his bodyguard and chauffeur.

"Keep going," Nona said. "I just want to get my purse."

The six men fell silent watching Nona as she swooped down upon them.

"If you're going back to the hotel," Kessler said in a nasty voice, "see if you can find Johanna. I seemed to have mislaid her."

Then he laughed loudly, and Nona reached down for her purse, remembering how the puns of Shakespearean fools always bridged the breach between insight and insanity. Without answering, she ran off to catch Cindy and Patsy who were walking toward the Parisian-style café on the terrace above the swimming pool. After a waitress in a bikini and high heels took their orders, they sat in silence around a red-checkered cloth-covered table, each avoiding the others' eyes, confronting her own private conclusions.

"Well . . . to the end of things," Patsy said, lifting her drink when it arrived. Goose flesh covered her bare, slightly sunburned shoulders, and she shivered as she spoke.

All around them classic Washington types were having their five-ish cocktails. Congressional staff and civil service people who had kept their jobs while the superstars soared, peaked, and disappeared were determinedly getting the most out of their summer vacations. "Oh!" Her voice hardened. "Look who's here."

Jay and Johanna were emerging from behind the construction site of the new wing of the hotel. Although there was a clear strip of blue sky crocheted between them, an air of conspiratorial intimacy transcended their separateness, and when they reached the terrace and saw the three women, they paused to speak to each other before sauntering innocently around the islands of café tables. Jay was wearing bathing trunks with a matching safari jacket, and Johanna was in a miniature yellow terrycloth outfit that exposed a strip of taut brown midriff winking below her swollen breasts. She sat down in the fourth chair at their table.

"Hi." First she smiled at Patsy. "We've been all over hunting for you people." She spoke with babyish petulance. "We couldn't find anyone anywhere."

"I thought we were supposed to have an editorial meeting at five, Jay," Nona interrupted. "Remember?"

"Sure. That's why I'm here," he said with a gallant self-introductory sweep of his arm. "Ready to get

263

started?" He began edging back away from the table where Patsy sat riveted with rage.

Nona stood up. "It shouldn't take too long," she said to the women. Then she swung her shoulder bag over her arm and moved toward the hotel.

"Let's go up to my room," Jay suggested once inside the hotel. They walked up the back staircase. "I suppose Patsy gave you a big earful," he said, disgust coloring his face. "She is the most hysterical bitch I've ever known. Her father spoiled her rotten."

Nona remained silent, but by the time they reached Jay's room he had whipped himself into a frenzy of anger about Patsy's jealous tantrums, and he dived at the whiskey bottle on his dresser with Kamikaze zeal.

"So? Didja finish it?" he asked, shoveling ice cubes out of the blue-flecked styrofoam bucket and tossing them into two nearby water glasses.

"Just about." Nona opened her purse and exchanged her manuscript for the drink Jay handed her. "I've only got the conclusion left to do. I wasn't sure how I wanted to end it until just a little while ago." She took a sip of Scotch. The drink she'd had in the café and the two double-duty gins that Dempsey had fixed her on the beach were producing a terrifying clarity of vision and conviction.

It was time to burn all her bridges now, finish all the dangerous liaisons. Now she had to cut loose, sever her link with *Metro* magazine, and kill off her last opportunity for an easy assimilated life.

"Actually," she said, "I ended up with a rather different kind of story than the one we had planned. I did write about the press but now I'm going to end my piece with a section on how you double-crossed us and told Kessler what we were planning to do. I think it's a terrific ending—how the big slick liberal editor went down for a fascist pig."

"What are you talking about?"

"Sam and Tony already met with Kessler, Jay. We

all know you told him everything. It's not very pretty."

Jay set his drink back on the bureau. Nona could see his face in the mirror. Usually soft with indolence, it was now wrenched out of shape with alarm.

Standing behind him, Nona could also see herself. Her hair was thick around her face and fell over the drooping shoulders of her blue denim workshirt. Now, with a rush of excitement that deepened the flush on her face, she felt her own strength. Driven by conscience, she would permanently eliminate any confusing contact with alternatives to a life of radical dissent and activism. She was high on deprivation and danger.

Jay turned around, nervously tightening the belt of his beach jacket, which only reached to his thighs and left his thick white legs protruding like helpless worms.

"Baby, you're looking for a lot of trouble," he sneered. "You're going to get yourself into a pack of trouble if you try to fuck me over. Whether you know it or not, you asked me to subvert a government official. You could do time for that. I'm not about to jeopardize my magazine for some revolutionary rip-off. I thought you were giving me a story and all I get is an opportunity to do time."

"I'm going to expose you, Jay," Nona said quietly.

"You're nuts," he jeered. But he stopped to light a cigarette, taking some time to think it through, figuring how to get her back into line before she went too far. "It's just your word against mine, sweetie. Mine and Eric Kessler's. Sam won't dare back you up, and I don't think Lewellen will either—since he sure won't want his old lady to find out about you. Your word ain't worth shit. You're out in the cold."

"That's exactly where I want to be—far out in the cold."

Despite her bravado, Nona felt some fear about standing only a few feet away from Jay. He was pulsating with anger, and his soft, bulbous body was quivering.

"You're really sick, aren't you?" he sneered, advancing a little closer to her. "You're just like all the rest of those weird sickies, aren't you? Oh, no, I take that back. You're worse. Because you're really a power-humper, too. You really like to see your by-line, and you really like all the little goodies you get off fucking big-name studs. That's how you got them to pull this crazy stunt for you, isn't it? Fucking them upside down and sideways. Isn't it? Shit! You'd sell out your own mother for a big story, wouldn't you? You people make me sick," Jay yelled.

Nona shrugged.

"Well, you're finished, kiddo. At least in Washington you are. You've written your last story for me, and I'll see to it you won't get an assignment from anyone else in this town. I can promise you that." He picked up her manuscript and tossed it at her. "You know what you can do with this, don't you?"

Nona bent over to pick it up.

"Now it's going to take me the whole fucking day tomorrow to find some puff piece to substitute for that piece of shit. I'm going to have to bust my balls looking for something to fill up the goddamn issue. And you can bet your ass I'm not going to forget that either, baby. You can bet your bottom dollar on that!"

"Really, Jay, you sound like a takeoff on one of those old Hollywood producers. . . ."

"You won't write for any decent magazine or paper east of the Rockies when I'm through with you."

"Worse things have happened to me," Nona laughed.

"You're finished, you're washed up, you're done."

Nona picked up her purse. "You're really out of touch, Jay. You really think that slick bullshit you publish means anything? It's nothing . . . it's just like *Life* and *Look* and *The Saturday Evening Post*. It's

266

worthless crap and you'll fold one morning just like they did."

"Get out," he yelled.

Then he came at her, his body bent murderously, and Nona turned, flinging open the door so it banged against the wall as she fled down the corridor to the empty stairwell.

Sixteen

As she moved out into the lobby on the first floor, hoping to hide in the bar alone, Nona saw a large crowd of people bending over a body on the floor, and she felt panic shoot through her. When the circle began to dissolve Tony and Sam emerged lifting Eric Kessler between them. Kessler's head hung down as though his neck were broken, and his chin kept striking against the top of his chest. The man who only a few hours before had crushed Michael's chances for freedom had deteriorated into an unconscious lump with a string of spittle dripping from his mouth.

A few minutes later a siren screamed outside the main entrance and everyone turned to watch two medics rush inside the lobby to confiscate Kessler, tucking their shoulders beneath his armpits as they took him into medical custody, carrying him behind the registration desk into the manager's office.

The crowd of people began tumbling around the lobby, grouping and regrouping as they discussed the identity of the victim, feeling close to the demise of the Nixon regime by having witnessed the collapse of one of his deputies. It was only when they began to disperse that Nona saw Cindy, hugging a huge beach towel around her leaning against a Coca Cola machine near the elevator.

"What's happened?" Nona demanded, rushing forward to grab her arm.

"I don't know for sure," Cindy said. Her blue eyes

seemed swollen. "Either he OD'd on something or he's having a nervous breakdown." Her flat, uninflected voice predicted hysteria. It was the same shrugging tone she had used during the skinny-dip in Sam's pool—she wasn't connecting with what was happening.

Nona turned to look at the blank face of the manager's office door. Sam was standing behind the reception desk, holding Johanna by the arm, and a few minutes later he led her over toward the elevator.

"O.K. Keep an eye on her," he said to Cindy. "She's pretty upset."

"Sam," Cindy said with totally inappropriate timing, "I heard what you did. Kessler told me what you told him."

"Oh, for Christ's sake, Cindy," Sam roared. "Lay off me, wouldja? Can't you see I've got my goddamn hands full right now? I've got to go call the goddamn White House."

He turned and ran back to the front desk. The three women remained silent for a few minutes.

"Do you think I should take Johanna upstairs?" Cindy said to Nona as if they were alone.

Johanna, who had a sulky expression on her face, pretended not to hear.

"Would you like to take a rest?" Nona asked her

The full pink lips fluttered but produced no sound.

Nona nodded at Cindy and reached over to press the call button. When the elevator arrived, Johanna walked inside, and Cindy slipped in behind her just as the door began to close.

Nona buttoned her shirt to the bottom and headed toward the cocktail lounge, relieved to be alone without an entourage that would orchestrate each drink into a party. She burrowed into a small booth in the farthest corner, watched the room fill up with boisterous drinkers, and tried to think. She had blown it. Perhaps some day news of Michael's

269

tape would surface and the court would supoena it for a new trial, but that could take years—or it might never happen. She finished a first and second drink and was surprised when Cindy suddenly appeared, fully dressed and sober, to summon her.

Without asking any questions, Nona followed her outside to the beach front. In the café a group of hotel personnel were clustered together. Patsy sat alone at one of the tables, and Cindy walked over to join her, but Nona continued walking past the café and down to the pink cabanas ringing the swimming pool. From there she saw Tony, Sam, Jay, and Dempsey guarding the shoreline, interrupting the dark horizontal smear where the sky reached down to the sea. Whipped by the ocean wind, the shapes of the four men seemed smudged and poorly drawn, shadowy sketches rather than outlines.

Feeling an ominous air of expectancy, Nona waited for something to happen and eventually became aware of a helicopter that had been buzzing the beach begin to descend, finally setting down on the sand and scuttling along the shore like a pudgy pigeon moving between park benches. Three men in army uniform climbed out of the hatch and walked toward the civilian welcoming committee, scanning the faces of Kessler's friends to ascertain, in their eternal search for authority, who held the highest rank. Gradually they focused in on Dempsey—either by instinct or orders—and talked intently to him for a while before disappearing into the hotel.

It seemed to Nona that the ocean skipped a beat, missed one of its regular pulsing waves and lapsed into a more irregular rhythm.

After a short while two of the officers reemerged through the terrace door, bracing Eric Kessler between them, and began hobbling across the beach toward safety. Kessler's head was still bobbing up and down as if it had been severed from his spinal cord, and his disobedient arms and legs danced lopsidedly.

A moment later, Johanna Dupres, wearing a white Mexican wedding shirt that billowed up around her thighs in the first rush of wind off the sea, moved into view. She stopped in the center of the terrace and wrapped her arms around herself, hugging her body as she watched Kessler being lifted up and loaded into the helicopter. Quickly Jay detached himself from the civilian honor guard and went over to put his arm around her. Startled, she recoiled at first, but then resumed her original position, turning her gaze toward the hotel as the third army officer came outside with the Secret Service man to run down and board the helicopter.

The propellers began to spin, spitting up curls of sand and making a whirling sound that zapped Nona's nerves. Then, as the helicopter began to rise, Nona flashed back to a quick kaleidoscopic review of a decade of network footage showing death-by-helicopter in Vietnam. A thousand images flashed before her eyes ending with a close-up of a Vietcong prisoner being shoved out of a helicopter hatch into TV-colored space. Suddenly she felt a strong, cathartic sense of justice that Eric Kessler was being carted off in one of the same whirlybirds that had descended like locusts upon the Vietnamese countryside.

When the men scurried back from the spiraling sand, Johanna disentangled herself from Jay and ran inside the hotel. Cindy and Patsy were still seated in the café, and Nona decided to join them just as she saw Tony cross the beach toward the cabanas where she stood.

"Well, that's that," he said in a reluctant voice as he moved in close to Nona. "This sure turned into a goddamn nightmare. Kessler berserked from the pressure. Would you like to go somewhere else to have a drink? Away from here? Back to Rehoboth?"

271

"No, thank you, but I wouldn't mind a walk on the beach."

They moved out of the floodlit area and down toward the surf. The wind bit at them in the darkness.

"Look," he began, "I want to say I'm sorry I got so rough. I just went nuts down on the beach this afternoon. I couldn't believe you were baiting Sam that way—doing him like that. He likes you, you know, Nona, and he tried to do right by you." His voice snagged as he spoke. He too seemed out of focus, fastening on irrelevancies, inverting the order of things to blur reality.

When they reached the shore Nona bent down to unstrap her sandals. As they began walking again, Tony reached out to take the shoes from her hand. Nona sighed. The seductiveness of his concern teased her and stirred her longing to continue being loved.

"I'd almost forgot. You almost hit me." She smiled into the darkness, concentrating on counteracting any impulse to regress. "You got my cherry on that one, Lewellen. No one ever roughed me up like that before."

"But you can understand, can't you? I mean . . . we practically lived at Sam's all summer. We ate there and used his pool and slept there and then you started doing him like that, putting him down as if he hadn't tried to help you, even if it didn't work out."

"I was wondering if I could borrow your car tonight," Nona inquired, curling her toes into the cool damp sand.

"What for?"

"So I can drive back to Washington."

"What are you talking about Nona? What are you saying?"

"I'm going back tonight."

"Why? What happened doesn't have anything to do with us. I know Kessler put the screws on Sam, and Sam knuckled under. But that's over. Kessler's going to be at Walter Reed for a long, long time. He's off our backs now, and Sam can run his story and that finishes Kessler off forever. That's it—we wrap it up."

Nona felt laughter start to simmer inside her, hurrying toward a climax. "Tony, I don't give a damn if Sam runs the story now or not. The tape's out of our reach. I could have had this all locked up. Now it'll take years."

"Nona, we tried . . . we really tried."

"Bullshit. You weren't going to take any real risks."

"What the hell are you talking about? All of this happened because we tried to get the stuff from Eric."

"I'm cold," Nona said, unrolling the sleeves of her shirt.

Tony stopped walking and reached out for her. In the moonlight his face looked tortured. "I didn't have enough cards in my hand, baby. I didn't have any trump to deal. I was dealt out the minute Kessler threatened Sam. I couldn't muscle Kessler with Sam's life at stake."

"Don't," Nona snorted, shaking his hands off. "I just want to go back and get my sweater. It's cold."

Tony took off his jacket, enveloping Nona as he engineered her arms into the sleeves, lifting the sides of the jacket over each breast so he could zip it, moving quickly like a crafty parent who had pushed thousands of thoughtless arms and legs into countless garments and finally lifting the length of her hair out from beneath the collar to spread like a fan behind her shoulders. Then his finger began to dig desperately into her arms again.

"Please," Nona begged, almost overcome by emotion.

Lewellen pulled her into his arms and held her against his chest, rocking her back and forth, rhythmically trying to cancel out his errors, repair his omissions, correct all the mistakes of their relationship.

"I'm sorry," he mumbled. "I'm sorry . . . I'm not just saying that. I really am sorry . . . about . . . a lot of things. You were right about a lot of stuff. . . ." He stroked her cheek, rubbed his face against the top of her head, tucked her body tighter against him. Then he bent his thumb and forefinger together, creating a little egg cup to cradle her chin and lifted up her face. "Please give us a chance, Nona. Please."

"I don't want to," she said looking away but still leaning against him, yearning to accept the oasis of love and security that he offered.

"O.K." He turned and started walking back across the beach. Nona trailed along behind him, but as they approached the hotel she slipped away from him and ran toward a steel-plated fire door on the side of the building. She waited inside the cinderbrick hallway for a few minutes, expecting Tony to come bursting in on her, but then she walked through the hotel basement to the service elevator and, suddenly feeling brave, impulsively pressed the number four button and a moment later walked along a dimly lit stucco-walled corridor to 420A. She knocked lightly on the door and listened carefully for sounds behind it.

Johanna Dupres called, "Come in."

Nona turned the unlocked door.

Stark naked, Johanna lay propped up against several pillows in bed. When she saw Nona, her mouth puckered into a rosebud of surprise that matched her large pink nipples, and without lowering her eyes, she reached down to pull the covers over her breasts.

"Oh, dear," she said, staring straight into Nona's face.

"Oh, I'm sorry," Nona said. "I just came to . . . I

274

lent Eric something, and I thought I should get it back."

"They took all his stuff away," Johanna said, her eyes still stretched from the shock of Nona's arrival. She lifted her hand tentatively to stir her hair back from her face. "Two of those soldiers came in here after they got off the helicopter and put all Eric's clothes in his suitcase and all the papers and books and his briefcase into a cardboard box, and they sealed it with tape and stamped something on top of the tape and took it away. They even sealed the suitcase."

Nona looked at the set of matched luggage lined up against the wall.

"They left my clothes," Johanna explained, "and those bottles. Would you like a Coke or something?"

"No, thank you."

"Do you have any cigarettes on you?"

Nona fished the Winstons out of her purse and carried them over to Johanna.

"I heard what Jay told Eric," Johanna said, looking cautiously at Nona. "Were you looking for that tape?"

"Yes. I'm going back to Washington in a little while so I just came by to see . . ."

"I never saw any tapes," Johanna said, tacking the sheet to her bosom with splayed fingers. "I don't even know if he really had them." She lit her cigarette. "Why are you leaving tonight?" She seemed genuinely curious.

"I have to . . . do something first thing tomorrow morning."

"How are you getting back?"

"I'm borrowing Tony's car."

"Oh. You could drive back with Jay and me. We're leaving at seven in the morning. The chauffeur's going to take us."

Johanna's invitation emerged so naturally that it took a few moments before either of them recognized the meaning of her disclosure.

"And Patsy, too," Johanna blurted.

Embarrassed, Nona walked toward the dresser mirror and began to smooth her hair, pressing it back from her face and doubling the rubber band so that it gripped the ponytail even more sternly. Somehow it seemed important to treat her hair severely in front of a woman who saw hair as an index of style.

"I mean, well, there's no reason for me to stay here," Johanna explained. "In fact, I should probably go visit Eric at the hospital tomorrow. If they'll let me. Do you know where Walter Reed is? Is it outside the city? I don't have a car."

But her tone contradicted her voiced intention. She would never see Eric Kessler again. His power had been their only mutual interest, and with that gone they shared nothing else in common. Simply and smoothly Johanna had shifted responsibility for herself over to Jay Lazar. She had psychologically moved—just one space over—on some invisible game board, carrying all her properties with her and re-settling in the territory of the next available man.

"Jay has to be back tomorrow morning," she explained. "Saturday is when the magazine goes to bed. He's not even sure yet if Patsy's going to stay on for the rest of the weekend or not." Johanna sent out her feeler with the impunity of a pragmatist.

Impressed by the show of audacity, Nona smiled again. "Actually I was sort of hoping that maybe Patsy would go back with me tonight so I wouldn't have to drive the whole way alone. Would you mind if I called her from here?"

With a dazzling smile Johanna Dupres bestirred herself to shove the telephone across the bedside table in Nona's direction.

Some of Nona's studied control began to disintegrate, but she started dialing without making any comment.

Patsy answered after one ring.

"Patsy. It's Nona. Tony's lending me his car, and I'm going back to Washington in about twenty minutes. I could use another driver."

"Oh, shit! I forgot my glasses back in the apartment so I can't drive. But I'm a hell of a rider. The last bus to Washington left at six so I was just going down to rent another room. I'll meet you in the lobby."

She hung up, and Nona replaced the receiver.

Johanna lay motionless on the bed, her face cleansed of any emotion. The sad half-circles waiting to spoil the skin beneath her eyes were only barely invisible.

From behind the curtain of her blond beauty, Johanna looked at Nona briefly with a quizzical expression as she walked out.

When Nona unlocked the door of 201, Tony was lying on the bed, arms folded beneath his head, staring up at the ceiling. He was listening to Cindy's voice, which floated into the room from Sam's adjoining balcony. Hysterical accusations were picked up and delivered by the wind.

". . . but if you were going to kill the Kessler story just so Joan wouldn't find out about us, why should I believe you, Sam? Why should I think you'll ever leave her? If you were so afraid of her finding out that you'd do *that!*"

"Oh, God," Tony said in a sick, stricken voice, grabbing the sleeve of the jacket Nona wore as she passed him. "Shut the balcony door."

"Why?" Nona asked. "Maybe I should hear this."

"You never planned to leave her," Cindy screamed. "You've been putting me on."

There was a slice of silence during which Sam must have spoken, but then Cindy's response came loud and clear above the groan of the sea.

"Because I want to get something out of this. Something."

Tony rolled to his feet, starting toward the balcony.

"How come I'm always supposed to be around for you, Sam, but I have to get scraps—whatever's left over you throw me. How come you get to have everything—a wife and kids and *The Week* and your goddamn friends, and *everything!* How come you think you're so great that half of you is enough for me?"

Nona heard a door shut. Then there was silence.

"You're leaving?" Tony asked.

"Yes." Nona went into the bathroom and dressed.

"So that's it?" he called out. "You're finished with me? Because you didn't get what you wanted, you're just walking out?"

Nona opened the bathroom door and came out.

"I love you, Tony. But that's it. Patsy's riding back with me. I can use your car, can't I?"

He shrugged and then sat down on the bed planting his elbows on his knees. "How you going to drive across the bridge?"

"Nervously."

"You'll never make it if you close your eyes and put your head between your knees the way you did this morning."

Nona knelt down on the floor. She zipped her suitcase and tilted the case of her typewriter to see if it was snug inside.

"I can't believe you," he said with sudden ugly scorn. "I can't believe you're doing this . . . that after everything you're just leaving this way."

"I'm going back to nothing, Tony," Nona said. "I'm going to be without a job or a friend or . . . a man. I'm going back to a great big zero. But this is too rich for my blood."

"Goddamnit, Nona! That political jazz of yours is just a smoke screen. Your whole goddamn radical spiel is just a bunch of bullshit—a hype to get attention. You don't really give a damn about any of that political crap. It's just a shtik. You're using it as a cover because you're afraid to connect with people. As long as you can outflank someone from the left, you can mock them and act superior. It's just a high school defense mechanism. You use that Marxist political stuff to cut people down because you don't know who you are."

"You're full of shit, Tony. You don't have any politics," Nona said.

"Why do you talk like that?" he thundered half-rising off the bed in a spasm of rage.

She turned around, untying the rubber band that held her hair so that the snarled strands fell loose about her face offering a sheltering veil. "Look Tony, nothing can happen between us, so what's the use. It isn't your kids or anything. It's you and me. We're from different planets," she said in a sad, quiet voice. "That was the turn-on. But our heads are too different. You've got too much to lose, and I have too little—or something." She shrugged and then began to canvass the contents of her purse checking for her wallet and keys.

"Look, Nona. I can help you. You're young and you're ready to take off. I've got lots of good connections in New York. Maybe you're ready to do a book now. Maybe you'd like to get a nice fat advance on some book that really interests you so you don't have to mess around with magazine articles anymore. I could help you get a contract, and we could just wait and let this thing play its way out. I love you, Nona. You know that. We could be together as much as you'd want. I could get away for a couple nice long trips with you every year. And I'll get you a nice apartment, or a house in Georgetown. Something at least that has some goddamn air conditioning."

"I don't want any air conditioning," Nona wailed, tasting bitter self-contempt in her throat. "I don't want an air-conditioned life. I want to be hot in the summer and cold in the winter. I want to be out front and a little bit scared all the time because otherwise I forget what the hell I should be doing or who the hell I want to be."

"Well what DO you want? Tell me."

"I'm not sure," she said letting honesty squeeze past her pride. "But I know we can't make it anymore."

"Let's see about that," he said coming at her, his arms curved open in a wide empty arc.

"No," she said darting aside. "I can't. Please, no."

He stopped. His face was frozen, but the fingers of age were digging at his eyes and around the edges of his mouth.

Nona recoiled with regret, but didn't recant. After a second she bent over to pick up the typewriter case.

He pushed the pain off his face with an elaborate grin. "What are you going to do? Put the suitcase on top of your head?"

She smiled, achingly.

"I could drive you back," he said.

She stopped smiling. "No. No thank you."

He picked up her suitcase and then looked down pleadingly into her eyes. "Don't leave my life," he said.

Nona watched the smudged erasures of his past smiles deepen into lines of age, and her heart pounded with ambivalence. He had been her friend. He loved her.

"I've got things I have to do," she said briskly, walking toward the door as loneliness and alienation sprang alive inside her again.

"Shee-it!" His hand reached out to encircle her arm. "What do you have to do? Blow up a Chase Manhattan bank or something?"

"I don't know," Nona said. "That's the bad news. I don't know."

They walked slowly down the hall to the elevator Nona pressed the call button.

"You know, Watergate's changed a lot of things,

Nona. If we keep after Nixon long enough, we'll get him impeached or make him resign. There's no way the Democrats can lose in seventy-six, and the party's going to move so far to the left you won't be able to recognize it."

"I'll believe that when I see it," Nona said, cynically.

The elevator door opened. They walked inside, and Nona punched L.

"We could get involved in a presidential campaign," Tony persisted. "We could travel with the candidate—do some speech-writing and PR—be together a lot of the time."

The door closed. Nona kept her gaze on the control board, watching the bulbs light up as if her concentration assured a safe descent.

"Listen," Tony said desperately, "I knew this adultery business was for the birds a long time before Cindy got the message. And I've been thinking . . . when my kids get a little older . . . go off to school . . . my wife might not mind . . ."

"If I moved into one of the empty bedrooms?"

"No. I mean. I don't think she'd mind working out some kind of an arrangement."

"You don't really believe Elizabeth Lewellen would buy that, do you?" Nona asked. It was the first time she had broken the taboo of mentioning his wife's name.

Their eyes met, echoing pain. Nona knew she was close to tears. Tony squinted and scanned the ceiling of the elevator.

The elevator door opened, and they stepped out into the lobby. Patsy was standing near the front entrance.

Nona set down her typewriter. "I'll leave your car in front of Sam's house tomorrow morning," she said. "I'll put the key under the front seat." There was a hot stinging sensation behind her eyes. She reached out to touch his face. "Take care of yourself."

281

"Are you going to leave Washington?" he asked in a formal voice while handing over her suitcase.

"I don't know yet."

He began to say something else but stopped. "Do you know where the car's parked?"

"I'll find it."

"Do you know the way home?"

Now her smile was genuine. "No. But I think that's the name of the game. Don't worry . . . I'll make it."

Nona drove with Patsy beside her, hands folded in her lap, as prim and proper as a little girl being taken home from a party at which she had misbehaved. After they became accustomed to the rhythm of the car on the black highway, Patsy would occasionally send out distress signals from the depths of her self-absorption.

"So you threw in the towel at *Metro?*" she said after one particularly long silence.

Nona laughed. "Did Jay tell you the whole story?"

"Did he ever! You're lucky you got out of the room alive. Me he was glad to see go," she added bitterly. "But I'm surprised he didn't beat you up."

Nona's right knee was quivering as she held down the accelerator. It would be another hour before they reached the Chesapeake Bay Bridge so she felt she had enough time to assess her phobia.

"Well, what are you going to do now?" Patsy asked. "I think Jay might really try to blacklist you around Washington. He's a very vindictive guy."

The darkness was flying up to beat against the windshield.

"Well, first I'm going to write an article about what happened today and get it published somewhere. Then I'll probably start looking around to find a commune to move into so my rent and food will be cheaper, and then I'll see if I can start up our newspaper again. I might even go back to a straight newspaper again."

"What newspaper?"

"Any newspaper. I'm a good reporter."

"You're really tough," Patsy said admiringly. "Me? I'm still getting kicked in and out of affairs, apartments, jobs, everything. It still all hinges on some prick. But you're something else. And I bet you kissed off Lewellen too."

"Yes, we're through."

"Aren't you . . . going to . . . miss him?"

"Yes," Nona paused, wanting to answer honestly. "I'm going to miss him a lot."

For many miles theirs had been the only headlights interrupting the darkness, but now, as another car approached and sizzled past, Nona chanced a quick look over at Patsy. The lean lovely face was twisted with anxiety, and the sight of it reactivated Nona's own fears. For a moment she tried to envision how the Bay Bridge would look at night. Would there be a chain of lights strung along that harpsichord of wires to indicate some pathway across the black stretch of sky above the void? What light was Nona to follow out of darkness into nothing across that deep abyss toward some unseen shore?

"I keep thinking," Patsy said slowly, "I mean, I don't think it exactly in words, but one idea keeps going through my head, like, who's going to love me now . . . who's going to love me now. Isn't that stupid. To worry about who's going to love me—instead of who I'm going to love?" she faltered. "But I don't even know where I'm going to live now."

"You'll stay with me," Nona said quickly. "For as long as you want to. It's just a one-bedroom place, and I don't have any air conditioning, but. . . ." She stopped herself from apologizing further, recalling that those objections were Tony Lewellen's and not her own.

"Hey, that'd be great if I could," Patsy said with husky relief. "I mean, if it's really O.K. with you.

You don't have to."

"Are you kidding? I can't stand living alone. I think it's socially immoral." Then, staring into the darkness, she decided to share her secret fear. "You know, Patsy, I'm. . . ." Suddenly afraid to provoke any panic, she changed to a slower track. "Did you ever see one of those big green signs they sometimes have on roads, right before you get to a long bridge, that says something like . . . Escort Service Available or something like that?"

"No."

"I wonder what they mean by that," Nona insisted. "Does an escort take you, or just go along beside you?"

"Well, if they're like most escorts, they probably sideswipe you and then leave you stranded."

Nona laughed. "I was thinking that maybe the highway department would drive people . . . who are afraid . . . across the bridge. I mean, that the state troopers would drive their cars for them . . . if they're too afraid to get across . . . safely."

"How would the cops get back?"

"Well, with people on the other side who are afraid to cross the other way."

"Are you afraid to drive across the Chesapeake Bay Bridge?" Patsy asked incredulously.

Nona laughed. "Oh, no! I was just wondering."

Now that she had severed herself from the entice-ment of Tony Lewellen it was easier to sound tough even if she felt afraid. Without the distraction that had diminished her independence and depleted her integrity she was forced back into her original posture of strength. She needed her strength in order to struggle. She needed to struggle in order to survive, and she needed to survive in order to struggle.

She turned on the radio with nervous fingers. The Beatles were singing "I Want to Hold Your Hand." The whine of the sixties filled the car, sucking her back into the past, pulling her down into other earlier times.

The Delaware disk jockey continued playing the Beatles' first album.

Nona let it happen. She let it come. The hot volcano of her memory began to heave up its lava, spewing out the burned ashes of her life. Time and distance fused with space and speed, music and memories blurred and blended. She ached from longing and wanting more.

And then, suddenly, they were on the bridge. There had been no advance warning. She had forgot there were no tollgates on the Delaware side. Gradually the road had begun to incline, and by the time Nona saw the Christmas string of bulbs strung out against the sky, it was too late—she was on an access road above the ground, moving inexorably higher over the water.

She felt her body coiling tighter and tighter, an unendurable vise constricting her soul. For a second a silent scream of terror possessed her, and her foot pressed down upon the accelerator. Then the fear began to disintegrate and dissipate itself. Soft panting breaths pushed from between her lips and she trembled as fear passed from her body, purging her of panic. She drove calmly down the outside lane, mindfully maintaining her speed as the sharply lettered signs posted along the guardrails requested.

Slowly and imperturbably Nona drove out above the black water through the dark night across a suspension bridge hung from the sky, supported only by faith and hopes of those coming from one place on their way to another.